BLAIR DENHOLM

Revolution Day

To the persecuted, victimized and powerless in this world.

Death is the solution to all problems. No man - no problem.

JOSEPH STALIN

Foreword

This novel has been a little over three decades in the making. From a couple of tentative pecks on the keyboard of a Mac SE in the early 1990s to a completed work in 2021. It is the novel I've always wanted to write and the first one I set about writing. In the meantime, I've put out seven other crime fiction novels, most since 2017. Revolution Day threw up so many challenges, it was easier at times to simply shelve the project for another day. Then another, and another. But, like all long journeys, the end has been reached. Finally…

Thanks, first of all, to my fellow students at the Pushkin Institute in Moscow, members of the 1987/88 cohort, many of whom remain friends today. John, Ilpo, Minna, Mika, Rob, Togo, the lads from Nigeria, my Aussie compatriots Irena and Alan, the list is long. That tiny window of time had a profound impact on me and the career path I followed. Thanks also to the many Russian friends, teachers from the University of Queensland the late John McNair, Lyndall Morgan and Masha Kravchenko, as well as work colleagues who have helped me learn the Russian language well enough to be considered fluent. But most of all, I'd like to thank Anders, the absolute epitome of loyalty and staunchness.

Chapter 1

'Are you there yet?' Burov barked, his words difficult to make out over the crackle of the two-way radio.

'Nearly, Comrade Colonel.'

'You'd better be, Voloshin. Recover the body, get it to the morgue as fast as possible.'

'ETA five minutes.' I quirked an eyebrow at my driver, Lieutenant Yegor Adamovsky. He nodded and returned his attention to the road.

'I want this case solved and put to bed. Understand? It's a potential PR disaster for Gorbachev, the Party, the entire country.'

'Yes, Comrade Colonel.'

'The Central Intelligence Directorate's asked us to conduct a quick preliminary investigation until they take over.'

'When will that be?'

'When they tell us,' said Burov. 'Over and out.'

Yegor chuckled.

'Shut the hell up and drive.'

Masses of red flags lined both sides of the highway. Our clunky Militsiya Lada sedan skipped across Leninsky Prospekt, slick with ice. Snow flecked with dirty grey gravel lay in thick drifts at the sides of the four-lane highway. Trolleybuses and trams stopped at regular intervals to pick up shivering commuters. We hurtled along a five-kilometre section of road that bisected a vast wooded parkland. Yegor wrenched the wheel left and right as the car fish-tailed down the highway.

1

'Oi!' The burr of the engine and static radio chatter compelled me to shout. 'I'd like to arrive in one piece if you don't mind.'

'We have to hurry, Comrade Captain. You heard what the Colonel said.' He gave me a wide-eyed stare. 'Only a handful of officers are at the scene. If word spreads about what's happened and we aren't there to lend our authority, well...'

'I know that.' I took a deep breath. 'But getting there five minutes earlier won't make much difference. Especially for the victim.'

'What do you mean?'

'He's already dead.'

Yegor nodded. 'Yes, of course. But there could be a panic if we don't...'

The car tilted, just missed a truck passing in the opposite lane. 'Watch out, you moron,' I spat. Yegor, teeth clenched, regained control of the swaying vehicle. 'Slow down immediately.'

'Sorry.'

My warning all but ignored, we drove the next 500 metres at 95 clicks an hour, an insane speed for the icy conditions. A concrete barricade blocked the road ahead. I stared at Yegor, his boot still firmly planted on the accelerator.

'Slow down, for God's sake.'

He slammed his foot on the brake, the vehicle slid sideways. The rear right wheel struck the gutter and the car bounced twice before landing with a clunk . I gripped Yegor by the forearm. 'You'll kill both of us. What's wrong with you?'

'Sorry, Comrade Captain. You know the old saying. *What Russian doesn't enjoy a fast ride?* Anyway, you can relax. We're here.'

Sergeant Anatoly "Tolya" Pronin waited for us on the side of the road near two Militsiya vans. In the highway's outer lane a squat, round cop from the Traffic Directorate Branch waved a striped baton like an orchestra conductor at drivers who slowed down to rubberneck. Probably anticipating a car accident in the icy conditions. Thank God they'd be spared the horrific crime scene a hundred metres from the highway.

'So glad you've arrived, comrades.' Pronin saluted, waited for my acknowledgement.

'Put your hand down, Sergeant,' I said. 'No ceremony needed with me. You should know that by now.'

'Yes, Viktor Pavlovich.' He dropped his hand, the tight lines at the corners of his mouth softened. After eighteen months at Yugo-Zapadnaya Militsiya station the men still treated me like a newcomer. Gavril Peskov, the man I replaced, a fixture at the station for thirty years, suddenly dropped dead at his desk. Massive stress-induced heart attack. He had a reputation for being a hard-arse, a stickler for procedure. By comparison, I was a free spirit and the crew were still trying to figure me out. 'Would you like some details?'

'I'm listening.' I raised a flap of my ushanka fur hat and pointed at my ear. Pronin smiled but I heard Yegor groan. 'Talk and walk. Time's ticking.'

As we set off into the forest, we passed a hulking, ruddy-cheeked officer who snapped out a salute, then thrust his hands behind his back. I smiled at Pronin. 'See, that's how you do it. Short and sweet. So, what else have you got for me?'

'Okay,' Pronin inhaled deeply. A furrowed brow told me he was anxious not to forget anything. 'I placed Sasha Kozlov on guard at the start of the forest path.' He glanced at his watch. 'About an hour ago. Kirill Gregoriev's manning the track where it exits to the Chekhov Institute, one of those colleges for foreign students, on Bolshevistskaya Street.'

'Anyone approach our men with information?'

'Kozlov's turned away a few brave joggers who don't give a damn about the cold. Otherwise, not too many eager to enter the forest with Militsiya about. The Traffic Division cop's been very diligent, too. One glare from him would scare off anybody.'

'And the guy at the far end of the path?' I sidestepped a puddle with little chunks of ice floating on the surface.

'Don't know, sir. I haven't spoken to Gregoriev for a while. Too busy keeping the dead man company.'

'Witnesses?' My hopes weren't high. A lonely track on a bitter winter's morning isn't the most pleasant place to spend time. Just after dawn, an anonymous male called in from a payphone. Reported the crime and promptly hung up. A potential A-grade witness scratched from the start.

'But there was one person near the scene when we arrived.'

'Who?'

'An old woman in a blind panic. She stumbled upon the victim just after first light. She buried a dog here.'

'She did what?' I stopped, spun around to face Pronin. 'When? This morning?'

'Uh, no sir. I should have been clearer.' He consulted a notebook. 'Let's see. Her name's Nina Petrova. Lives in an apartment block less than 300 metres away. Apparently, her terrier died last summer. Couldn't afford to dispose of the little fella properly, so she and her son, Vasily, dug a hole and buried him here. The dog that is, not Vasily.' He laughed uneasily, checked his notes again. 'She visits every week. Probably goes without saying, but she's a bit loopy.'

'People can't go burying animals in public parks.' I gestured for Pronin to lead on through the forest. 'Has to be a public health violation. She could've buried the bloody thing in the cemetery down the road.'

'I'm pretty sure that's just for humans, Comrade Captain,' said Yegor. He leaned in closer to my shoulder as the path narrowed. 'Should we see the victim before we interrogate her?'

I ignored Yegor's question. '"Where is she then?' We need to interview her in depth.'

Pronin coughed into his fist, steam from his breath poured between his fingers. 'Gone home, sir.'

'You have her address, I take it?'

'Of course.' Pronin pointed over my shoulder to the northern edge of the park. 'Her apartment's over there. Did you really expect a 90-year-old babushka to wait in the freezing cold until the chief investigator showed up?'

'Yes,' I replied. 'Obviously.'

'Viktor Pavlovich, with respect, she'll be more inclined to answer questions in the comfort of her own apartment.' As if confirming his argument, a gust of wind shrieked through the power lines.

'Witnesses have better recall when the time between the incident and the interview is minimized,' I said flatly. 'That's basic police work. Something you should know.'

'We couldn't keep her here. She was raving, struggling not to lose it. Deep shock. Rita Vasilyeva took her home before she passed out in the snow.' Pronin nodded towards a uniformed woman standing about 30 metres ahead, hands behind her back, her gaze fixed on something hidden in a dense thicket of birch trunks. 'The old woman's son was home. He's with her now, waiting for us to return.'

'Any other civilians see the body?' We continued to shuffle along the path, skirting ice-encrusted puddles and slippery mud.

'Yes, Comrade Captain. Some schoolkids were hanging around when we arrived, but they scarpered. Vasilyeva and Gregoriev gave chase but the little bastards pissed off.'

'How many?'

'Three.'

'You saw them?'

'No, not me. Rita and Kirill spotted them standing around the corpse. When the officers called out, the children took off like startled deer.'

'Fitness standards have certainly dropped since I joined the Militsiya. I can't believe two adults couldn't catch them. We need their statements.'

'There are things you haven't considered,' said Yegor.

I gave him my fiercest glare. 'Your tone is verging on impudent, Lieutenant. What haven't I considered?'

'Trauma.' Yegor persisted.

'Elaborate.'

'Like Pronin said. The kids saw the body. It could mentally scar them for life.'

'True. Pronin, make sure Rita and Krill provide a full description of those kids. Finding them'll be next to impossible, but we've got to try.'

'Yes, Comrade Captain.' Pronin stepped over glittering shards of smashed vodka bottles, held out his hand in warning. 'Watch your step, comrades. Popular route for drunks, this. We've gathered pieces of glass near the crime scene. For forensics. But the place is littered with...well...litter. I reckon it's a pointless exercise.'

He was right. The area was strewn with all kinds of garbage, much of it slimy and fetid. 'That's it for witnesses?' I asked.

Pronin shrugged. 'Maybe there were more. Who knows? No one has come forward apart from the man who called it in.'

'Is it him?' I pushed branches aside as we edged ever closer to the murder scene.

Pronin stopped, eyebrows arched. 'Who?'

'You know who I mean. The missing student.'

'Hang on a second.' Pronin reached deep into his coat pocket. 'I found this near the body. He held out a dark green foreign passport. I went to take it, but he tightened his hold.

'Come on, man,' I growled. 'Give it to me.'

'Is the missing student a Nigerian, by any chance?'

'Stop playing games and hand it over.'

'Name of Aaron Adekanye? Date of birth 5th of January 1964?'

'Yes, damn you. I should have you sacked for such insolence.' Of course, that would never happen. Pronin was efficient, loyal and tough – one of the best officers I'd ever worked with.

Pronin released his grip and I snatched at the document, kept walking to where the path widened slightly to a small clearing. A quick scan of the passport confirmed what was until now a supposition.

Yegor stopped suddenly, grabbed my elbow. 'Captain, look.' I glanced in the direction his trembling index finger was pointing. I now saw what Rita Vasiliyeva had been staring at. 'Oh my god,' I mumbled. It was all I could do to not to throw up.

Chapter 2

A man's mutilated body hung limp from the bough. Higher up, strong gusts whistled through high-voltage power lines and support towers that marched across the parkland. Even this far into the woods, the wind punched through the bare, tightly bunched birch and larch trees. The corpse swayed almost imperceptibly in the wind, as if the man still had some life left in him.

I stepped closer, a metre from the body. Simmering anger at the brutal treatment of the victim fought with my professional curiosity. For me, facing this kind of murder victim was unusual. The cases I deal with are mainly related to domestic violence. Women beaten to death by alcoholic husbands. Lovers knifed in fits of jealousy. Hit over the head with a rolling pin. Most cadavers I see are already at the morgue. I take people there to identify relatives. Accident victims. Drunk vagrants who passed out in the snow and died from hypothermia. Or drivers who refused to wear a seatbelt and ended their lives as human missiles flying through windscreens. Those dead souls looked at peace compared to the man on the end of the rope. His final moments would have been the stuff of nightmares. I tilted my head 45 degrees to the left.

'Any clearer at that angle, Captain Voloshin?' Yegor quipped over my shoulder.

'I hold my head like this when I'm concentrating.'

'Dogs do that when they're curious.'

'Are you comparing me to a dog, officer?'

'No, of course not, I...'

'I find it helps me determine the complexity of a problem. Figure out what's the best way forward.'

'Has it helped you now?'

'Not really.' I stood. 'This act is so heinous, I can't comprehend the mind of a human that would do this to another. Fucking monsters.'

Yegor scratched his cheek. 'That's an understatement. Not sure there's precedent for this.'

'There is.'

'Really?'

'More than twenty years ago. A student from Ghana was found dead. Like this guy, in a forest.'

'You're kidding.'

'I'm serious. 1963 to be exact. It was a huge scandal. Embarrassing for the Soviet Union. There was plenty of press coverage abroad, but not here. Hushed up like you'd expect. There were even protests in Red Square. African students marched about with placards. They accused Moscow of being a city of racists, like Alabama in the USA.'

'Holy shit. Was the killer caught?'

'The official verdict was accidental death. The coroner declared the man drank too much, wandered into the forest, collapsed and froze to death.'

'Do you believe that version? Sounds way too convenient.'

I shook my head. 'To guarantee impartiality, a Ghanaian medical student attended the autopsy. To make sure there was no funny business.'

'But do you believe it was death by misadventure?'

'No. He was found far from his registered address. His institute was in another city altogether. The Ghanaian student could have been paid off, threatened. But it doesn't matter what I think. Whatever the truth hundreds of Africans were pissed off, convinced the guy had been assassinated.'

'This man definitely was. I mean, it's not suicide.'

I gave a sharp nod, plucked a cigarette from a packet sporting a portrait of Laika, the first dog in space. I struck a match, cupped my hands hunched over and tried to disappear into my greatcoat. Cigarette lit, I eyed from the coat, expelled a cloud of smoke into the crisp morning air. 'Burov was right, the ramifications of this are massive.' I took a drag on the cigarette, the cheap tobacco tasted so foul it probably contained traces of Laika's fur. 'I'm nervous about what lies ahead.'

'Don't stress, Viktor Pavlovich. Remember, Burov said the CID would take over after we've completed the preliminary work.'

We both fell silent, refocusing on the victim. He was a big specimen; over two metres tall and broad in the shoulders.

'It must have taken a great deal of strength, numbers, or both to hoist the fellow up and secure the noose.'

'Got any theories about who might've done it?' Yegor shuffled his feet in the snow. 'Could it be someone involved in that incident you mentioned? Twenty-four years ago, but you never know. What if it was a relative of the real killer from 1963? Continuing the racist legacy.'

'Can you stop rambling?' I crushed the cigarette under my boot. 'Give me a few minutes to examine the scene before we embark on any speculation.'

'Sorry,' said Yegor. 'Just trying to help.'

'No. I'm sorry. I shouldn't have snapped like that.'

'That's OK, Viktor Pavlovich. Understandable given the circumstances. Not every day you're confronted by something like this.'

'Thankfully.'

A few metres from the victim's feet a wooden stool lay on its side. Those poor feet. Bits of toe and ankle bone protruded from the ruptured skin like gristle in bacon.

'They gave him a serious beating.'

'Unbelievable.' Yegor sniffed. 'Sick bastards.'

'The killers must've overpowered him or threatened him with a weapon. Then stood him on the chair and pulled it away. Left him there until he choked to death. I wonder why they didn't take the stool with them?'

'Maybe he was dead when they slipped the noose around his neck and the stool's got nothing to do with it. Could have been lying there the whole time.'

'Perhaps. The perps might've killed him first. But it's a lot harder lifting a dead man than a live one. I suspect he was still breathing before they strung him up.'

'Why harder?'

'Oh, for God's sake! Are you really that stupid?'

'Everyone knows you did a special KGB course. Learned some tricks.'

'Like someone asleep, a cadaver weighs no more than a live person. Basic physics. When you pick up a conscious man his centre of gravity shifts, weight distribution changes, muscles tense. Inadvertently, he helps you pick him up.'

'I hadn't thought of that.'

'If I try to lift my seven-year-old daughter after she's nodded off, it's like she weighs more than a refrigerator.'

Yegor rubbed his jaw. 'Maybe the killers beat him as he hung there.'

'Pointless if his neck was snapped. Perhaps they got perverse pleasure out of it. Anything's possible.'

'Fuckers.'

'Now, let me examine the scene thoroughly. I'm not standing around in the cold doing nothing waiting for forensics.'

'Of course.' He made two exaggerated steps to the left and a be-my-guest gesture with his hand.

'Have a poke around the woods for clues.'

'Will do, Comrade Captain.' Yegor marched off towards a well-worn side track.

Dark clouds threw a shadow over Adekanye's body, strung up like a sack of chaff. His face was a mass of bloody flesh around eyeballs swollen to the size of small potatoes, his head twisted at an unnatural angle, no doubt due to snapped vertebrae. His tongue lolled from his mouth, fat and long, his hands tied together behind his back with old rope. A wound – red, ragged and raw – framed the area where his genitals had been hacked off. Jesus, what kind of person would do this to another human being? Behind the body, his clothes lay in a disorganised pile: winter boots, thermal underwear, blue-and-white beanie, woollen jumper, gloves. Dressed for the outdoors. Most likely he hadn't been kidnapped from an indoor location. Poor bastard, out and about, living his life, suspecting nothing. A ragged Christian cross was carved into his back; a vertical line from the base of his neck to just above the coccyx. The horizontal line spanned his shoulder blades and looked to be a centimetre or two deep.

'Yegor, come back.' He turned and trotted back, splashing mud as he ran. 'Look at the cross.' I pointed to the wound.

'Jesus Christ!'

'In his honour, do you think?'

'What?'

'Not what. Who. Jesus.'

'Sorry. Didn't get your meaning. I'm an atheist, like most right-thinking citizens. But this is outright blasphemy whatever your beliefs.' Yegor doubled over like he was having an attack of appendicitis, took a couple of deep breaths. 'I mean…hell. What a thing to do to a man. Disgusting. And cutting off his dick and balls. Holy shit.'

Bile rose in my throat. 'There's symbolism attached to this.' I covered my mouth with my hand.

Yegor regained an upright posture, brought his breathing under control. 'Perhaps the killers were fanatical ultra-orthodox types and the cross means his existence was an offence to God.'

'And castrating a man is not an offence to God?' I shook my head.

'Hard-core racists believe black people are subhuman. Killing this guy would be of no more consequence than swatting a fly.'

I took a step back and marvelled at the outrageousness of the scene. Mahogany-coloured blood caked on the chest, stomach and legs. Again, my attention was drawn to the raspberry jam patch where his penis and testicles were supposed to be. Under him, more blood splatter – patches directly underneath, droplets of various sizes in a circular pattern around him.

I pulled a notebook from my coat pocket, made some quick notes and started to sketch the scene. I'd drawn a couple of lines when the crime scene photographer, Sergey Morozov, appeared from nowhere. He jumped about like a nervous rabbit, looked for the best spots to snap off a few shots.

'Excuse me, Viktor Pavlovich,' he stuttered, spittle flying through yellow teeth. 'May I take a picture from the front, right about where you're standing?' How fucking blasé could the man get? Had he no feelings? It was like we were at a model train exhibition rather than a murder scene.

'Wait a minute. I'm not finished drawing yet.'

Morozov frowned. 'You don't need to do that. My photographs will be good enough for the CID's investigation.'

'That's a matter of opinion.' I kept my eyes on my notebook. The little diagram was my form of insurance. Accidents occasionally happened in the dark room with film spoiling. Or negatives went missing. 'Come back when I'm done, okay? Then you can take all the pictures you want.' Morozov slinked off with a grimace, puffed away on a rancid papirosa cigarette. His black Zenit-19 camera bounced on his hip.

'We'll have to get the body down soon, Comrade Captain.' Yegor pointed to a pair of crows hopping about in the treetops. Two others squabbled on the ground nearby. Their cawing grew louder. The pallid sun peaked through the blanket of clouds momentarily before disappearing again.

'They sound hungry.' I jammed the notebook back in my pocket. 'And there's the man's dignity to consider. It's indecent to leave him there. We have to get the body to the morgue as quickly as possible. That was also Burov's directive. District Medical Examiner Ivanov's on standby for delivery, apparently.'

'Yes, Comrade Captain.' Colour was returning to Yegor's face.

'Where the hell are forensics, dammit? If they don't show in the next 15 minutes, I'm making the call for a truck to come and fetch the corpse.'

'Pronin, you combed the scene here before we arrived. I'm guessing no note was left claiming responsibility for this atrocity?'

'Sadly no.'

Wind gusted through the birch trees and I grabbed my hat to prevent it flying off. 'Maybe the killers did leave a message somewhere and it blew away in the wind.'

'With all due respect, I don't think we'll find anything apart from the stool, his clothes, the rope and more filthy trash. If they'd left a note, it would've been nailed to the tree he's dangling from or pinned to his person.'

'He's naked. How could they pin it to him?'

'Viktor Pavlovich, for a seasoned detective you are quite naïve at times.' Pronin had been at the station nearly as long as the dearly departed Peskov and wasn't afraid to voice his opinion to a senior officer. An insightful man, I was never offended by his directness the way others might be. 'People capable of doing this aren't going to baulk at pushing a safety pin through a man's flesh.'

My skin crawled. 'You're smarter than you look, Tolya. I can't understand why you haven't moved up in the ranks.'

'Never been one to aspire to your level, Comrade Captain. All that stress gives you wrinkles.'

I rubbed my forehead, feeling the network of furrows.

'Reckon we'll catch the killers?' Yegor squatted on his haunches like a peasant in a potato patch, patted his gloved hands together.

'Doubtful. Colonel Burov pulled me in for a briefing before we left the station. Said don't waste time on the matter if the body turned out to be the missing Nigerian. Gather evidence to hand over to CID and leave it at that.'

'Why?'

'He's the one who got me up to speed about the 1963 incident. Like you, I hadn't been aware of it.'

'Not exactly the kind of thing the Party would want taught in history classes, hey?'

'Indeed.' A light sleet swept across my eyes. 'Burov reckons there'll be massive pressure from the top to keep this case quiet. My opinion – they've already got to him.'

'What makes you say that?'

'Because this is clearly murder. If there was doubt about the cause of death 24 years ago, there is none here.'

'Surely Burov's interested in finding the culprits.'

'A repeat of the '63 protests is unthinkable with Perestroika and Glasnost in full swing. It might sound ironic, but the ideal of "openness" would be threatened by a public display of anger.'

'That doesn't make sense.'

'Think about it. Any protest today would be reported not just overseas, but here. Widely. Editors of the new liberal magazines would get an erection just thinking about publishing a story on protesting students. TV station executives, too. On the other hand you've got the old-school hardliners in the CPSU who'd claim all this openness has led to chaos. They'd say "We're not ready for it. We must return to the old ways." Bad publicity would put the entire program of reforms under imminent threat.'

'You can't believe what you're saying. A man's been murdered and the killers must be brought to justice. Simple as that.'

'I agree. But Burov said unless there's immediate and compelling evidence pointing to actual suspects, there'll be a quick autopsy and the body will be shipped back to Africa. In any event, we're to keep our investigations low-key.'

'Bloody hell.'

'He said there might be alternative scenarios. Internal squabbling or a black market deal gone wrong.'

'They may be plausible explanations, sure. We have to check all possibilities, right?'

'Of course. I reckon the insistence on discretion is to avoid spooking the foreign students. Averting public disorder is a worthy aim, I agree with that. This may turn out to be an isolated event.'

'I should bloody well hope so.'

'Burov's a good man at heart. If he tells us not to look hard for a racist motive, it's got to be pressure from above.'

'How high do you think? Politburo?'

'Possibly. The Ministry of Foreign Affairs would definitely have a vested interested in stalling our efforts. Then again, the victim's a student, meaning the Ministry of Education would be shitting bricks about adverse publicity. There's a ton of prestige attached to educating kids from the Third World. It's a matter of honour for the USSR. Besmirching that's gonna cost the country dearly.'

The distinct sound of marching boots sounded from down the path. Two Militsiya privates I didn't recognise emerged into the clearing. Probably seconded from another station; all our scant resources were either here at the crime scene or preparing for Revolution Day deployments.

One of the newcomers produced a hacksaw from a vinyl duffel bag and gestured towards the victim. 'We've been ordered to take him to the morgue immediately.'

'Where the hell are the forensics team?'

'There's been a massive traffic accident outside Sheremetyevo Airport. Tourist bus cleaned up by a train at a level crossing. Mangled bodies everywhere.'

'Oh my God.' Reporting of a disaster like that would test the boundaries of Glasnost.

The man stared at me with pale grey eyes. 'Want us to cut him down now?'

'No, leave him there as a decoration for New Year's Eve. Of course cut him down, you idiot. Get him to the ground as gently as you can.'

One officer leap-frogged onto the shoulders of the other like a gymnast, and quickly sawed through the rope. The other chap stood flush against the cadaver, side on, wrapped a protective plastic sheet around the thighs, took a firm grip. Once the rope was cut, the man with the saw flung it to the ground. He snaked arms around the victim's neck to stop the body toppling forward. The first officer bent his knees, taking most of the weight of the body, while his companion dismounted from his mate's shoulders, never letting go of the neck. The two eased the dead man to the ground, stood to one side to let us take a closer look.

Morozov appeared again, snapped away from all angles. This time I said nothing until he'd used up the entire roll of film. He rewound the spool, popped it out and fished another from his pocket. I held up a hand. 'I think you've taken enough shots now.'

'But–'

'Enough, I said.' And, like mist, he was gone again.

On the ground the body seemed even bigger than when hung aloft. 'Bloating's a factor, but this is a larger-than-average human,' I said. 'At least two, maybe even three or more, were involved in his death. If it took these two strong lads to get him down, getting him up there would've been a struggle.'

'Sounds about right.' Yegor extracted a cigarette from his coat pocket. He offered me one and I took it. 'But who the hell did it?'

'That's what I'd like to find out.'

'So young.' Yegor shook his head as the shadows of the body and its two-man escort disappeared from view down the track . 'What was he doing in the USSR?'

'Medicine,' I said sharply. 'We know that.'

'Yeah, but was that all? We know foreign students are up to their eyeballs in illegal activities. Money changing, for example. Could be linked with that.'

'You're right. We have to rule things out before we rule things in. Let's talk to his classmates first. Break the bad news. And ask some questions.'

'What about interviewing babushka?'

'She can wait. Actually, I've got a better idea.' I waved to Rita Vasilyeva. She crabbed her way to me through slush and ice, probing sections of the path with the toes of her boots. 'Think you can get some useful information out of the old dear?'

'Doubt it, Comrade Captain. But I'll give it a try.'

'Take Pronin with you. Two is always better than one. Take notes and make sure to–'

'I can handle interviewing babushka,' she insisted gruffly. 'The old woman seemed to trust me when I took her home.'

'Sorry. We need more resources in this country to conduct investigations. The FBI would have put up crime scene tape all over the place. Squads of grunts in protective suits would be combing the area for clues, not to mention–'

'Yes,' said Yegor, a bit too curt for my liking. 'However we don't have their levels of violence.'

'Not yet.'

'We never will.'

'I hope you're right.' He wasn't. Violent crime was escalating in Moscow. Official statistics said otherwise, but government numbers were not to be trusted. In coming years the Militsiya would be found wanting when it came to fighting crime. Even now, our miserable rough-and-ready stockpile of equipment would make an American cop laugh his head off.

'Vasilyeva, you're a competent officer. Forgive me for questioning your abilities.'

She gave a nod and stared at the ground.

'Before you go, post Kozlov and Grigoriev by the tree. Morozov, too. He can be of use for a change.' There were thousands of trees all around, but everybody knew which one I meant.

Vasilyeva squared her shoulders. 'Yes, Comrade Captain.'

'Tell them to shoo away nosey parkers, forensics will be here shortly. I can't believe they weren't here before us. But I guess with that bad accident across town.'

'And it's extremely early, Comrade Captain,' Rita ventured. 'Extra manpower will free up soon.'

I nodded. 'Maybe. Anyway, all of us will chip in later to help Medical Examiner Ivanov conduct a methodical search. I suspect we'll have to wait until he's finished the autopsy.'

Disappointment clouded Pronin's face. 'That could take all day, Comrade Captain.'

'Do you have better things to do? More important than finding the sadistic pricks who tortured and murdered a man?'

'Well...'

'Didn't think so.'

'Stay here with the others until further notice.'

Pronin frowned.

'C'mon, Yegor. Let's get a move on. Do you know where the Gandhi University of Peace and Friendship is?'

'Of course. Not sure it's going to live up to its name, though.'

'Me either.'

Chapter 3

Yegor gave me a pained look as I clipped on my seatbelt. 'You've never trusted my driving, have you?'

'Just get us to the university in one piece.'

'Don't worry. I'll take it easy this time. Not so urgent now, is it? What with the body on its way to the morgue.'

As I shook my head he crunched the gearstick into first, floored the accelerator. I closed my eyes and did the standard mental count to ten.

'Surely Yevgeny Nikolaevich isn't being serious about not conducting a thorough investigation, Comrade Captain,' said Yegor when I'd reached six and stopped hyperventilating. 'Did he actually say, *Don't investigate this crime?*'

'No.' I opened my eyes and breathed a sigh of relief. Stopped at a set of traffic lights. 'I told you already. We're to hand the matter over to the CID.'

'I get that. But did he say anything else about why it's so sensitive?'

'He told me about a recent case involving foreign students. I think to reinforce his theory this murder's an inside job, as they say.'

'What case? I've heard nothing.'

I stifled a yawn. I was dog-tired. A tattoo pulsed incessantly inside my brain, the effects of the bottle of cheap vodka I polished off last night after a heated but ultimately pointless argument with my ex-wife about our daughter's education. We shouted obscenities at each other over the phone and my voice was hoarse by the end of it. At no stage could I recall topping up my glass, but by midnight the bottle was empty and so was my heart.

This horror case wasn't going to help me turn to clean living and sobriety. Handing it to another agency was best for all concerned. 'Burov said two Africans were beaten up a fortnight ago. Way off our patch. Zelenograd District.'

'That's 50 kilometres away. The point?' Yegor absentmindedly caressed the gear stick.

'Turned out to be a disagreement over illegal business. One faction cheating another. The guilty parties were caught, they confessed. All expatriated to Uganda on the next available flight. No Russians involved.'

'And Burov thinks this might be a similar case of payback?'

'Yes. Or it's a coincidence.'

Yegor frowned and swerved to avoid one of the millions of potholes dotting the city. 'I'm inclined to agree. In-house stuff.'

'What about the cross carved on the victim's back?' The genital mutilations? Adekanye's own people wouldn't do that.'

Yegor changed gear. 'If he double-crossed someone, pardon the expression, why not? Maybe it's not his own people, but another faction involved in black marketeering?'

'Again I have to ask, why the cross and the mutilations?'

'I can think of two reasons. One, to throw us off the scent. Make it look like a racist crime when it isn't.'

'Makes sense. A red herring. The second reason?'

'Many nationalities attend the Gandhi University. It could just as easily be Vietnamese or Venezuelans pissed off over a business deal gone wrong.'

'There're Russians studying there, too, don't forget. Meaning, again, a possible racist motive with domestic roots.'

'True.' Yegor fell into deep thought. Either that or he was finally concentrating on driving properly.

An endless line of light-grey panelled apartment buildings abutted the road, hulking sentinels dominating a slightly greyer sky. The dreary cityscape was brightened by red banners festooned for the Revolution Day celebrations, just two days away. I ran things over in my mind. The rattling Lada struck a pothole, momentarily putting a couple of centimetres of air between our backsides and our seats.

'Sorry, Viktor Pavlovich. Couldn't avoid them.'

'Be careful.' I tightened my seatbelt a fraction. 'If this thing breaks down, Burov will dock your wages to pay for the repairs.' A thought struck me. A revelation. I thumped a fist into my palm. 'Wait a minute. The Latin Americans are Catholics, right?'

'Mostly, I'd say.' Yegor half turned his head towards me, then snapped eyes forwards as a horn blared. 'Apart from the Cubans. And atheists from other Central American countries who we're trying to turn into card-carrying communists.'

'Wouldn't they be the contingent most likely to send a message via a symbolic crucifix?'

Yegor shrugged. 'Sounds like a logical connection. But, like I said, it could be someone trying to send us down the wrong path. Make us focus on Latinos instead of the real culprits.'

Thanks for shooting big fat holes in that theory. Then he made it worse. 'I'm not confident we'll ever find who's responsible for this, you know.'

'Me neither,' I sighed. Yegor was the perfect sounding board, unlike the arse-kissing yes-men I'd previously worked with, and I knew which I preferred. Straight shooters who question everything. 'At least let's go through the motions. We might get lucky.'

'Yeah. And there might be meat in the shops tomorrow.'

We both laughed. The only meat in town was at the outdoor bazaars. Carcasses of unidentifiable beasts heavy on bone and light on flesh. Brutally butchered and wrapped in yesterday's edition of Pravda by swarthy gents from the Caucasus region. Even that miserable fare was unaffordable on our wages.

A military lorry zoomed past in the opposite lane, sent a spray of dirty water all over the windscreen. 'You fucking goat's arsehole!' Yegor shook a fist at the driver. 'Punks,' he said. 'Or some other kind of social degenerate.'

'Actually, I think they're soldiers.'

'I mean the possible culprits.' He flicked the wipers to clear the mess. Half of it clung stubbornly to the glass. Yegor pushed a button to squirt clean water onto the windshield, only to be met with a prolonged, forlorn whine from under the hood. And no water. 'I'd bet on it being skinheads.'

'They're not really a threat, are they? As a movement, I don't give them a long life. I've only seen one or two. Late at night on the Metro. Arrogant little shits. But they're no danger to anyone. Like the saying goes, the breast milk hasn't dried on their lips yet.'

'Don't be fooled, Viktor Pavlovich. When they get together in packs, they're damned dangerous.'

'Come off it.'

'It's true. My Georgian friend, Irakli, you've met Irakli, right?' The tall fella, hairy as a bear and just as fat. The one with the gorgeous brown-eyed sister you can't look at without Irakli pulling out a *kinzhal* and threatening to slice your ears off. You met him last winter when we were investigating those Leningrad guys selling fake lottery tickets, remember? When the weather was worse than Siberia.'

'Yes, yes, I remember Irakli. He doesn't ramble on as much as some people I know. Get on with it, we haven't got all day. The killers will be eligible for the old age pension before you finish your story.'

'Well, you may or may not remember, but he sells fruit at the local markets. Pomegranates, oranges, grapes...'

'And?' My headache was getting worse.

'They've been getting grief from a skinhead gang in that area. Turning over fruit stands, throwing bottles at stall holders, frightening off customers. There's a racial element for sure. Leaflets of Nazi propaganda strewn all over the market for decent citizens to read. Irakli pulled down posters saying *Black bastards fuck off back to the Caucasus*. People who do that need to be sent to the Gulag for re-education.'

'You're joking, aren't you? Nothing scares those Georgian guys. They rule the roost at all the markets in Moscow.' The passenger window fogged up. I rubbed it with my cuff, watched a packed tram disgorge passengers and swallow up new ones. 'Those hooligans are either brave or stupid. If the Georgians catch them, they'll end up in the bottom of the Moscow River.'

'That's my point exactly, Viktor Pavlovich. Everyone's scared of the

Georgian mafia. Even us!' He smacked both palms on the dashboard and gripped the edge of it, which left me wondering how he was steering the car. 'So, yes, a gang of spindly skinheads carrying out hit-and-run operations against a feared section of society is cause for concern.'

I scratched my cheek. Feeling the scraping sensation on my skin reminded me of the deficit of razors in the stores. Along with bread, vegetables, eggs, milk, everything else.

'When you put it like that...'

'What's worse, you can't spot 'em so easily in winter with hats covering their shaved heads.' Yegor chuckled. 'Anyway, they're a growing problem all over Moscow.' He stopped for a red light. 'Immoral foreign influences are filtering through to our kids,' he said as the light turned green. Yegor launched into his pet propaganda piece about disaffected youth. His face was smooth as a baby's backside even though he was near 30. Unlikely the man picked up a razor to shave more than once a week. 'But as to the root causes of this,' he glanced at me until an irritated driver leaned on his car horn. 'I blame the anti-social messages in modern music, books. Our teenagers are emulating Western degenerates. Home-grown bands like DDT are – if you don't mind the pun – poisoning the minds of our youth. Telling them to rebel against authority, the Party. And it's only going to get worse with this Gorbachev fool running the country.' Yegor wound down the window and spat. 'Perestroika, my arse!'

'There's another group to consider,' I said.

Yegor nodded quickly. 'You mean the Lyubers?'

'Exactly.' Lyubers were disillusioned young men from the town of Lyubertsy, about 25 clicks or so from Red Square as the crow flies. Obsessed with pumping iron, practising martial arts, staying fit, living a healthy lifestyle. They held the abuse of vodka and tobacco in contempt. All well and good, even admirable, if you don't throw a whacko ultra-patriotic ideology into the mix. 'Their tentacles are starting to stretch far beyond home base.'

'Didn't you travel there recently?' Yegor rubbed a smudge of condensation from the inside of the windscreen.

The memory of the excursion made my flesh crawl. 'Yes.'

'What for? Isn't there enough to do around here?'

'Special assignment. You know I used to work at a station in Lyubertsy, right?'

'Yeah, you've mentioned it once or twice.'

'Worst three years of my life.' I ignored his sarcasm. 'I couldn't wait to get out of the place.'

'I've heard it's a shit hole.'

'You're not the only one. Anyway, I went there with some officers from the Yakimanka station. A gang of Lyubers had taken a late train to central Moscow for a bit of fun. In other words, serious assault and destruction of property. The plan was for us to grill the hooligans, make them confess.'

'Did they?'

'You're joking.'

'What did they do that was so bad?'

'One of them has a second cousin who runs a *stolovaya* stand-up café off the Garden Ring road. A Jewish family set up one of those new co-op style restaurants next door to it. The guy related to the Lyuber wasn't happy about the competition. You can guess the rest. Like Kristallnacht. Smashed the place to bits.'

'Did you arrest the scum?'

'Easier said than done. They denied all involvement. When we called in a witness who heard them conspiring to commit the act, he retracted his original statement. Too scared to speak up.'

'A wasted trip, huh?'

I mulled this over for a second. 'Perhaps not. I know where the main gang hangs out these days. It'll save time if the investigation into Adekanye's murder leads us in that direction. And if we can get some proof.'

'What do you mean *we*? You said the CID's taking over the case.'

'Something tells me they won't investigate it properly and the killers won't be brought to justice.' My initial inclination was to hand the investigation over and leave it at that. Now, I sensed a massive cover-up was on the cards. One day I'd do my own digging around and see where it led.

We turned the last corner before the Gandhi University, foot and road traffic appreciably heavier now with morning peak hour approaching.

'I heard something interesting the other day, again from my friend Irakli at the markets.' I felt my brain throb as Yegor got on a roll again. 'He reckons the Lyubers have been making their presence felt around our patch, just like the skinheads.'

'Just what we need. Two factions of morons hell bent on upsetting the apple cart.'

Yegor shrugged. 'Irakli sells oranges, not apples.' He smiled, pleased with his little joke. 'Anyway, he's seen a few of these meatheads strutting about the market like peacocks, giving the stallholders filthy looks. It was only in February they beat up those dissidents.'

Innocent Jewish refuseniks bashed senseless while the authorities – us – stood by and let it happen. Things often happen in this country that make me ashamed of the uniform I wear, the authority I represent. My own family has dirty secrets buried deeper than the permafrost. I will never shake the belief my own mother was a victim of repression. The story she died giving birth to me is bullshit. She wasn't "working class" by strict Bolshevik definitions. Her blood was tainted by ancestors of the merchant class. Papa's eyes glaze over when I ask about how Mamma really died. He fobs me off with stories of her poor health, weak lungs. I know he's lying. Too proud to admit his cherished system was evil at its core, willing to sacrifice those who didn't fit the mould perfectly. Unable to look me squarely in the eye and admit the truth. One day, though, I'll find it.

'I have a horrible feeling there's only going to be more of these incidents with the new freedoms.' Yegor shook his head.

'Probably. But having the freedoms is better than not having them. We'll just have to deal with the side effects when they arise.' I stared out the car window at a gang of generic workers carrying crimson Revolution Day banners on their shoulders. The irony, celebrating the victory of socialism while the system barely functions.

'The Lyubers must be crushed.' Yegor interrupted my musing. 'They're worse than the skinheads because they're better organized. The skinheads are opportunistic anarchists without a plan. The Lyubers have purpose.'

Yegor kept talking, but his voice was now merely a humming sound. I needed this day to end. I knew what motivated the Lyubers. Their hatred of everything different, foreign. African students, especially males walking around with attractive Russian girls dangling off their arms, would make a magnetic target for their hatred. Yegor's droning finally pushed me too far. 'Stop your babbling for a minute, will you? And wind the damned window up, it's freezing.'

'Sorry, sir. Don't worry, you'll be out in the cold again in a second. We're here'. He turned the steering wheel to the left and, counter to form, sedately guided the Lada into a vacant car parking spot.

Chapter 4

Once you're out of the cold in Moscow you can sometimes sweat like it's the middle of summer. Central heating in most buildings is a hit and miss affair: it's either on the blink or cranked up to max and there's nothing you can do about it. The rector's office fell into the latter category. He'd be sweating out of worry once we brought him up to speed on his missing student. An angry campus, a repeat of 1963, was something he'd surely be anxious to avoid.

After introducing myself and Yegor, I made a cursory assessment of the rector. Comrade Vadim Fedorovich Kuznetsov, scholar and academic, was a friendly looking soul. Erudite, broad forehead and white strands of hair neatly arranged to optimise coverage of his expansive scalp. Scholarly black-rimmed glasses with thick lenses.

'Good morning, gentlemen. I'm not sure I'm going to enjoy this little chat.' Kuznetsov rose from his seat, wedged tight behind his huge office desk, extended his hand to me, then to Yegor. Several tomes he'd written on economics sat on the desk. One of them looked like just the thing to cure a bout of insomnia. *The Socialist Transformation of Economy: Past and Present (A Marxist Perspective).* How predictably tame and boring. A party apparatchik of the highest order. He motioned for us to sit opposite him in a pair of leather armchairs.

'Neither are we,' I said flatly. 'It's my duty to inform you your missing student has been found.'

'Where?'

'Not far from this very building.'

'Passed out drunk, was he? The man has a reputation for being a party animal, as the young ones put it these days. A penchant for our beautiful Soviet women, too, so they say. Is he in the lockup waiting for someone from his country's embassy to come bail him out?'

I fixed my gaze at the portrait behind Kuznetsov's right shoulder. The leader of the Proletariat and the great Soviet Bolshevik Revolution, Vladimir Ilyich Lenin, watched over us. The man with the goatee and bulbous brow was a ubiquitous presence in government offices. And in the private homes of died-in-the-wool communists. The revered leader's expression remained impassive at all times, a calming influence on the people he'd led out of the clutches of capitalist tyranny and enslavement into the light of glorious socialism.

'I'm afraid the news isn't as good as that.'

'Oh?'

I decided being direct would be the best policy with an intellectual type like Kuznetsov. 'The man is dead.'

'Excuse me?'

'I said the man is dead.'

The rector's face turned ashen, like he'd seen a ghost. He rubbed his face with a chequered handkerchief. A jug of cloudy Moscow tap water stood on the desk. I poured Kuznetsov a full glass and handed it to him. He took it in shaky hands and downed half the contents, rubbed his lips with the same handkerchief he'd used to wipe the sweat off his face.

'Are you OK, comrade?' asked Yegor. 'Do I need to call a doctor? A nurse?'

The man looked up, eyes suddenly weary. 'No. I'm fine. It'll just take a moment or two to sink in.'

'Of course,' I said. 'Quite a shock.'

Kuznetsov coughed into a trembling fist. 'You can say that again. The African Student Union has been at my door constantly since the chap went missing at the start of October. This could send them over the edge. Just like...' He grabbed the glass of water, drained what was left.

'Just like in 1963?' I said.

He gave a slight nod. 'Exactly. Not sure why I couldn't bring myself to say it. I wasn't rector at the time. But still…The incident occurred before my time. I took charge here in 1970.'

'Nothing like this has happened while you've been rector?'

'There have been plenty of dramas, of course. When you're dealing with students and their raging hormones and bad attitudes, it can't be avoided. How long have you got?' He laughed uneasily.

Yegor folded arms across his chest. 'If you have information you think can help us solve the mystery, then we've got all day.' He turned his head to look at me, raised his eyebrows, seeking my approval of his boldness.

'My colleague is correct, Comrade Kuznetsov.' I took out my notebook and pencil. 'Feel free to divulge all you know. Even the most inconsequential detail can turn out to be vital.'

'Forgive me for saying, but you've told me nothing of the circumstances surrounding Mr…. oh dear. What was it again?' He clicked his fingers. 'I've forgotten his name.'

'Mr Adekanye.' I prompted. 'Aaron Adekanye.'

'Yes, of course. The medical student from Nigeria.' So, the rector wasn't completely ignorant of the details. Instinct told me he wasn't being entirely candid either. A missing student with his classmates *constantly at his door*, plus him remembering what the man studied and when he disappeared, meant Kuznetsov must've been keeping a closer watch on developments than he pretended. Not remembering the name was bullshit. 'And when you say *solve the mystery*, well, that's setting alarm bells off in my head right away.'

'He was murdered,' I said.

'My God! How? Where?' He gripped the edge of the desk with the smooth fingers of a lifetime office worker, pushed back. The chair scraped loud enough to set my teeth on edge. Yegor inhaled sharply as Kuznetsov scrabbled for the jug. The rector splashed more water across his blotting pad than he poured into his glass, which he upturned and emptied like he was drinking a shot of vodka at a wedding party. His chest heaved as he fought for breath. Eyes wide as bread plates, he grabbed at the lapels of his jacket, tugged on the knot of his tie. Surely not a heart attack. That would make a shitty day even worse. But I sensed it was all so much acting.

'Comrade Kuznetsov,' I said. 'Calm down, for heaven's sake. I'm going to call an ambulance.' I reached across to his telephone, lifted the receiver and started dialling.

A hand darted across the desk, grabbed mine. 'Please, no need for that. Just give me a minute.' I placed the phone back in the cradle and leaned back. Kuznetsov pulled a small bottle from a drawer, tossed a little white pill into his mouth, washed it down with another sip of water. He'd probably wanted me to think it was heart or blood-pressure pills. I saw the label. Plain old aspirin.

'One minute. Then I'd kindly request you start telling us all you know.'

He gave an apologetic nod. 'Of course.'

I watched the clock. Its loud insistent ticking reminded me of my limited allotted time on Earth. Time I'd invariably spend entirely inside the borders of the Motherland. Dealing with ideological zombies like Kuznetsov. Even Yegor to an extent. I'd been reading some of the liberal articles in the emergent press, so I know there are people in the country capable of independent political thought. Everyone I knew was so old-school. I needed to find friends outside the job. Soon.

'Right. I think I'm feeling better now.' The rector's deep voice snapped me out of my reveries. 'Shall we proceed?'

Yegor gave a little start in his seat. He'd almost drifted off waiting for the interview to recommence. 'Yes, let's do that,' I said.

'First, can you tell me the circumstances of the young man's demise?'

I thought for a moment. Should I inform Kuznetsov or not? I decided against it. 'I've not received clearance from my boss to divulge that information,' I said. 'Right now we're gathering as much background material as we can that might be germane to the case.' Out of the corner of my eye I saw Yegor scrunch up his face. I wondered if he knew what germane meant. I turned back to Kuznetsov, whose expression showed a mixture of relief at not having to hear the details, and disappointment, for the same reason. 'So, please Comrade Kuznetsov, tell us what you know about Aaron. Nothing is irrelevant at this stage.'

'Not sure how much I can tell you, really. So hard to know what to include, what to leave out. Some things will need to be checked. Documents, records and the like.' My word, he knew how to fluff about. This was going to take some work.

'Let's start with the victim's personal life. What –'

'Sorry.' Kuznetsov interrupted. 'Before we continue, I'd like to invite my assistant, Galina Sokolova, to observe this interview. Do you mind?'

Yegor and I exchanged a questioning look. We both shrugged simultaneously as if it was a choreographed move. 'No objection from me.' I turned back to Kuznetsov. 'You aren't suspected of anything.'

'I understand,' he said. 'I'd just prefer someone to be a witness. Make sure I don't get myself into trouble.' Another nervous laugh.

'Fair enough.' I nodded.

With the fine-featured Ms Sokolova – armed with a bulging manila folder – by his side, Kuznetsov appeared more relaxed. The anxiety lifted from his eyes. Colour returned to his cheeks. Looked like we were just about ready to proceed. To be honest, I wasn't sure how best to approach the matter. As my father always says, though, life has no rulebook. I decided to wing it. I passed my notebook and pen to Yegor so I could concentrate on Kuznetsov's responses to my questions.

'The victim. What can you tell me about him? Apart from the fact he was a medical student from Nigeria.'

'Not much, really.'

His first mistake. 'I find that hard to believe.' I narrowed my eyes. 'You already stated he was a party animal and he liked Russian women. That's pretty specific, if you ask me. I contest you knew more about him than you care to admit.'

I expected the faux heart attack again. But no, he remained calm.

'That's not a question, it's harassment.' He picked up the telephone. 'I'm going to call your superior. What's the number?'

'There's no need for that,' said Yegor. *Good boy, be the good cop.* 'I'm sure Captain Voloshin didn't mean to imply, you know, that you're hiding something. It's been a distressing day for us, seeing the body in the state it was in. Simply horrible. The way they'd–'

'That's enough, Comrade Lieutenant,' I said. 'No need to get into the nitty gritty. But yes. My colleague is right. We've had a thoroughly awful morning.' Time to feed him a teaspoonful of information. 'I can tell you this: your student was killed in a brutal way, a way no human being deserves.'

Kuznetsov squinted, trying to process, imagine the scene I was only prepared to describe in the most general terms. Perhaps I should give it to him with both barrels, as the Americans say. Stir him up, see what apples of truth fall. Ms Sokolova was shaking slightly. No need for her to hear it, poor thing. On second thoughts, neither should the rector. Keeping him in the dark might prove more prudent. 'Please rethink your last statement. You know more about the victim than you're admitting. Why is that?'

'Ah...'

'Have you been pressured by a higher authority to deflect inquiries about the missing student?'

He held up a finger. 'You said he was dead. Now you say missing. I'm confused. What do you mean?' Galina also looked genuinely puzzled. 'And no! I have not been pressured, as you put it. There have been phone calls and letters from his family via the Nigerian embassy, questions from his fellow students, but no influence from anywhere about what I should say or do or how I should act. The country is different now.' He took another drink of water. 'Why on Earth would you even suggest such a thing?'

'Just a feeling.' I imagined the word LIAR in bright green neon hovering above the man's head.

'My personal view, Comrade Captain, was the man would turn up sooner or later, ready to resume his studies. Happens sometimes. I'll grant you, it's usually only after a day or two's absence. But still, I was sure...'

I wanted to press him further about his previous statements about Mr Adekanye's character. His penchant for partying and fancying Russian women. I tapped my knuckle on the edge of the desk. 'Comrade...'

A firm knock rattled the door in its hinges.

Kuznetsov glanced at his assistant. 'See who that is, will you? Tell them to go away.'

I could hear a low hubbub coming from the corridor. Almost menacing in its low timbre, a rumble of voices. Galina opened the door a fraction and was hurled backwards as three black men and one woman burst into the room.

Kuznetsov was on his feet in a flash, face flushed pink. 'What's the meaning of this intrusion? Get out at once. You have no right to barge into my office without an invitation.' His bulging eyes appealed to me and Yegor. 'Arrest these people.'

Yegor and I had leapt up, too. Clearly sensing trouble, my partner spread his arms wide. The largest man of the trio shouted words in English – at least I thought it was English. His companions shook fists, angry grimaces narrowed their eyes. Our Militsiya uniforms had no effect on their behaviour, which gave me great cause for concern. They were desperate and unafraid of authority. Lieutenant Adamovsky and I waved our arms and legs about like basketballers on defence, to protect Kuznetsov and Galina. I barked at Yegor: 'You speak some English, don't you? Find out what these people want before they tear the place apart.'

'All I can remember from school is how to count to ten and say good morning.' His eyes darted about. 'Not sure that's going to do much good in this situation.'

The woman in the group pushed her way to the front of the men, quelled the ruckus with some decisive hand movements and short, sharp words. I noticed how her large, round eyes sparkled, how her skin bore an even, satiny sheen. She struck me as rather beautiful. I had to ask myself: Why do their men chase white women when their own were just as attractive? The cynical and perhaps true answer to that was that our women are instigating most of these relationships. Less for love than simply looking to marry a foreigner. Any foreigner. To escape the Soviet Union. Didn't even matter if it was to the middle of Africa. A place where the culture shock for a Russian woman would be as great as it was for Africans coming to stay in our freezing land. I'd heard no stories of black women seeking out white Russian men, or the other way around. The entire phenomenon was in need of sociological study.

I quickly assessed the woman and her escorts. She wore a bright yellow head wrap I guessed was part of her national costume, a stylish woollen coat and shiny red leather boots. Fingers were adorned with a variety of bejewelled rings. Such an ensemble must have cost a packet. The logical question arose: how could a state-sponsored student from the Third World afford clothes like that? Her male colleagues weren't far behind her in the fashion stakes: leather jackets, tailored jeans and sneakers our own petty crooks would drool over. Perhaps even kill for.

The woman turned to her companions, put a finger to her lips. The men obediently backed down. I expelled a sigh of relief and Yegor's face brightened. The intruders weren't going to attack us after all. Student riot averted. I was packing a standard issue Makarov pistol, but I hadn't fired it in the field in years. I didn't want today to be the day.

'Don't worry, officers. I speak Russian.' Her accent was so faint as to be almost non-existent. I doubt I was able to hide my shock. Then again, it was only six words. Not much to gauge a person's fluency. 'You are surprised, yes? Don't be. The teachers here are excellent. It's why we Africans are so eager to secure a place at a Russian university.' She paused. Thrust out a proud, strong jaw. 'Until now. We're fed up being kept in the dark about what's happening. Especially when it comes to our personal safety. We know many of you do not welcome us.' She fired a glare at the rector, whose mouth morphed into a rictus of shock and indignation.

This time I caught it. The common problem foreigners have pronouncing Russian's soft "L". Apart from that, the woman spoke almost like a native Muscovite. 'Were you born in Russia?' Curiosity about her remarkable language skills put all other questions on the backburner.

'No, I was not. I have an affinity for languages. I also speak adequate French and passable Italian.' Her expression hardened. 'But we aren't here to talk about that.'

I nodded. 'Yes, I know. But yelling and screaming is not appropriate behaviour.'

'Fuck your mother!' snapped one of the men. The richness of profanity in our language is a matter of pride for us Russians. To hear it from an outsider was too much.

I jabbed an index finger at him, then at the other two men, and finally their charismatic female leader. 'I will have you all arrested for using foul language in a public place. It's still on the books, you know, and I won't hesitate to charge each of you. Now, can we please sit down and discuss things calmly?'

'Comrade Captain,' said Yegor. 'I think that's going to be problematic. Not enough chairs.'

'We stand,' said the third man. He folded thick arms across his chest, gave me a look that dared me to suggest otherwise. 'We also speaking well Russian.' He pointed at the woman, a look of deep respect etched into his pockmarked face. 'But she talk on our behalf. Literature students like her taking more interest in Russian than we.'

'OK.' I addressed the woman. 'Please tell me what it is you want, and I'll see what I can do. Please state your name.'

She bowed slightly. 'Flora Madenge.' She introduced the men as Samuel, Daniel and Justin. Nevertheless, I asked to see ID. I examined their student cards with the acute interest of a border control officer. I handed them to Yegor and ordered him to jot down all details – one never knew what information might prove decisive in solving a case. The men gave empty smiles of acknowledgement as they heard their names read out aloud by Yegor. 'These men are second-year medical students and close friends of Aaron.' Flora continued. 'We believe you are here about him. Is that true?'

For a moment I doubted myself. I glanced at Yegor, who gave a tiny tilt of the head in encouragement. *Tell them, boss.* 'Yes, we're here regarding the man you named.'

'What's happened to him? Is he alive? Where is here?'

'Yes!' said the middle-sized man, Samuel. 'Where is he? Fuck your mother!'

'Hey!' Yegor slapped the notebook on Kuznetsov's desk. 'Have you forgotten the Captain's warning to you about swearing? I won't hesitate to arrest the lot of you. You can cool off overnight in a cell with some local drunks.'

The biggest man, Daniel, held out both hands, palms up. 'I am sorry for my friend's behaviour. Please, tell us what has happened.'

Before answering I eyeballed the rector and Galina. Both sat meekly, hands in laps, observing the spectacle unfold. Kuznetsov's wide-eyed stare told me he wasn't used to arrogant students making demands, virtually mocking the institution that was giving them a first-class education. He'd rarely get his hands dirty dealing with the minutiae of student life on the sprawling campus.

'What I'm about to tell you will come as a shock.' They were gearing up for the worst possible news. The men clenched and unclenched their fists, jaws twitched. Flora stood up and down on the tips of her toes. Itching for a fight, the lot of them. I pinched my nose hard, trying to find the words, to be the diplomat. I had to gain their trust. 'Before I do, I need an assurance from you. Otherwise I won't be able to help you to help us get to the truth.' I weighed up Burov's and Yegor's theory that the killing may have been an inside job. If they were right, telling the Africans everything might be a mistake. *Take the middle road, Viktor.* More of father's words of wisdom.

'Yes.' The smallest man, Justin, spoke for the first time. 'What you want from us?' His Russian wasn't great. Not terrible either. Good enough for communicating with cops on less than esoteric subjects.

I fixed my gaze squarely on Justin. He had a more serious mien than his two male buddies; temperamentally I pegged him similar to Flora. I sensed she'd be the most valuable asset, and not only because of her language skills. She had a leadership quality I'd rarely seen in a woman before. My next words were addressed to her. 'No panic. You must remain calm. From the hysterical behaviour I've seen so far, I'm not sure you can give me that assurance.'

I paused to let the message sink in.

'All right,' said Flora. 'But remember, we Nigerians are an emotional people. Our culture, music, is all about expression. When we are sad, we cry. When we are happy, we laugh and sing. When we are angry...'

'You must not be angry. Anger can only lead to more anger and...' I almost said violence. 'Fear.'

'We not guarantee anything,' said Daniel, meeting my gaze manfully.

'Then we are done. Please leave and allow us continue the interview with Comrade Kuznetsov.'

'Don't listen to him,' piped up Flora. 'He will toe the line and do as I say. My father is an important man in Nigeria. A high-ranking official in the government.' She turned to Daniel, spat something in English. I managed to make out the words *go home*, perhaps warning them about possible deportation. He shrugged, but the sour, twisted mouth remained.

'Aaron was murdered,' I said bluntly. 'Sometime last night. Until you answer our questions – designed solely to find who killed your colleague – I can't go into any more detail.'

The men stood frozen to the spot, as if they expected this news but hoped to hear something else. No angry outbursts, just glares, bubbling hatred for the white people in the room, as if we symbolised a racist country.

'Why not?' asked Flora, firm but unflustered. She seemed to be fighting some incredible urge to express her resentment and grief. 'Someone needs to identify the body.'

'He had his passport on him,' said Yegor quickly. 'We compared the photo and other details in the document with the man himself. There's no doubt, I'm afraid. It was Aaron Adekanye.'

Instead of more tantrums, the mini delegation responded by nodding solemnly. Perhaps the calm before the storm. I glanced quickly at Kuznetsov. His eyes flitted about as he tried to avoid looking at me. Or anyone. God only knew what was going on in his head. Right now I wanted to get as many answers as I could from the students, see if their information could lead us to the killers.

'I demand to see him.' Flora set her hands firmly on her hips, elbows at right angles. She put me in mind of a kettle about to hit boiling point.

'Did you have a personal relationship with him?'

'What kind of impertinent question is that?'

'Well, did you?'

'Yes.' She hesitated for a split second. 'He was my...lover.'

The three African men's eyebrows arched at once. Another Russian word they understood. *Lover.*

'I don't believe you,' I said with a rapid shake of the head. 'You should have got your story straight with your friends here. The looks on their faces tell me you're lying.'

She delivered me a stare of absolute loathing. It's what people do when caught out lying. She doubled down. 'Aaron and I were going to get engaged. All the...' she couldn't finish the sentence, tears poured down her cheeks. Her breathing grew ragged, a hand shot up to cover her eyes.

I reached out, gently touched Flora's upper arm. 'There, there.' Stupid words of comfort, but nothing else came to mind. Instead of flinching, telling me to piss off, she snuggled in. I instinctively put an arm around her. Completely inappropriate, an assessment backed up by Yegor's rapid one-two head shake. I disentangled myself from her, took a step back. A good metre or so. 'Please, don't persist in telling lies, Flora. It won't do any good, and it won't bring back Aaron.'

She looked up at me with tear-stained eyes. 'I'm sorry. I...we're all scared. There's been some terrifying incidents around the city lately. Bashings, harassment on the street. We're too frightened to go out alone. Always in groups. Now this! What are we meant to do?'

'I suggest that we retire to somewhere quiet where we can discuss the matter further. In confidence. You will tell me everything you know about Aaron. Who he associated with on campus, what he did in his spare time, his hobbies, any suspect activities.'

'Suspect activities? For God's sake, the man is dead, and you want to turn this into some kind of political investigation?'

I felt my nostrils flare. Flora wasn't going to be easy to handle. 'Of course not. I'm only concerned about one thing. Finding the culprit.'

'Fine,' she relented. 'We can go to my dorm room.'

'What about your roommates?'

She shook her head. 'I have a room to myself.' Her father *did* have influence. Most of the kids here would be sharing five to a room, two if they were lucky. In a land where privilege was a dirty word, having a place to yourself in a dormitory was exactly that.

I ushered the students into the corridor, turned to have one last word with the rector. I noticed him slowly close his eyes, take a deep breath. 'We may come back to ask you more questions.'

He nodded.

My gaze shifted to Galina. She held her hands in her lap, fingers rolling over each other. 'We might interview you, too. Separately.' She winced. Her position close to Kuznetsov gave her the perfect opportunity to eavesdrop, pick up signals. She might have a better handle on what the students are up to than the rector.

My entourage and I headed for the exit under the watchful eyes of a handful of students and teachers milling about in the foyer. Our Militsiya uniforms stood out like sore thumbs. I gave silent thanks for the early hour.

'How far away is your room?'

'Not far. On the other side of The Cross.'

'The what?'

'The Cross. It's the nickname for the big open space in the middle of the buildings.'

The irony of that circumstance felt like someone had slammed me in the guts with a sledgehammer.

Chapter 5

Compared to my old college accommodation at the Militsiya academy, Flora was living in five-star luxury. Not quite, but as the Russian saying goes, you learn things by comparison. In other words, she was living like a princess in high-grade shit.

The floor wasn't the usual ubiquitous two-toned, poorly laid wooden parquetry. She had carpet. A massive patterned Central Asian rug, tucked under her bed, wardrobe, desk and sofa. It didn't look like a rug at all, but wall-to-wall carpet. Elaborate, intricate patterns. It would have a price tag equivalent to a couple of months of my wages. All the mod cons were on display: a mini refrigerator, small television, even a telephone.

Then there was the sheer size of her digs. On par with Kuznetsov's office. On one wall hung a kind of triptych of portraits. A trio of revolutionaries: V.I. Lenin, Ho Chi Minh, Che Guevara. The hypocrisy of her comfort contrasted starkly with the modest garb on the heroes of the proletariat.

'You think I'm a spoiled brat.' Flora half closed one eye, the way people do when they throw out a challenging statement.

'It's irrelevant what I think. What matters is finding out who killed Aaron.' I said slowly and clearly, refraining from employing even the mildest slang. I wanted Flora's compatriots to understand as much as possible without having to rely on her interpretation.

The men were squeezed up on the couch. Yegor and I stood by the window, our hostess sat on the edge of her bed. Outside, oblique snow flurries under iron-grey clouds. Inside, glowing tungsten.

Flora stood, walked to a fancy glass display cabinet. On top of it stood a shiny silver samovar. 'Tea anyone?'

I accepted. Yegor nodded enthusiastically. The other men declined, preferring to puff away on cigarettes. With so much nicotine-laden gas floating around, I felt no need to light up myself. Yegor reached into his pocket to fetch a smoke and joined in polluting the atmosphere. A particularly stinky Bulgarian brand. The wall-mounted radiators were chucking out plenty of heat; enough to allow some external air inside. I turned the handle of the window up and pulled, opening it a few centimetres in vertical mode. Streams of smoke got sucked out of the room into the cold morning air. Gripping a steaming glass of black tea inside an ornate filigreed holder, I continued the questions.

'Are you going to admit Aaron was *not* your boyfriend?'

Flora looked wistfully out the window. I followed her gaze to see a crane on the horizon sweeping back and forth. Construction never ended in this city. Quality was poor, but quantity, you got it by the bucketload. More characterless panel boxes for the proletarian hamsters to live in.

'He wanted to be.'

'Pardon?'

'He was in love with me. At least infatuated. At every student party we attended, he was all over me.'

'You didn't reciprocate?'

'No, I did not. I felt no attraction toward Aaron. I hate to speak ill of the dead, but he was a bit sleazy.'

'Then why did you say he *was* your boyfriend? What was the point of that?'

'I don't know, it came out reflexively. Maybe the idea of a girlfriend left behind would make you act more urgently.' She fell silent for a moment, lit a cigarette. 'Are you going to tell us more about how it happened?'

'What makes you think I'd do that?'

'Because he was a part of our lives. His death has scared the hell out of all of us.' She took an extra-long drag on her Marlboro, flicked the ash into a metal ashtray, fixed me with a look that could turn butter into concrete.

Flora stood, chest heaving. She was able to turn her emotions on and off like a tap. 'We deserve to know!'

I took a deep breath, made a face as if I was about to relent, like I was weighing up my words. The three men edged forward on the sofa, eager to hear the details. They studied me so intently it made me uneasy.

'I'm afraid I to have to say no.'

'Why?' Daniel exclaimed, eyes protruding and fists balled. 'What is your problem, man? We are his friends! We have a right to know!' Samuel and Justin's twisted expressions mirrored Daniel's.

'I understand your anxiety and rage. That's precisely why I can't tell you. If you lose control of those emotions and reveal key information to the wrong people, it could hamper our investigation. You don't want that, do you?'

'Ridiculous,' said Flora. 'The killers already know how they did it. How could us having that knowledge compromise the investigation?'

Yegor gave me a look that said, *she has a good point.* And she did. Still, I wanted a bargaining chip. Something to ensure their co-operation. Give them full details and they could cave, walk away and refuse to speak to me or anyone else investigating the case. Or worse. Start a full-scale riot. Drag the rest of the African student body into it. A repeat of 1963. 'OK, Flora. What you say is valid, up to a point. But I'm not willing to divulge details at this stage.'

'Please, sir.' It was Justin this time. 'Can you answer one question for me? Did Aaron suffer before he died?'

'No. I believe it happened quickly.'

The men hung their heads. Samuel made the sign of the cross, kissed his fingers then looked to the heavens. Flora's face hardened like flint. 'You're just saying that so we don't start rioting.'

I shrugged. 'That's my assessment. It's your choice to believe me or not.' I hated lying to these people; pragmatism dictated my thinking.

Justin mumbled something in English. The other men nodded.

I turned to Flora. 'What did he say?'

'He said at least Aaron's earthly suffering is over and now he is with God.'

'Are you devout Christians?' I scanned all their faces. Perhaps here was a link to the cross carved on Adekanye's back.

'Of course not,' said Flora. 'We are in your glorious country training to be communist revolutionaries, learning to take over our country and install a dictatorship of the proletariat. To ensure the complete victory of socialism!' The sarcasm was barely hidden. 'Of course we are Christians. Maybe not devout, as you say. We lack somewhat in our adherence to the teachings of Jesus, but we are Christians nonetheless. Like Russia once was. What you saw Samuel do and Justin's words were more a sign of respect than religious acts. Don't read too much into it.'

'I see,' was all I could say.

The interview wasn't revealing anything particularly useful. I'd press on for another few minutes, perhaps one of the Nigerians would provide a vital piece of information. I'd go back to Kuznetsov when I was done here, ask to see the students' files. They might contain some significant information about the victim, possible enemies. Maybe about the people I was sitting with at that very moment. 'Let's just get one thing straight,' I said. 'You *may* be informed of all the circumstances if and when I decide there's no risk of you leaking confidential information all over campus. Answer my questions and I'll leave you in peace, unless and until I need more from you. Understood?'

'I agree, but with reluctance,' said Flora. 'We'll do our best to co-operate.' I took the silence from the others to mean yes.

I side-eyed Yegor, who'd been frantically scribbling in my notebook the whole time. 'Are you getting all this down?'

'Every word, sir.' I doubted it, but he was clearly doing his best.

'Firstly,' I continued. 'What were Aaron's economic circumstances and was he involved in illicit economic activities?'

I sensed them all trying to avoid my gaze.

'He received a stipend from the Friendship Society,' ventured Samuel. 'I don't think he was into anything shady.'

'Of course he was. All of you are. I wasn't born yesterday.' I mouthed to Yegor *'Leave that bit out'.* He nodded. I continued. 'Everyone knows it's going on all over the city. It's just the degree of involvement that varies, right?'

Silence. Empty stares.

'So, I'm curious. What was he buying, selling, trading or stealing?'

Again, nothing but the ticking of the clock on the wall.

'Let's try another tack, shall we? Did Aaron have a girlfriend? A real one, I mean. Not his unrequited infatuation with Flora.'

'He was seeing a Russian girl,' said Justin without hesitation. 'He met her at a party at the Chekhov institute. It's just up the road from here.'

'I know very well where the Chekhov Institute is. It's been a source of trouble in this district for a long time. Who is she?'

'All we know is her name's Olga,' said Daniel. 'Don't know the last name.'

'Have any of you seen this woman? Can you describe her for me?'

Blank looks greeted my inquiry. Honest blank looks. I took another sip of tea as I pondered the follow up.

'Surely he told you something about her? Where she worked, studied, things like that?'

'Not to me he didn't, maybe to the boys.' Flora gave a hopeful shrug, lit another cigarette, wriggled her backside until her spine was against the wall, legs stretched straight out in front. She brought the ashtray to her side, tapped her cigarette on it.

'He said she did anything to please him,' said Samuel, suddenly sheepish. 'You know, in bed.'

I felt my eyebrows rise involuntarily. Quite a candid response.

'Did he say he was in love?'

Samuel shook his head. 'No sir. I took it to be a flirtation on his part. He hooked up with the Russian girl because Flora wouldn't have him, I guess. My theory is the local woman wanted to get married and flee the USSR. It's a very common motivation for Russian girls to seduce our men for this purpose. I have no proof, it's just a hunch.'

'How long had they been seeing each other?'

Justin rubbed his jaw. 'About three months. But it was only maybe once a week.'

'What else can you tell me? That can't be everything. He said he was going out – occasionally – with a Russian girl called Oksana. Brilliant.'

'No, sir. Olga,' corrected Justin.

'Right. Olga. No last name and she was a great lay. Not much to go on.'

More silence. Smoke curled towards the ceiling as the students sought refuge from my sarcasm in nicotine. I took a business card from my pocket, flung it on Flora's writing desk, tapped Yegor on the shoulder. 'Come on. We aren't going to get anything useful out of this lot. They act all aggrieved, and when they get the chance to actually do something about it, they clam up. I'm not sure they really want us to do our jobs properly. They're just looking for an excuse to be pissed off and cause trouble.' I stood, brushed a speck of dust from my trousers.

'Hey, wait a minute.' Daniel stood, blocked the doorway. His mates stood either side of him. I felt the pistol nestled under my coat. Its heaviness instilled confidence, even though we were outnumbered in extremely close quarters. 'We haven't told you the important part, yet.' It struck me that over the course of this brief and unproductive interview, the quality of the men's spoken Russian had improved to an intermediate level. Fewer grammatical mistakes, good use of idiom. Was I imagining it? All kinds of alarm bells were going off in my head.

'Damn straight. You've told me nothing useful at all. What is it that's so important? And it better be good.'

Daniel folded his arms across his barrel chest, feet shoulder width apart. 'Aaron was a spy,' he said. 'Working for the government.'

'Shut up, you idiot!' Flora leaned forward, eyes afire. 'Don't talk nonsense.'

'Oh, yeah?' I ignored her. It sounded like fantasy, but I had to hear him out. Test his mettle. 'Which one? Ours or yours?'

'Stop talking!' Flora again.

'Yours.' Daniel took no heed of the princess. 'And the Americans.'

I burst out laughing. A double agent. Not the answer I expected. 'And you have proof of this?'

'No, sir. He would get drunk sometimes. Quite often, actually. He had a stash of vodka that'd put a Russian to shame. Aaron would ramble about his contacts in the US embassy. How he told them about African students recruited to spy for Russia. He also said he'd been approached by one of the teachers here – wouldn't say who – got offered money and an upgraded room to work for the KGB.'

'A room like this one, perhaps?'

'Shut up!' Flora was frantic, eyes darting. 'I told you, my father has great influence. I'm no spy. You have to believe me.'

I did believe her. Why would she invite me into her privileged world if she were a spy? Plus, she just wasn't the type. Too over the top. It was the man blocking the doorway I didn't believe.

'Sorry, young man. Unless you have proof of your claims, I have to treat your words with scepticism. I need names, witnesses, photographs, recorded phone calls and the like. You understand?'

'What if I can tell you where you might be able to get your hands on stuff like that?'

'Sit down again and start talking. You've got five minutes.'

Chapter 6

The trusty Lada edged gracefully into a vacant car parking spot. Until it struck the inevitable pothole abutting the edge of the main campus building. The Chekhov Institute of Russian Language and Literature was a boutique-sized operation compared to the sprawling campus we'd come from.

The drive from Gandhi to Chekhov took less than five minutes, sparing me elevated blood pressure and possible injury. For now. Yegor switched off the clunking engine and pocketed the key. 'What did you make of that spy nonsense?' he asked, opening the sticking driver's door with a shove.

'Not sure. I half believe it. First we have to find that Canadian student Daniel claimed was Aaron's contact. What was the name again?'

Yegor fished out the notebook. 'Michel Lacroix.'

A grim-faced woman stood guard at the front entrance of the institute. She studied us for a moment, stepped aside without demanding our documents. Our uniforms generally allow as unquestioned access to everywhere and this was no exception. A quick turn to the left brought us to the reception desk.

'We placed a call about ten minutes ago from the Gandhi University.' I said to the top of someone's head. 'The rector should be expecting us.'

A narrow mousey face popped up; its owner put a women's fashion magazine to one side. Pale blue eyeshadow caked on thick as buckwheat porridge, mascara-laden lashes like twigs. A pair of bright-red lips parted. 'Yes, he is. Please follow me.'

The youthful brunette, wearing the standard female teacher's attire of polo-neck sweater, pleated skirt and mid-length black boots, appeared from behind a glass partition. She turned a key and locked the booth behind her. Her eyes ran up and down both of us, assessing our bona fides based purely on visuals. She gave a micro nod and set off towards the end of the foyer. We ascended a set of concrete stairs to the mezzanine floor. Yegor and I struggled to keep up with the speeding woman and maintain our dignity at the same time. Already dozens of students had clocked us; those in pairs or groups whispered to each other behind their hands.

'Quickly please,' said the woman. 'We don't want to alarm the students with uniformed Militsiya marching about the premises. It's not often we get a visit from law enforcement.' A quick rap on the rector's door; she pushed it open without waiting for an invitation. 'Inside, gentlemen, hurry up. That's the way.'

No sooner were we inside than the door slammed behind us. I heard the click-clack of her retreating boots on the tiles quickly go from loud to soft as she scurried back to her post.

'Please, comrades.' The rector stood and gestured for us to sit.

I'd already phoned Vadim Ivanovich Shukhov from Kuznetsov's office. His tone during the brief conversation bore no trace of anxiety about our impending visit. Calm as a millpond, the hint of defiance even. I both distrusted and disliked the man sight unseen. His supercilious voice had been enough. Seeing him in person didn't change my mind.

'Thank you,' I said. What were the odds? Interviewing two rectors of institutes teaching foreign kids in the space of a few hours. The first one a ham actor, this one an arrogant son of a bitch. We took our seats, Yegor with notepad and pen poised at the ready. 'I'm not going to waste your time with unnecessary chitchat, comrade Shukhov.'

'No? Not even a cup of tea?' I shook my head. It was already nearing midday and we hadn't even returned to the station to see if there were any forensics results yet. I'd obtained a Xerox copy of the dossier on Adekanye from Kuznetsov. I read it on the drive to the Chekhov Institute, but the thin tome contained nothing of any apparent value. On top of that, we'd spent far too much time and effort placating the Nigerians, albeit with this possible lead via the Chekhov Institute. 'Perhaps I can offer you a Cuban cigarillo?' Shukhov winked. 'We confiscated these from a lad who was getting up to a bit of no good.'

I held up a hand, even as Yegor accepted the offer with a beaming smile. I glared at my partner and he dropped the cigar back in the wooden box. 'No thanks,' I said. 'I'd rather get down to business.'

Shukhov nodded slowly, sparked up a match and lit his cigar. The sweet aroma of the smoke was intoxicating. 'Of course.'

Physically, the man sitting opposite didn't match up with his vocal qualities. Young to be holding such a responsible position, perhaps mid to late thirties. A mop of abundant black hair and stylish glasses you don't normally associate with academics. Everything about him said coddled communist party functionary.

'I believe you have a Canadian student here, name of Michel Lacroix.'

'Quite possible. I know very few students by name. My role is basically administrative. Keeping an overall watch over the institute. I do believe we have a medium-sized contingent from Canada this year.'

'Think you could check for me?'

He puckered his lips. 'You could have given me the name when you called. Saved a bit of time.'

He was right. It would have. But, if Daniel was correct and Lacroix was part of some spy network, it could also have given Shukhov time to warn the man we were coming. 'Must have slipped my mind.' I said. 'So, if you could please fetch your enrolment records, that would be most appreciated.'

His opened his mouth to say something, but quickly closed it again. Placed his hands on the desk palms up.

'I haven't got all day. If you like, my partner and I can gather up all your records, take them back to the station and look through them at our leisure.'

'That won't be necessary.' He picked up his phone, dialled a three digit extension. 'Masha, please find the file on a,' he looked straight at me, lying through his perfect teeth, 'what was his name again?'

'Lacroix. Michel Lacroix. Canadian.'

Shukhov repeated the name. He placed the receiver back in the cradle. 'Why do you want to speak to one of my students?'

'It's in connection with a very sensitive and confidential matter.' I wasn't giving the prick any more than that.

'Can you at least give me a hint?'

'Afraid not.'

A minute later there was a timorous tap on the door. 'Enter!' Shukhov commanded. A frumpy middle-aged woman entered with the requested document, dropped it on the desk and shuffled out again, eyes downcast.

I picked up the file. The thin folder contained the student's enrolment form, completed in a neat, careful hand, and a couple more sheets of paper. Russian handwriting by non-natives is easy to spot, and Lacroix's – assuming he filled out the form himself – was no exception. Many of the joined-up looping characters had spaces in between rather than running together. A small passport photograph was attached to the top with a paperclip.

'A handsome specimen, don't you think?' I held the folder open for Yegor to see.

'Indeed, Comrade Captain. He's a good looking man.'

The Canadian student of interest could have passed as a male model. Classically symmetrical features, leaning towards Nordic rather than Gallic as his name would suggest. Cold, clear blue eyes, no smile. Perhaps indicative of a calculating nature. A pair of wire-rimmed spectacles added an air of studiousness. I glanced back up at Shukhov. His glasses were almost identical to Lacroix's.

'Where'd you get those expensive glasses?'

'Oh, ah, my uncle's an optometrist. Has access to all kinds of stock not available to the general public.'

'Only it's interesting that young Michel here is wearing a pair strikingly similar to your own.'

Shukhov shrugged. 'Perhaps he also has an uncle?' *Smarmy prick.*

Behind the enrolment form was a second sheet of paper. Lacroix's class timetable, dormitory room number and medical information confirming he was fit and healthy. Clear of the horrific new disease marching across the globe. AIDS. I flipped over the second sheet. Tucked behind it, attached with a paperclip, was a scrap of note paper. *Character profile. February 1987. Michel Lacroix: 22-year-old French literature major from Montreal, father known to have affiliations with Canadian leftist organizations. Never been in trouble with Canadian or other authorities. A man with charm, boyish good looks. Outgoing and confident. No steady girlfriend but has had brief liaisons with two women at the institute (language teacher Irina Gordeeva and East German student Katrin Keller). Keen interest in ice-hockey. Plays socially with friends in Montreal. Here in Moscow he has made friends with a social team that plays occasionally at Malaya Arena. Believed to be acquainted with members of top-level Soviet league teams.*

'Interesting character. Are these your notes?'

'No.' He relit his cigar, which had gone out. 'I've got no idea where that came from. I assume KGB or another security agency. We have them here, of course. Planted in the institute. I don't know who did this. I assume they wanted us to know the kind of chap we've got staying here.' He reached out a hand. 'Mind if I take a look?'

I gave him the file.

He scanned the text, eyes darting left and right. 'Nothing compromising here. Just a normal, red-blooded male who's popular with the ladies and likes sports. His dad's got a good pedigree, ideology wise. In short, just the kind of student we like to have at the Chekhov.'

'Do you think if we looked at other students' files we might discover similar character assessments?' I pulled the file back from Shukhov's grasp.

He waited a few moments before answering. Glanced upwards and expelled a series of smoke rings. I watched as they ascended, touched the ceiling and dissipated to nothing. Then he fixed me with a stare, eyes aglow behind the fancy glasses.

'I'm sure you're aware of the reality of the world we live in, Comrade Captain.'

'What the hell are you talking about?'

'People are watched, studied, followed. Even – perhaps in particular – foreigners. Tourists, business people, students.'

'I'm fully aware of the fact. Pretty sure it happens in free societies, too. When someone is suspected of a crime, for example.'

'Indeed. A properly functioning society depends on vigilance. Which leads me to ask again. Why are you here and why are you interested in what's his name, Michel Lacroix?'

'We understand your curiosity, and your concern. You'll be informed if and when it's deemed appropriate.' Yegor looked up from his note-taking. I was grateful for his intervention. I was tired of Shukhov's evasiveness. 'We're conducting a highly sensitive investigation. Public order and the safety of the city of Moscow depends on us being circumspect.' Gilding the lily, but I nodded my support.

Shukhov shook his head. 'You people are beyond belief. You come barging in here...'

'We made an appointment.' Yegor again. I was enjoying his initiative. 'No barging.'

'Whatever.' Shukhov adjusted his glasses, pressed down a stray lock of hair. 'I'm reluctant to co-operate with you if I'm in the dark.'

'I'm afraid you have to co-operate.'

'And if I don't?'

I don't like making specific threats I can't back up. Better keep it vague. 'There could be professional consequences for you.'

'Bullshit.' Another cloud of smoke headed upwards. 'I have every right to protect my students' privacy. I suggest you try the young gentleman's embassy if you need more information. I already went too far in handing over that file.'

'Is this file all you've got on him?'

'It is.' He coughed. 'Everything you could possibly want to know is there in front of you.'

'According to whoever made those notes, you mean. Perhaps there's more the mysterious author omitted.'

'Well, you can't describe a person's life and personality on one page, can you?'

I sighed, handed the file to Yegor. 'Jot down all the names in here. Teachers,

51

students, the lot. Also his room number. Time to find this guy.' I turned back to Shukhov, who was grinning inanely. Thought he'd got one over on the dumb cops. 'We're done here,' I said. 'Thanks for your valuable time.' I opened his cigar box and extracted two exquisitely rolled brown cylinders. 'Oh, and for these lovely tokens of your generosity.' I pocketed one, handed the other to Yegor.

'May I have the file back, please?'

'I'll return it later.'

'We do have a Xerox machine, you can–'

'I'd rather take the original.' I flapped the file about nonchalantly. 'You'll get it back.'

'You have no right to–'

'Do NOT tell me what my rights are, understand?'

Shukhov nodded. 'Very well, Comrade Captain. But I warn you. Be very careful. I have contacts who can have you removed from your job in the blink of an eye. And worse.'

'Don't threaten me, you pathetic little man!' I ushered Yegor out of the rector's office and slammed the door behind me. If Shukhov thought he was getting that file back he was badly mistaken.

Chapter 7

'Hello? Anybody home?' I bashed again on the door of Lacroix's room, No. 902. I cupped my ear to the keyhole – silence. A one-eyed squint through it revealed no sign of life in the darkened space.

'Make some enquiries round the other side of this floor, behind the elevator shaft,' I said to Yegor. 'If you gain admission to any dorm rooms, keep the door open so I know which one you're in.'

'What's the plan?'

'Obvious, isn't it? We knock on every damn door until we either find Lacroix, or someone can tell us where the bastard is. You go left, I'll go right.'

'With all due respect, Comrade Captain, there's over a hundred rooms in this building. It'll take us all day. Plus it's a school day. Many of the students will be in classes.'

'So we interrupt them.'

'Lacroix's got no lessons today, according to his timetable. His lecture load amounts to a measly seven hours per week.'

'Doesn't matter. The other students might know something.'

'What about keeping this low key?'

'I'll pretend you didn't say that. Until Burov orders us off the case officially, we find out as much as we can.'

'I still think going around every floor will take too long. I agree with interrupting classes. There'll be more students in the one place and it'll save time.'

Yegor was right. If Shukhov was mixed up in this, he'd do all he could to alert Lacroix we were looking for him. Especially after the way I'd just spoken to the rector. 'Let's at least try the floor he supposedly lives on. Someone here has to know something.'

Yegor nodded and headed for the other side of the elevator shaft. I knocked on six doors before one opened. A female Asian face peered at me from behind a security chain. 'Yes?' came a nasally voice.

'May I come in?'

She clocked my uniform, slid the chain off and let me inside. Spicy aromas filled my nostrils. Unfamiliar smells I couldn't place, but which set my mouth watering. A man in grey pants and white singlet sat on a bed, a bowl of steaming noodles on his lap. A portrait of Ho Chi Minh adorned one of the walls. Cardboard boxes stacked high across another wall supported half a dozen bottles of Stolichnaya vodka and maybe twenty cans of black caviar.

'What you want?' said the woman in a clipped tone that left the consonants off the end of each word. She saw my eyes drift to the vodka, a slight twitch developed in her left eye. She must have thought I was here to look for contraband.

'Do you know the Canadian who's staying in 902?' I spoke as slowly and clearly as I could.

'I no understand nothing,' the woman answered in the worst possible Russian. The look of relief that washed over her face told me she understood me perfectly well.

'Do...you...speak...Russian?'

A head shake and a shrug of the shoulders. The man ate his noodles with slurping sounds, one eye raised as he observed the interaction between me and the woman. This was a waste of time. Maybe Yegor was having more luck with his enquiries.

'How'd you go?' I asked when we met outside room 915.

'Spoke to a Bulgarian guy. He claimed no knowledge of Lacroix.'

'Didn't even know the name?'

'No.'

'You believe him?'

'Yeah. Bulgarians have a reputation for behaving themselves, less likely to be involved in anything shady.' Yegor glanced at his watch. 'Viktor Pavlovich, it's 12:30, lunchtime. There's probably a break in classes right now. There was a canteen on the ground floor. How about we question some people at random, try and shake some information out of one or two of them?'

'Excellent idea. We can get a bite to eat there too.' The smells of cooking in the Asians' dorm room had kicked my hunger into overdrive.

The hygiene standards in the dining area were slightly better than at the filthy Kazan railway station. I couldn't see cockroaches, but I felt their presence. Yegor and I shuffled along in the queue. Groans of frustration from the students in front and behind us didn't make the line move any faster.

'Viktor Pavlovich, why don't we just cut in? That's what most cops I know would do.' Yegor's eyes sparkled with hope.

'It wouldn't be fair on everyone who's had to wait their turn.'

'Dammit, Comrade Captain. Now's not the time to get all egalitarian. I'm bloody hungry.'

'Oi!' The interjection came from a red-faced woman behind the counter. She wore a white smock splattered with brown stains. Curly grey hair jutted out from a white cap, slightly less grubby than her apron. She waved a ladle around for added authority. 'Who's swearing in the line? Behaviour like that will be rewarded with slow service!'

'Slow? Any slower than it already is and we'll starve to death,' Yegor whispered.

A male in front of us turned and chuckled. 'You aren't wrong. Luckily, the line's pretty short today.' Four students stood in front of the young man, maybe a tail of twenty behind Yegor. I glanced around the cavernous dining hall, dotted with people eating alone and in small groups. Plenty of empty seats and tables. Apart from the guy talking to us, the rest seemed to have little interest in our presence. Or they were anxious to keep a low profile.

'Is this the way it usually is?'

He nodded. 'Very slow. The saddest part is, when you finally get served, the food is disgusting.' His Russian was far from perfect but good enough to converse with us.

'Then why do you eat here?' asked Yegor.

He shrugged. 'What choice is there? We can't afford restaurants, there's nothing in the shops, and the vendors at the markets charge crazy prices for their produce.'

'Have you been a student here long?' I asked. The kid liked to talk. Let's see if he knows anything.

'Six months. Came for the winter course. Back to France in February.'

Not Canadian. Still, he and Lacroix could hang out together in some kind of mini French-speaking diaspora.

'You happen to know of a Canadian student called Lacroix?'

'First name Michel?'

'Uh huh.'

We shuffled forward as some lucky customer got their lunch order slopped onto their plate.

'Yeah, I know him. Is this about that African guy who went missing?'

I stopped as the next customer got to interact with the charming ladle waver. 'Why do you ask?'

'Oh, just that he, Lacroix I mean, does some trading with students from the Gandhi University. I saw him walking to the bus stop a week ago deep in conversation with a couple of black dudes. Dunno if they were from here, the Gandhi or some other institute.'

Yegor was already selecting his meal. 'Hey,' I said to the French kid. 'Would you like to join us?'

'Why?'

'We need to find Michel Lacroix as a matter of urgency. I'm afraid I can't go into detail at this stage.'

'Is he in danger? Trouble?'

'Again, I can't say.'

'Why not?'

'It might compromise our investigations if we tell you something and later on you let it slip to the wrong person.'

'Oh, come on! Who am I going to tell?'

'How would I know?'

He went quiet for a moment.

'You paying?'

'Sure.'

'In that case, I'll join you.'

I stared at my lunch. A thin brown gravy with minuscule chunks of meat floating in it. The chalk board said beef, and I took it on trust. Some pungent buckwheat kasha swimming in rancid butter on the side, plus a bread roll about the size of a large hen's egg. I picked it up, gave it a squeeze between thumb and forefinger. It had no give, solid as a lump of quartz.

'We call those things rocks.' The student nodded at my plate. 'Break your teeth if you're not careful.'

I put the bread back on the plate, scooped up a spoonful of kasha. I chewed fast, eager to swallow the revolting sludge and wash the taste away with tea. I gulped a mouthful of the sweet, hot tea, wiped my mouth with a napkin. The student laughed gently. 'Ha! See how they try to poison us.'

'Mmm.' Yegor tucked into a slushy potato puree. 'Don't know what you're talking about. This is delicious. Just like my mother makes.'

The man's taste buds must be on the blink.

'What's your name and where do you come from?' The way the student responded to direct questioning would show me the kind of person I was dealing with.

'Nicholas Dubois. Call me Nico. I'm from France, like I said before. Lyon to be specific.' He stirred a bowl of bright purple beetroot soup, slurped some down. 'I'm on a scholarship from the Charles de Gaulle Institute.'

'I'm not surprised, Nico. Your Russian is quite good.'

He blushed slightly at my overstated assessment. 'That's a real compliment. Especially coming from a cop. To be honest, I've never spoken to a *ment* before.'

I bristled slightly at the derogatory term for a policeman. At least he didn't use the even worse epithet of *musor*, the filth. I raised my eyebrows at him and he grinned. 'Sorry about that, comrade...?'.

'Voloshin. Captain Viktor Pavlovich Voloshin. This is my partner, Yegor Adamovsky.'

'Rank?'

'Does it matter?' I blinked.

'No, but since you gave yours...'

'Listen, sonny. We haven't got all day. If you have something to tell us, don't hold back. Your information could help us solve a terrible crime.'

'So it *is* about the missing black guy?' Nico barely flinched at my reproach. Cheeky brat. I liked him. I had to trust someone; my gut told me this French lad was the most trustworthy person around at the moment, aside from Yegor.

'Yes. But I implore you, don't say a word about this to anyone. Understand?'

'Sure. I thought it must be about him. Rumours are flying thick and fast about what happened.' He dunked his rock into the soup. 'By the way, this is the only way you can eat the things. Soften them up first, fuck your mother.'

The breadth of his lexicon was impressing me more and more. As did the culinary hint. I followed his example.

'So,' said Yegor, giving me the opportunity to eat the roll, which I'd now managed to get to a chewable consistency. 'What do you know about Lacroix hanging around with illegal currency traders?'

'It's weird,' said Nico. 'Lacroix flouts the system, running his little empire of economic crime, and gets away with it. At the same time he's got this reputation of being a staunch communist. Hypocrite if you ask me.'

'Interesting.'

'What's even stranger is his association with a French guy called Laurent. Can't remember his last name. Anyway, this dude's to the left of Stalin ideologically, if you get my meaning. Believes heart and soul in the inevitable triumph of socialism. All that bullshit.'

'Is it bullshit?' asked Yegor.

Yes, it's bullshit, I wanted to say.

'Of course,' said Nico, taking a slug of milky coffee that looked and smelled remarkably palatable. 'Yeah, I know I shouldn't be saying shit like that here, but Gorbachev gives me the confidence to be honest with my views. I mean, no one's going to have me arrested for saying I think this country's system is a crock of shit, are they?'

I watched Yegor's eyes narrow as the young man spoke. Yegor's opinions and mine were diametrically opposed on a range of political matters, but he was professional enough to keep his cool. This was a murder we were investigating, not crimethink. I wondered for a second whether Yegor was acquainted with Orwell. Might have to lend him my secret copy of 1984.

'No,' I reassured Nico. 'You can speak your mind with us.'

'I can tell you the guy's not liked by many other students at the Chekhov. We're sure he's a spy. There are others, too. But they're better at staying under the radar.'

'How so?'

He shrugged. 'Less audacious. I mean, Lacroix is a womanising show pony who...' Nico clammed up, turned his head sharply to the left. I spotted Shukhov at the entrance to the cafeteria, chatting amiably to another man. Looked like a teacher: rollneck sweater, pleated grey slacks, mandatory cheap briefcase. Both extinguished cigarettes in a sand-filled urn and made for the queue to the food service area. I looked around to ask Nico to finish what he was saying, but he was already gathering his things together.

'I'm outta here,' he whispered. 'Gorby might be OK, but that arsehole will have me expelled for talking to you guys.'

I grabbed his wrist before he could scarper. I quickly reached into a pocket, pulled out my wallet, extracted a business card, placed it in his palm.

'Call me when...' was all I could say before he was out of his seat and striding for the exit, shielding his face from Shukhov with his satchel.

Chapter 8

'Did you believe Kuznetsov? Or the other guy, what's his name… Shukhov?' Burov asked. Before either of us could answer, the chief lit himself a cigarette, offered the packet of Camels to me and Yegor. We each took one of the foreign smokes without hesitation. You never pass up a Western cigarette when it's offered. Burov leaned across his desk. In his hand he held a chunky silver Zippo. His wide thumb flicked the ignition wheel. We dipped our heads towards the dancing orange flame and inhaled. Burov tapped the packet. 'Left behind by a grateful visitor.' He smiled broadly. 'As a token of appreciation.' Everyone was on the receiving end of tobacco-related good fortune today. I felt in my top pocket; the cigar I'd expropriated from Kuznetsov. I'd enjoy its exotic flavour later with some cheap vodka in my shabby apartment.

'For?' I asked.

'Not arresting the arsehole for public disorder when he was clearly asking to be locked up.' The chief leaned back in his chair. 'Now, getting back to my question. Did you believe what Kuznetsov told you?'

'Maybe fifty percent of it. There was something about his demeanour that struck me as…I don't know…'

'False.' Yegor suggested through a cloud of smoke.

'He's covering something up,' I added.

Burov shook his head. 'Why, though? What would he gain by it?'

I patted my notebook. 'No idea. Probably nothing. Except his reputation, perhaps. Or he's carrying out orders from higher up.'

'Elaborate.' Burov flicked an ash-tail into a tin ashtray embossed with a red hammer and sickle. 'I fail to see how the murder of one student could impact on the man's reputation. As far as I know, he's a respected academician. He's even got the title of honoured scientist.' Burov stretched his arms out, interlocked his fingers and bent them till a loud crack resounded in the operations room.

'I'm with the Colonel,' said Yegor. He'd rolled up the sleeves of his blue shirt, like he was about to plant potatoes in the garden of his dacha. 'The death won't be blamed on him, so how could it affect his job?'

I ignored Yegor's question. 'The histrionics when I told Kuznetsov Adekanye was dead were completely disproportionate to what his reaction should have been.'

'I disagree.' Burov waved his hand as if a fly was about to land in his glass of black tea. 'News of death can knock some people off their feet.'

'You should have seen the way he regained his composure so fast. The whole thing was a fucking act!'

'Looks like histrionics coming from you now.' Burov pointed his index finger at my forehead.

'Hang on, Yevgeny Nikolaevich.' I wasn't going to let him get away with that. 'Raising your voice is one thing, carrying on like some over-the-top actor in a Chekhovian play is quite another.'

'Viktor Pavlovich has a good point there.' *Thanks for backing me up, Yegor.* 'I saw a performance of *The Three Sisters* at the Maly Theatre a while back. Kuznetsov could've played Andrei in that show for sure.'

I burst out laughing. Yegor looked pleased with his comment, Burov remained impassive. 'Come on, Comrade Colonel. Where's your sense of humour?'

'I bring it out of its box when something funny happens.' His face was granite. Apart from the tiniest smirk playing about at the corner of his large mouth.

'And the African students themselves?' said Burov.

'Aha,' I replied. 'This is where we might make some headway.'

'Why?'

'Because of a certain Nigerian female student, Flora Madenge.'

'How so?' Sparked interest gave Burov's voice an upward inflection.

'She's like a black version of Margaret Thatcher,' I said. 'Only more attractive.'

'Excuse me?' Burov twirled a pencil on blotting paper. 'You've lost me there, Voloshin.'

'Maybe not the best comparison, but I can't think of another woman capable of putting men in their place like this one can.'

'Haven't you met my wife?' said Burov.

Yegor doubled over in his chair. 'Out of the box, sir. Well done.'

The Colonel grinned broadly for an instant, before his expression returned to its default impassive status. Reminded me of a mannequin at the State Universal Department Store, known to all as GUM. 'Tell me more about this black Thatcher, Voloshin. Sounds intriguing.'

I settled back in my chair. 'She's taken it upon herself to be a kind of spokesman for the African student body.'

'Woman.'

'Sorry sir?'

'Spokeswoman, please be accurate.' The prick was playing with me. For Yegor's benefit. Judging by the smirk, my partner was enjoying my discomfiture.

'Whatever.' *Fuck you, Burov.* 'She's demanding we tell them exactly what happened to Adekanye or there could be a repeat of the 1963 protests you told me about this morning.'

Burov rubbed his oily forehead. 'Exactly what we don't want.'

'So we'd better figure out who did this and bring them to justice as soon as possible, don't you think?' I enjoy stating the bleeding obvious to the chief.

'Indeed.' Burov lit a fresh cigarette with the butt of one still burning. He winced as a stray curl of smoke got in his eye.

'If I can liaise with her and her...followers...I might be able to keep a lid on emotions. Keep them in the loop, only divulge as much as necessary for our investigation.'

'It's true, Comrade Colonel,' said Yegor. 'Viktor Pavlovich was able to build a rapport with the woman. She was hostile to begin with. Her acolytes, too. Looked like they were ready to rumble for the slightest reason. Commendable how the Captain kept them calm if you ask me.'

'I didn't.' Burov tapped ash. 'I'll be the one handing out commendations, Adamovsky, not you.' He drew deeply on the smoke. 'But as it happens, that's a huge bonus. If you can keep the peace with them, we'll be able to avert charges of a racist coverup until we can pin the murder on someone.'

'Pin it on someone?' I could feel my jaw dropping.

'You know what I mean.'

'Do I?'

The colonel stood to his full height of nearly two metres. I pushed further back into my chair. 'Do not question me like that again! You know very well I wouldn't stitch up some poor sod just to make the case go away. What do you take me for, Voloshin? It's just a figure of speech.'

'I apologise, sir. I thought...'

'I don't give a toss what you thought.. I misspoke, perhaps, but you must know the kind of man I am. Credit me with some integrity, man!'

I hadn't received a bollocking like this from the chief since I'd taken up my role. I turned to gauge Yegor's reaction to the fireworks. His head hung down, concentration focused on the floor between his boots.

Burov sighed, held out his crumpled packet of Camels. 'Here, both of you. Sorry for the outburst. I'm under a ton of pressure over this case.'

Exactly as I expected.

'The Director of the MVD wants this wrapped up before the Revolution Day celebrations,' Burov continued. 'Either we find who did it quick sticks, or we sweep it under the carpet.'

'I'm assuming your view is that the second option is not an ... ah ...option,' said Yegor.

'Eloquently put, Comrade Lieutenant.' Burov raised an eyebrow, brushed non-existent lint from his epaulettes. 'So, as part of ongoing investigations, I'd like you, Voloshin, to liaise with this Nigerian woman. Let the students know we're doing everything in our power to bring the culprits to justice. If they keep pressing about details, send her to me. I'll placate her.'

'I knew you'd push for a result,' said Yegor.

'I can't believe you would think otherwise. Anything else to report? What happened at the Chekhov Institute?'

'That lead came from the Nigerians. One of the male students claimed the murder victim was engaged in spying activities under the eye of a Canadian student at the Chekhov. Name of Michel Lacroix.'

Burov pressed his lips together thoughtfully. 'Great work. You think it's worth chasing this guy up?'

'We tried to find him at the institute, but nearly all avenues were blocked.'

'Nearly?'

I dropped Lacroix's file on the desk. 'I got this from rector Shukhov.' Burov snatched at it and started scanning its contents.

'Yes. I know about that arsehole rector.'

'You do?'

'I've got dossiers on all the Communist Party hack puppets at these colleges.'

I shouldn't have been surprised. There were many such institutes in the south-west of Moscow.

'Apart from this,' Burov tapped the file. 'The visit to Bolshevistskaya Street turned up nothing?'

'Not quite. We spoke with a Frenchman studying at the Chekhov. Nicolas Dubois.'

'The lad was eager to spill the beans on Lacroix,' said Yegor. 'Reckons the other students hate his guts.'

'Did he tell you where to find him?'

'He was about to give us something when Shukhov turned up and the lad took off like a startled elk,' I said.

'Very unfortunate.' Burov smiled ironically.

'I managed to slip him my card. I've got a feeling he might call or drop by the station.'

'Well, that's something. Anything else?'

'Not that I can think of.'

'What about Olga?' said Yegor.

'Thank you, Lieutenant.' I hadn't wanted to tell Burov everything, but there was no getting around it now. 'The Nigerians told us Adekanye had a casual sexual relationship with a woman called Olga. No other details, just the first name. Hard to chase up such a vague clue.'

Burov nodded. 'Hard, but necessary. She's possibly a key figure in all of this.'

A tap on the door. Rita came in wearing a blank expression.

'Yes, Sergeant Vasilyeva?'

'Babushka came up empty. I did get a nice warm bowl of soup out of her, though.'

Burov smiled and nodded. 'At least that's something.'

'The search for the kids?' said Yegor.

'Useless at this point,' said Burov. 'You know how many children live in this area? How many schools? We didn't have a proper description to go on; the odds of finding them are astronomical. Hours would be wasted knocking on doors. Hours I'm not willing to assign to a wild goose chase.'

I nodded. 'Fair enough, sir.'

'In the meantime, try to track down this Olga. Have another talk with the Nigerians, go back to the Chekhov and see if you can locate this Lacroix fellow. If Shukhov argues or tries to block you, arrest him.'

'Comrade Colonel?'

'For obstructing a murder enquiry. I don't give a fuck who he thinks will come to his rescue. Mouthy little apparatchiks like him make big claims about their influence. In reality, they have none.'

The olive green phone in the middle of Burov's desk gave a long beep. He seized it before the second ring. 'Yes? Who are you?'

A pause while the person on the other end spoke.

Burov placed a hand over the mouthpiece. 'Some foreigner. Says he'll only talk to you.' He handed me the phone.

'Captain Voloshin here.'

'It's Nico Dubois.'

That was quick.

'You have something to tell me?'

65

'Yes. I can't talk for long over this payphone. It's probably bugged. Meet me tomorrow at the Exhibition of National Economic Achievements. By the fountain in the central square. 9:00am.' Before I could reply, he'd hung up.

'Who was that?' said Burov.

'The French kid we met today. Wants a rendezvous tomorrow morning at VDNKh.'

'Excellent. When people come forward, they've often got good information. Let's...'

The phone vibrated on its cradle again. Burov snatched at it. Silence for a minute, punctuated by occasional head nods and ah-has from Burov. Then, his expression changed. The colour in his cheeks grew redder as the seconds ticked by. He played with the telephone cord, wound it around his wrist, unwound it, coiled it again. After another minute or so, it was his turn to speak to whomever was on the other end. 'Where the hell are these orders coming from?' Ten seconds. 'I don't believe it. It's impossible!' Five seconds. 'Oh, don't you worry. I will call and confirm.' He jotted something down on a scrap of paper. 'This is an outrage!' He slammed the receiver down hard. Extracted another Camel and started smoking furiously.

'Well?' I said.

'We've been ordered to drop our enquiries. Do nothing about the African.'

'Nothing?' Yegor squeaked like he'd just been castrated. 'What does that mean exactly?'

'It means precisely that. The matter is to be handled by the state security forces, apparently.'

'Who were you speaking to just now?' I was incredulous at this turn of events.

'Chairman Chebrikov at the Lubyanka.'

Holy shit. KGB headquarters. The guy who called was its boss. 'You said you were going to call and confirm. Who would that be? Chebrikov's at the top of the tree. The big pine cone, as the saying goes.'

'He gave me Gorbachev's private number.'

I felt my pulse racing. 'No way. Are you going to call him?'

Burov burst out laughing. 'Are you kidding? Chebrikov would have me exiled to Siberia for the rest of my life. I can't believe I challenged him like that.' He reached into a drawer, pulled out a bottle of Swedish Absolut vodka and poured us all a shot. 'That may very well be the end of my career, ladies and gentlemen.'

I shook my head. 'Surely not, sir. You didn't insult him or anything.'

'The man's capable of retribution. I shouldn't have fired up like that.' He rubbed his forehead before slamming down the vodka and pouring himself another. Rita, Yegor and I hadn't touched our glasses. 'Remember that passenger plane shot down in '83?' Burov continued, eyes blazing.

'The one with the James Bond flight number?' said Yegor.

'KAL007,' said Burov.

'What has that got to do with the murder of an African student?' I asked.

'Nothing. But it was Chebrikov who took charge of that whole clusterfuck. We claimed the plane was on an intelligence gathering mission, spying on the USSR, but of course it wasn't. Innocent people were killed over a mistake.'

Time to take that drink. Yegor and I chugged the vodka. Rita abstained, although her goggle-eye expression of bewilderment told me she needed it.

'And that's not the worst of it,' Burov continued. 'That group of paranoiacs, Andropov and his military chiefs, were all shitting themselves Reagan was going to nuke us. For fuck's sake! When will common sense prevail in this country?'

'What specifically happened? And how do you know?'

'I *don't* know. It's all rumour, but that's all you can go on, isn't it? This so-called Glasnost campaign of openness is nothing but window-dressing. Chebrikov was behind a disinformation campaign at the time. We've apparently recovered the black box that proves it was an innocent passenger flight, but our side isn't letting up with the lies.'

'Jesus Christ,' I said. Time to end the history lesson and swing Burov back to the matter at hand. 'So you think the KGB is going to conduct a proper investigation of the Adekanye murder?'

The laugh that burst from Burov's mouth was an assault to the ears. 'Are you fucking serious? Chebrikov described for me the steps they are taking.

All the newspapers and TV stations have been told, unequivocally, not to broadcast a single word of this to the world or their licences will be revoked. People will lose their jobs.'

'What about the new free press?'

The second laugh was even louder than the first.

'You...you can't be serious, can you Voloshin? There is no *free press*. Merely mildly contrarian views that are just tolerated. They'll also be swooped upon and shut down before you can blink an eye.'

I shrugged. 'Who knows, though? Maybe the KGB's decided it has more resources, a better ability to get to the truth.'

'You and I know the words KGB and truth don't belong in the same sentence.'

Something didn't ring true with Burov's indignation. I recalled this morning's conversation with him prior to departing to the crime scene. I couldn't let it rest. 'Yevgeny Nikolaevich. With all due respect, this morning you said...'

'Never mind what I said this morning! I've changed my mind, OK?'

I jumped in my seat; I sensed Yegor do the same. 'This is paramount to a declaration of war from the Centre. No way we're backing off. I want you two to continue this investigation, if only to satisfy my curiosity. I'm still of the view it's an inside job, some clan trouble or whatnot. But it's a horrific crime on our patch.'

'Yes, sir!' I said. 'I'd hate to think a man could be killed like that and the culprits go unpunished.'

'Well if you hate it that much, why are you still sitting here in my office?'

'Comrade Colonel?'

'Go and find out who did it!'

Yegor and I rose to leave when the phone rang again. We waited to see if it was Chebrikov again.

'Hello?' said Burov. 'What? No! You must be fucking kidding me!' He slammed the phone down so hard a crack appeared in the receiver. Burov slumped in his chair, cradled shaking hands to his head. When he looked up, I had a sudden urge to be somewhere else. Anywhere else.

'What the fuck did you do, you moron?' he roared, banging both fists on the desk. Loose papers fell off the edge, fluttered to the floor. Some tea spilled from a rattling cup. Out of the corner of my eye I saw Rita flinch, like a shot had been fired over her head. I imagine Yegor and I reacted the same way. I glanced at Yegor, opened my mouth like a goldfish, not a sound came out. I turned back to Burov. Who was he balling out, me or Yegor?

'You!' he stabbed an index finger at me, repeatedly, like a piston. 'You didn't check their identification, for God's sake.' He stood, paced back and forth. 'What a tragedy Peskov croaked on the job.' Burov's voice was calmer. Marginally. 'For us, I mean. Replaced by an inattentive numbskull like you, Voloshin.'

That was one question answered. Who the Colonel was mad at. Now I had another. 'Who's ID, sir? What are you talking about?'

'Those men who came to take the body to the morgue.'

I shuffled in my seat. I felt my face flushing. A prickly heat rose in an awful wave, ran from the pit of my gut to the top of my head. I wanted to be sick. It was worse than when I first saw poor Adekanye on the end of the rope. I reflexively defended myself. 'Didn't need to check, sir. They were in uniform. They were definitely Militsiya.'

'Like hell they were!'

'Sorry?'

'The body never turned up at the morgue. Adekanye's gone missing.'

Chapter 9

Thirty seconds later, when the tension in the operations room had dropped to sub-thermonuclear levels of palpable heat, Burov snapped his fingers.

'Voloshin, Adamovsky. Get your useless arses back to the crime scene. It's still roped off, I understand. Hopefully with a couple of men standing guard.'

'But what–' Yegor stammered.

'Just get there. As fast as you can. Find something. Anything that can lead us to the killers. Take the Medical Examiner with you. Since he's got no body to examine, he may as well make himself useful helping you clowns.'

'Yes, sir.' I stood, grabbed my hat and coat and dashed out the door before Burov could take another swipe at me.

How the hell could I have neglected to ask for ID? At least made them tell me what station they were from. I'd never heard of anyone impersonating Militsiya officers. Who would have the audacity to do it? The punishment for it was…What the hell was it? I had no idea, surely it was severe. Years in a Siberian prison with hard labour, most likely, or execution.

I gnawed my index finger, stared out at the bleak streetscape as Yegor tore up the asphalt. Red banners waved in the wind. Portraits of lunatic ideologues who'd transformed a country with endless potential into an economic basket case.

I didn't give a shit any more about Yegor's erratic driving. He was talking, rambling, but I heard none of it. All I could think about was Aaron Adekanye's grieving relatives back in Nigeria. He was someone's son, uncle, cousin – dead and disappeared. Gone from the physical world, no body to bury, to send off to the next world.

'Snap out of it, Viktor Pavlovich. You have to make things right now.'

'Sorry, what?'

'You can't dwell on the mistake. I mean, those guys looked for all the world like cops. No one else at the scene asked if they were legit, did they? We all assumed they were the real thing.'

He was right. We all fell for it. But so what? Guilt and shame gripped me like a vice. My voice was thick as I spoke. 'Be that as it may, I was in charge of the scene.'

Then there was my own situation to consider. I'd be subjected to disciplinary action over the blunder. Demotion, maybe fired from my job. Pension cancelled. No future. Although on the other extreme, the KGB would probably like to give me a medal.

'I'll vouch for you if there's an enquiry, Viktor Pavlovich. I'll say anyone would have acted the same as you.'

'Fuck it, Yegor. Do you realize we actually *helped* them get the poor sod into the body bag? We assisted the criminals steal the cadaver. If the African students ever find out the body's been snatched, my God, the '63 protests will seem like a Pioneers' picnic.'

'They won't find out.'

'How can you be sure?'

'I'm not going to tell them. Are you?'

I shook my head.

'And with the threat of retribution against any press who leaks information, there's a chance we can keep a lid on it.'

'I guess there's that glimmer of hope,' I sighed.

'That's the spirit, Comrade Captain.' He flashed me a smile of encouragement.

'If we get anywhere with this case it'll be a bloody miracle. I'm doubtful even threats from the KGB will keep all the media outlets quiet. American journalists would risk everything for a scoop like this.'

'Hmmm,' was all Yegor could add.

'Are we nearly there?' Pathologist Ivanov's timorous voice came from the back seat of the UAZ-452 van we'd commandeered from the vehicle pool. He'd not said a word until now.

Yegor craned his neck over his right shoulder. 'Just another two minutes or so.'

'I hate to speak out of line,' said Ivanov. 'But do you have to drive so fast, Comrade Adamovsky?'

'Aha! See, it's not just me who thinks you're a maniac behind the wheel.' I said. 'Slow down at once. We need CME Ivanov focused, not shitting his pants.'

Yegor nodded. 'Sorry about that.'

Despite his apology, the speedometer needle failed to retreat. I grabbed Yegor's forearm. 'I said slow down! We all need to be in a fit state of health to do our job.'

Only then did he ease up on the gas. But it mattered little. We'd arrived. Private Yanin greeted us with a crisp salute as we clambered out of the van.

The crime scene depressed as it did this morning. Cold, slushy, windy. Minus the body. An officer still posted at either end of the track, one at the tree. No need to check their IDs. They were from our station and I knew them by sight.

'Good afternoon, Comrade Sergeant.' I shook Kirill's hand. 'You can join us in the search.'

'Haven't we already done a search?'

'I'm afraid Burov's requested one more sweep of the area.'

'Why? It's pointless.'

'I fucking know!' I snapped. 'Perhaps he thinks there might be a vital clue we missed under all this garbage.'

Kirill nodded.

'The four of us will spread out, search in quadrants. I'll take from twelve o'clock to three, Yegor – three to six, Kirill – six to nine, Ivanov – nine to twelve.'

'Should we call in the men on guard to assist?' asked Yegor.

'No. I still need them to turn away sticky beaks. We can't have inquisitive members of the public getting in our way.'

The three men shook their heads.

'Right,' I continued. 'Let's make a start.'

It felt like the temperature had risen a fraction since the early morning. A pale, dipping sun shone weakly through the upper tree branches, cast soft shadows presaging nightfall in a few short hours. The frigid air pinched the nose, the breeze harassed, nipped at the lips. Underfoot was a hiker's nightmare – rough ground, mud, slush, slick ice. The scraggly birch trees stood so close together I couldn't examine the area thoroughly even if I wanted to. A light snow had fallen around lunchtime, maybe two centimetres. Not enough for us to cancel this fool's errand, but enough to cover up potential clues.

I pushed my way through the trees, bending thinner saplings and slalom-stepping around thicker trunks. Some branches cracked and split like kindling, others bent and flicked back annoyingly. I copped a stray one in the eye. I rubbed it hard, wiped tears away. When my vision returned to almost normal, something made me stop in my tracks. A glint. A knife used to goad Adekanye into the noose, covered in dabs perhaps? In my haste to get to it, I stumbled on a patch of ice, fell to my knees. My hands landed in a puddle. Damn it to hell! Not a knife, but a discarded silver candy bar wrapper, half of it sticking out of the snow. It flapped in the breeze, taunting me with its irrelevance. I picked up the item, spat to one side. I stuffed the thing in my pocket anyway. To show Burov we tried. Half an hour and a dozen other pieces of crap later, I trudged back to the starting point. The others were already there, vacant expressions like lost sheep.

'Nothing obvious in my section,' I said. I turned out my pockets. 'Grabbed these in case. Just the bigger items.'

Ivanov frowned. 'Probably a waste of your efforts, Comrade Captain. But I'll bag them up just the same.'

The others had each brought back a handful of detritus equally as uninspiring. Ivanov gathered our harvest, sorted the items by type, put them in separate paper bags. 'I'll give this the best analysis I can. I doubt it'll turn up anything of value.' His smile was as weak as the sun's feeble rays.

'Come on then,' I said. 'Let's get out of here. Kirill, return to the station. See if Burov's got any other jobs for you.' I called the other two officers on my walkie talkie, told them they were no longer required at their posts. Golytsin joined us at a jog from the Chekhov Institute end watch point. We'd meet up with Yanin at the Leninsky Prospekt end, debrief and head back to the station to figure out our next move. Right now, I had no idea what that was going to be.

As we neared the car, Ivanov handed me his tattered satchel. 'Bring this to the lab,' he muttered.

'But you're coming with us.' It was half statement, half question.

'I'd rather take the Metro, if you don't mind.' He glared at Yegor who shrugged an apology the coroner ignored.

Before I could object, Ivanov turned on his heel and meandered off in the direction of Yugo-Zapadnaya Metro station. I watched him limp along the sidewalk, favouring his left side. I remembered Ivanov telling me he'd caught a bullet in the thigh six years ago in Afghanistan. His job as a medical orderly had taken him to the most perilous war zones. I shook my head slowly, incredulous that a man who survived the hell of war was too scared of Yegor's driving to ride back with us. He hadn't walked five meters when an almighty crack rang out across the sky, echoed back from the amphitheatre of apartment blocks on the other side of Leninsky Prospekt.

Ivanov dropped like a stone, limbs jerking like he'd been electrocuted.

Then another. Boom!

A third. Boom!

I hit the deck, one eye focused on the other side of the highway. My service pistol dug into my ribs. Useless when you don't have a clue where the shots are coming from. I turned my head to see where the rest of my team were. Next to me, Yegor kissed concrete, fingers interlocked behind his head. Wouldn't stop a bullet, but I understood the protective reflex. The others were also lying prostrate, waiting for a command to get up. I prayed no one else had been hit.

I counted to ten. Twenty. No more shots.

We had to get to Ivanov. I jumped to my feet. 'Everybody up.'

In a semi-crouch, I spun around, gun gripped in both hands, scanned in every direction. My colleagues did the same. No sign of a shooter.

We raced over to where one of Moscow's top pathologists lay in a crumpled heap. I knelt next to him, the others formed a screen around me and Ivanov. A bullet hole just under his right ear. Blood pissed out like a busted tap. The shot must have come from across the highway.

I tore off a glove, handed it to Yegor. 'Press this against the wound. Hard as you can!'

My CPR training kicked in. I pumped his chest, breathed, counted. Did all the steps. For ten minutes.

But it was as useless as the search we'd just conducted.

The coroner was dead.

Chapter 10

Seven vehicles arrived in a thunderous convoy, sirens blared. Spetsnaz trucks and an ambulance van. When one of our own gets shot, no resources are spared. And they arrive in less than thirty minutes. An African student gets lynched – don't make a fuss.

Priorities.

Up and down Leninsky Prospekt, all hell had broken loose. Spetsnaz Tactical Unit officers fanned out in a wedge-shape. Maybe thirty of them. The synchronized stomping of running boots set my heart racing.

Yegor and I stood watch over Ivanov's lifeless body as a heavily armed officer ran towards us. He looked more like a soldier than a cop. Black helmet, body armour, AK-47 slung over his shoulder. A belt with all manner of gadgets dangling from it. Handcuffs, riot baton. The only thing missing was a rocket launcher. He crooked his finger at us. 'Come on. Look lively.'

'Excuse me?' I said.

'We need every available officer scouring that building over there.' He jabbed a finger across the highway. 'And the area behind it. Buildings to either side.' I suddenly envied the other officers I'd relieved of duty and sent back to the station. *Yegor and I can handle it*, I'd told them, not anticipating the firestorm we'd be caught up in.

'What about the body?' I gestured toward Ivanov. 'Someone has to stay with him.'

'It's too late for him.' The man's tone brooked no argument. He barked a few words into his walkie talkie. 'Zolotov. Get a move on. Bring a stretcher.'

A scrambled reply.

'Now, dammit!'

Two men, one of whom I assumed to be Zolotov, appeared within a minute, gathered up the cadaver. They quickly loaded him into the ambulance and screeched off towards the city centre.

The Spetsnaz goon stood with legs spread wide, shoulders back. His dark eyes shifted from me to Yegor, back to me again. 'I'm Lieutenant Filatov. I acknowledge you outrank me, Comrade Captain. But in this emergency you must obey my instructions.'

I nodded. 'I agree in principle. But do you expect us to charge over there and join the hunt? We haven't got the equipment you have. We'd be sitting ducks if the shooter decided to fire on us.'

'Sorry. Orders are to mobilize every available man to find whoever's killed the coroner. And that includes you.'

'Whose orders?'

He pretended not to hear. 'Just stay close to me.'

We followed Filatov to the back of a van. He threw open a dented door, reached inside and grabbed two bullet-proof jackets from a basket, tossed them to me and Yegor. Then he handed us a couple of steel riot shields.

'You've both got pistols, I take it?' he said impatiently.

We both nodded. Yegor's face had turned white, I'm sure mine was similar.

'Good. We've no more weapons or ammo, just the protective gear. Get those jackets on and follow me.'

Out of habit I looked left, right, left. Unnecessary, Leninsky Prospekt was barricaded off 250 metres in both directions. Clear as an airport runway. We took off across the road at a trot. I glanced up at the hundreds of windows. Curious faces peered through cupped hands pressed to glass. Could one of them be the shooter?

Other Spetsnaz operatives scurried across the road either side of us, headed for entrances to the apartment block in groups of three. I felt relatively safe in my flak jacket, but my ears were on the alert for more shots. My mouth was dry and I fought to maintain even breathing. Yegor's jangling nerves were almost palpable to me; his running gait was unsure, uncoordinated. The man was bloody terrified.

We ran through a passageway, navigated a vast, empty courtyard. Here and there skip bins overflowed with rotting garbage, crows poked about looking for a snack. Filatov picked out an entrance-way to a section of the block, waved for us to follow. We stepped inside. Deathly quiet. Smashed up green letter boxes, graffiti, glued handwritten notices. Rectangles cut into the bottom half with phone numbers on them, to be torn off by anyone interested in the advertiser's products or services. The stench of apathy and urine. A typical Moscow apartment block foyer. A quick glance at the elevator panel told me there were eighteen floors. Christ, how many apartments was that? Filatov pressed the elevator button, cocked an ear. The slow grinding of gears. 'Sounds like the lift's at the top. You,' he pointed at Yegor. 'Get up to the sixth floor. Bang on every door. Search every apartment. If you see anything suspicious, call me on your walkie talkie. Frequency 500 Mhz. Got it?'

'Yes,' he said, barely audible.

'Well? Why are you still standing here. Go!' Yegor legged it like a frightened hare.

'What do you want me to do?' I asked Filatov as he adjusted his belt.

'Come with me, Comrade Captain. You'll get off at the top, search from floor 18 down to 13. I'll cover the middle section. Chances are you won't encounter the shooter. He's probably well clear of the area by now. But you never know.' If he intended his words to instil confidence, they failed.

The rattling elevator arrived at the ground floor with a thunk. Inside the cramped space stunk of stale piss and body odour. Hints of vomit added a degree of complexity to the bouquet.

'If you feel your life is threatened, shoot.'

Holy shit. I'd only ever fired at the range. And I wasn't a particularly good shot. If I got close enough to an armed attacker, I felt confident I could disarm him. Or anyone. But shooting at a human being, even in self-defence, that was another matter altogether.

Filatov and I rode up without saying a word. The only sound was the clunk of the elevator cable and faint, scratchy radio chatter from our two-ways.

We arrived at the twelfth floor and my temporary commander shouldered the door open, gave me a thumbs up. 'Good luck, sir,' he said.

I pulled the heavy steel door closed, punched the button for the top floor. My mind raced. What if I encountered the shooter? Would there be more than one of them? Would help arrive in time if I needed it? My entire body shook.

Smells of cabbage cooking flooded the landing at the "penthouse" level. Four upholstered, reinforced doors. No answer after bashing on three of them. A frightened middle-aged woman in an apron opened the last. Her eyes widened as she took in my battle gear.

'See or hear anything suspicious, madam?' No time for pleasantries. Five more floors to cover after this one and not all day to waste.

'Just the loud bangs. What was it?'

'Can't say. May I have a quick look inside your flat?'

She waved me inside. As I suspected, nothing.

Next floor down. Same process.

By the time I met up with Filatov and Yegor, I'd spoken to two more females and one male. Their apartments were clean as whistles. Leads wise, that is. The man's place was a pigsty. But not a whiff of cordite or anything else to indicate a link with the crime. Filatov and Yegor's efforts proved equally as fruitless.

We trudged back to the operational control point with Filatov, returned the riot gear and clambered back into our own vehicle. Conflicting emotions coursed through me: relief at not confronting the shooter and frustration for the very same reason. And not a small dose of shame for being so afraid.

'My God,' said Yegor, voice ragged and hands shaking as he somehow inserted the key into the ignition. 'What else can happen to us today, Comrade Captain?'

'I'm sure we'll find out soon enough.'

Burov neared a state of apoplexy as he paced the floor like a caged bear. 'I can't believe what a shitstorm you two imbeciles have created. And look at me when I'm speaking to you, fuck your mother!'

'No need to shout, Yevgeny Nikolaevich.' I wouldn't let him steamroll me.

'I beg your pardon?'

'I said no need to shout.'

'Or swear,' added Yegor quietly.

I'd never seen a human face acquire the exact shade of boiled beet. Until now. Burov clutched the edge of his desk, leaned over until his body was almost horizontal from the waist up. 'I will speak at whatever volume and use whatever language I see fit!' He took a mighty breath and sat down slowly. Swept some stray paperclips onto the palm of his hand and dropped them in a saucer. I braced myself for another onslaught, but he'd regained a modicum of calm. With his sudden mood swings, the man was harder to read than Old Church Slavonic.

'OK. Listen up. This appalling incident with Ivanov has kicked off some serious manoeuvring at the top levels of power. And, of course, on a human level it's an absolute tragedy.'

'And the lynching of Adekanye isn't?' I challenged.

'I'm not suggesting for a second his murder isn't a tragedy, too.' Burov continued. 'What do you take me for? It was a heinous crime. The worst thing ever to happen in our precinct under my watch. But surely you must understand how things are being prioritised at MVD headquarters.'

'Naturally,' I said. 'Probably all the way up to the Politburo.'

Burov lowered his voice. 'I also understand your desire to make things right, Voloshin. You've cocked up big time. If you want to dig deeper, I won't stop you.'

'Don't worry, I will.' Losing Adekanye's body was going to haunt me for the rest of my days. I simply had to find out the truth.

'You'll be acting without my endorsement.' Burov tapped a well-chewed pencil on a blotter. 'Officially, there are no enquiries being carried out by us.'

'What a joke,' I said.

'The CID's taken over both murder cases as of now. They've told us to butt out. Go back to normal duties, they said, like getting hooligans and drunks off the streets in time for the Revolution Day shindig.'

I sighed. 'Not surprising.'

'You'll probably be called into HQ for questioning about Ivanov.'

'There's nothing more I can tell them. He got shot from across the street and no one saw anything. They'll get the exact same answer from everyone else who was there. Besides, I've given you my report.'

Burov nodded. 'Which I'll approve and pass along in due course. Doesn't mean they won't haul you in, though. You too, Yegor.'

Yegor breathed in sharply. I shuddered. The CID has some original investigative techniques that I didn't particularly care to experience.

'Furthermore,' Burov continued. 'You'll both have to undergo a psychological assessment. You've experienced extreme trauma today. Only on medical clearance will you be allowed to carry out further duties. In any capacity.'

'And when is that to take place?'

Burov reached for the phone. 'I'll arrange it right now.'

'I don't think so, Yevgeny Nikolaevich.'

'You damn well will!'

'Are Vasiliyeva, Gregoriev, Pronin, all the others seeing a shrink?'

'Ah...no. It's been determined that...ah.'

'Stop. Just stop with the bullshit. Time's getting away.' I glanced at my watch. 15:45. 'We need to get on the road, chase up the few leads we have. With all due respect, sir, you can stick your psych assessment up your arse.' I stared at him hard, dared him to reprimand me. I was past caring. If he wanted to report me higher up the food chain, get me fired, sent to a concentration camp in Irkutsk, let him. But Burov didn't flinch, unmoving as the Kremlin wall. The silence in the room was so acute I could hear the blood coursing through my head, pulsating in my eardrums. I nodded at Yegor. His darting eyes told me he'd rather be anywhere else than the boss's office. I pushed my seat back with a squeak, stood, marched towards the door. Yegor shuffled two steps behind me. I reached to turn the door handle. Burov finally spoke. 'Oh, one more thing.'

'What now?'

'You and Yegor will be using public transport from now on.'

'What the hell!' said Yegor, eyebrows knitted. 'I'm the designated driver.'

'Not anymore you're not. The vehicle's been requisitioned for other purposes. Most cops use the Metro. Deal with it.'

As much as I hated Yegor's erratic driving, getting about on the subway and trams was going to slow us down. For a second I thought about arguing with Burov. 'C'mon Yegor,' I said. 'Let's get out of here.' Once he'd passed me into the corridor, I turned back to the chief, held his cold gaze. 'I'm going to do everything I can to find Adekanye's killers. Ivanov's murder has to be connected.'

'Of course it's fucking connected, you ox! Find the link. Keep me informed of everything you find out.'

I mulled this over for a moment. 'I don't get the separation of the cases. Surely if they're linked, as you believe, the CID would be desperate to crack the Adekanye case if it would lead to Ivanov's killer. Or am I missing something?'

'What if they've had a hand in it, working with the KGB? The black kid's murder, I mean. Not Ivanov's. Not even the KGB would sanction knocking off a District Medical Examiner.' Burov stared at the portrait of the CPSU General Secretary hanging on the wall. Perhaps trying to divine meaning in the port-wine birthmark.

'Those cunts would bump off their own grandmothers,' said Yegor over my shoulder. Exactly what I'd been thinking.

'You have a point, Lieutenant Adamovsky,' said Burov. 'However in this case I think you're wrong. Why would they send in the Spetsnaz to find the shooter if it was someone working for them?'

'Any suggestions on what we should do next?' I ignored the boss's question. There were several answers to it, but I was keeping them to myself for now.

'Get out on the streets and start sniffing around. I'm sure the idea's crossed your mind, but don't bother disobeying the CID order to steer clear of Kuznetsov and Shukhov. They'll clam up the second they see you.'

'Sir.'

'One last piece of advice. Change into civvies. You, too, Yegor. Smart-casual.' He gave a tiny smile. 'Be circumspect, tactful, but most of all, be fucking careful.'

'Of course.' I saluted with an exaggerated flourish. I'd only tell him what I thought he needed to hear. I was starting to wonder if I could even trust Burov.

Yegor was already at the exit to the street waiting for me, lighting a smoke. 'Come on, comrade. Cheer up. Here's our chance to prove ourselves.'

'But he won't let me drive...'

'Suck it up. Look, here comes our trolleybus to the Metro station.'

'Terrific. Where are we going?'

'To see your Georgian buddy.'

The Cheryomushkinsky market was busy for late afternoon. Strains of shouted conversation echoed in its cavernous belly. Vendors called out to passers-by. *Try our delicious apples, have a bite of these juicy pears!*

Citizens eagerly stuffed their string bags with what they could afford, haggled over prices. *That's too dear for cabbage, fuck your mother! Don't like it? Go somewhere else. There's nowhere else to go, the shops are empty! Change the system then, ha ha!* They all had a point.

Fearless sparrows ducked and dived around overhead support beams, pigeons sought out crumbs on the ground. The feral birds shat all over the place, including on the produce. Hygiene standards aren't what they used to be. Come to think of it, they were always rubbish. We passed a butcher in a blood-stained apron, laying into some bones like he was chopping up the remains of his worst enemy. The coppery stench of blood punched me in the olfactory nerves.

As Yegor led me towards Irakli's stall, two young women lost in their own conversation blocked the narrow aisle. Both toted plastic shopping bags bearing ostentatious names – Stockmann from Finland, Harrods of London. The bags bulged with produce. Feathery green carrot leaves and exotic herbs poked out of the top. They had enough grub between them to feed a large family for a month. The women were dressed like fashion models, sable hats and coats. I coughed to alert them of our approach. They ignored me. 'Excuse me, please,' I said. They kept talking. No way they didn't hear me. I tucked my elbows to my sides, raised them and pushed them backwards. I parted the women out of the way like a ship forging through pack-ice.

'Watch where you're going, dickhead!' one of them said, her entitled voice laced with venom.

I stopped, opened my mouth to educate them in good manners. Yegor grabbed my arm. 'Tact, Viktor Pavlovich. Remember what Burov said.'

He was right. No point getting angry, even though it would have been the perfect opportunity to let off steam.

'Where's Irakli's stall?' I asked Yegor. 'All these operations look the same to me.'

'Just over there.' He inclined his head towards a stand groaning under a mound of plump oranges. 'But that's not him. There's another guy behind the counter.'

'Where's your boss?' Yegor asked. He selected an orange, fondled it lovingly. I couldn't blame him. When was the last time I'd eaten an orange? My diet these days consisted of macaroni, mouldy potatoes and stuff in cans.

The short, chubby man behind the counter grunted, rubbed fingers calloused from hard graft over a chin covered in black stubble. 'Who wants to know?'

'This bloke's new,' Yegor whispered to me. 'Perhaps Irakli's sold on his business.'

'I want to know.' I ignored Yegor's remark, flashed my Militsiya ID at the man. He frowned, nodded, folded arms across his aproned chest.

He barely looked at my ID. 'Is it about the skinheads?'

'Might be.' I took an orange, started to peel it. Fuck it, why not enjoy one of the tiny perks of the job? The sweet citrusy oil cut through the miasma of smells hanging in the air, neutralised them for a moment. The man looked at Yegor. 'You, take one too! We're happy to assist the Militsiya in their work. Irakli's fetching some stock out the back. He'll be back soon.'

I couldn't wait for soon. 'Take us to him.'

Clouds of sweat-induced steam pooled around the big Georgian's head. Flakes of sawdust and bits of straw were sprinkled through his stubble. 'I can't leave the stall unattended.'

'Not necessary,' said Yegor. 'I know where the loading zone is.'

When we got there, teams of bent-backed burly men and women with sinewy arms loaded their produce. They all bore the darker features of folk from the Caucasus.

'Hey, friend.' Yegor called out. 'How's business?'

Irakli greeted us with an affable, open-mouthed smile. I nearly recoiled from the metallic glare. I quickly assessed the value of his gold teeth to be equal to the price of a brand-new Lada Sputnik.

'Hello, Yegorchik.' The Georgian embraced my colleague in a fearsome bearhug. Looked like he didn't want to let go; when he did I heard Yegor inhale like a suction hose. 'Business is booming. I've even bought myself a new VAZ 2108. There it is. Ain't she a beauty?' He pointed at a shiny raspberry coloured sedan parked further up the snow-lined alleyway.

'I fail to see how selling fruit and vegetables at a market can earn you enough money to buy a car,' I remarked with all the irony I could muster. 'How is it possible?'

'Are you kidding me, comrade? We grow about 30,000 tonnes of oranges a year in Georgia. My share of the sales is enough to buy a new car every year for myself and one for my parents back in Tbilisi.'

'I think I'm in the wrong business,' I held out my hand. He took it in his fleshy paw. I flinched as he squeezed. I couldn't tell if he was proving his strength or he always shook hands like he was trying to crush them.

'I'm not sure about that, comrade. I know cops who make pleeenty of money. On the side.' He winked. 'If you know what I mean.'

I knew exactly what he meant. Bribery was a national sport in the USSR. Traffic cops were the worst. They probably let off more drivers in exchange for a pack of smokes or a few roubles than they actually booked for violations. But detectives also gave in to temptation.

'Well, I'm not one of them,' I said, squaring my shoulders.

Irakli grunted as he loaded the last wooden crate of oranges onto his trolley. Patted his hands against his overalls and pulled back on the trolley handle, one foot at the base for leverage. He looked me directly in the eye before setting off for his stall. 'Wouldn't you like to make a few extra notes?' he chuckled.

'I beg your pardon?' I said. 'We're here to ask you about the trouble with the skinheads.'

'Excellent.' Irakli's tone became serious. 'Those little shits are starting to get on my nerves.'

'Surely you can handle them,' said Yegor. 'Everyone knows the reputation Georgians have for being tough guys.'

'Yes, we do.' The trolley's wheels squeaked as we arrived back at the stall. 'We are all fearless warriors. Also amazing lovers with giant cocks women can't get enough of.' He laughed, fished a Rothmans out of a soft pack. 'Of course, this is gross exaggeration. We only repeat it because our fathers and grandfathers fill our heads with such nonsense. The average Georgian man is...well...an ordinary person. Like me.'

'What about the organised gangs, the syndicates? Everyone knows about them.'

'They exist, yes. But do you believe every Georgian businessman is part of that scene? Many are, not me. I run a clean operation. Those skinheads are giving me grief and I want *you* to do something about it.' His index finger dug into my chest and it bloody hurt. '*You* are the upholders of the law and public order in this city.' He drew hard on his cigarette. 'Not me.'

'Yegor,' I said. 'Please take down the good citizen's details and his official complaint.'

Irakli held up a hand. 'Come on. No need to get all bureaucratic. Just a word in their ear will be fine. Put the frighteners on them, so to speak. And like I said, for a few notes...'

'What was that about running a clean operation, Irakli?' I said, shaking my head slowly.

'What I meant was–'

A woman screamed.

Then another.

Glass smashed. Metal clanked as shelving toppled over.

More shouting voices, louder and louder. Pigeons and sparrows scattered, the flap of their wings like gun shots. Feathers fluttered down like indoor snow.

'There they are!' Irakli's face flushed red. 'The fuckers are back. Go get 'em!'

Yegor had already taken off, his boots a blur at ground level. I was a step behind him, sprinting as fast as my middle-aged legs could carry me. 'Don't alert them we're coming,' I huffed. 'Let's catch the bastards by surprise.' I saw the back of his head bob up and down as he nodded.

On the very far side of the market, just by the expansive entrance, I made out a group of four youths. They postured like roosters, swore at a quivering old man in a traditional Armenian fur hat. 'Fuck off, you dirty bastard,' spat the first kid. He was the biggest. Broad shouldered and a boxer's stance. I clocked him for the leader.

The old man held his hands up defensively, probably expecting to be struck by something.

'Go back to wherever you crawled from!' said another.

'Russia for Russians!' cried a third at the top of his lungs.

The fourth stood silently menacing, waved a long stick. Looked like a tyre lever. The lot of them wore ripped denim jeans and matching jackets. Despite the freezing weather, they were hatless, showing off shiny bald heads. None of them had any idea we were onto them. Burov had been right about wearing civvies.

Finished with terrorizing the Armenian vendor, the skinheads turned their attention to the next victim. A woman in a black scarf tended a wine stall. We were about twenty metres away now. A swarthy gent with a long, hooked nose appeared from behind a screen, put a protective arm around the woman. He waved a green bottle by the neck. 'Get away from here, you bastards!' he said. *Please don't throw it at them!* I thought to myself, as I coaxed my legs to keep up with Yegor. People got in our way as they ran in the opposite direction, fleeing the trouble. We pushed and shoved them aside.

'Stop! Militsiya!' I screamed. Four snarling faces turned towards us.

'You're not cops. Piss off,' the leader scoffed and spat on the floor. Childlike dimpled cheeks contrasted with glassy eyes glowing malevolence. His mates glared in support, shouted obscenities.

Yegor and I exchanged a quick glance and a nod. Outnumbered, but I was confident we could handle them.

'Come along quietly and no one gets hurt,' I said. I held out my hands, palms exposed. 'You've done enough damage. You'll get off with a caution if you cooperate.'

'Fuck off!' Dimples pulled out a knife with a fifteen centimetre blade. Rusty and serrated teeth you could saw a log in half with.

That was it.

'Yegor, take him!'

'Sir!'

Before the lout knew what was happening, Yegor grabbed him in a fierce wristlock. The knife fell to the ground with a clang. The lad screamed in agony and buckled at the knees as Yegor bent his wrist at an obscene angle.

'Let go, you bastard!' he screamed.

'Why should I?' Yegor grunted in his ear. 'Give me one good reason.' Another push on the wrist and the poor lad hollered like a bear caught in a trap.

Two of the lads legged it, vanished in an instant. The one brandishing the tyre lever stuck around to defend his companion. I stared at the youth, daring him to take a swing. He waved it at me like he was wielding a sword. 'Go on, son,' I said. 'Try me out.'

He snorted, drew the lever back. His hips engaged, twisted his body in a half-turn, like a discus thrower about to unleash. Deep blue eyes and feminine lashes, rather beautiful, focused straight at his target – my head. Before he could swing, I crouched low, sprang at his knees in a rugby tackle. I heard a sickening crunch as my shoulder connected with one of his patellas. The lad cried out, dropped the lever on the nape of my neck. Better than copping a full blown swing, still painful. Enough to push up my anger levels.

I roughly pulled the vanquished kid to his feet. He wriggled mightily, like a possessed demon. 'Fuck off, pig!' he spat.

'Right. That's it.' I dragged him back to the ground, applied a headlock. I quickly adjusted my grip. Now my forearm pressed firmly against his throat. His face started to turn purple, his eyes widened. He'd had enough. I reefed him back to vertical, copied Yegor's move and slapped on a wristlock. The youth stood a full head shorter than me, about Yegor's height. But he was stocky and strong as a bull. Yegor's detainee was closer to my height. For a fleeting moment I felt bad for creating the mismatch and siccing Yegor onto the big fellow. But the feeling passed; Yegor had acquitted himself superbly. Not that I'd be bringing that up often in later conversations.

'Your friends are cowards,' I hissed at Blue Eyes. 'Running away like that.'

'Fuck those pussies. They're not my friends, they're traitors.'

A curious crowd had gathered around us. 'Someone call the Militsiya!' cried a babushka.

'I'll go,' said a middle-aged man in a cheap business suit.

'No need, sir,' I said. 'All under control. We're plain clothes officers.'

I growled at Blue Eyes. 'Come along quietly, sonny, and we won't hurt you. Resist and we'll break your fucking arms.' I turned to Dimples, who grimaced and squirmed under Yegor's expert wristlock. 'You too, arsehole.'

Pity we had no vehicle. And no handcuffs. Escorting them back to the station on the Metro was going to be a barrel of laughs. I had another idea. We'd interview these louts on their own turf.

Chapter 11

Black Spider, he called himself. After the famous Dynamo Moscow football goalie Lev Yashin. I'd asked the kid on the train if it was because he was a great athlete. No. He simply shared the Hero of Soviet Sport's surname. Baby-faced, blued-eyed Yuri Yashin was a brainless, directionless thug. His stocky buddy was just as thick. Gennady Belikov, nicknamed Krokodil. I guessed for his slightly bucked teeth. Or because the diminutive form of his name was "Gena", like the popular kids' cartoon character. The idea of interviewing the pair didn't exactly fill me with joy.

Following a tense subway and tram ride to the heart of the grim Belyaevo district, we arrived at young Yuri's family home. A five-star shithole. Introduction to mum, already three parts paralytic, was short and laconic. The fact her son had turned up in the company of a couple of cops didn't faze her.

'Wanna cup of tea, gents?' she asked perfunctorily. 'I'd offer you vodka, but I've only got a little bit left. I'm saving it for the glorious Revolution Day celebrations.' She cackled, evidently pleased with her sarcasm.

'No thanks, Vera Stepanovna.' I surveyed the flat. A mountain of unwashed dishes and cutlery filled the sink. Bottles full of cigarette butts occupied every inch of floor space not already taken up by tattered cardboard boxes, food scraps, dirty clothes or skittering cockroaches. The cramped one-room apartment sat halfway up a characterless block of panelled apartments in an undesirable neighbourhood on Moscow's sprawling south-west. It stunk of generic filth and cheap cigarettes smoked with the windows permanently shut.

'I wouldn't mind one,' said Yegor.

'Your funeral, comrade' I said.

'Waddaya mean by that?' said the woman. She rubbed a dirt-encrusted fingernail under her red-raw nose, scratched down an arm dotted with faint needle tracks she didn't try to hide. Hair matted, hadn't seen shampoo in weeks. Pasty skin, red eyes veined like a road map, pin-prick black pupils barely visible.

'I mean your flat isn't fit for human habitation. I can't believe you and your son live like this.' I gestured around the tiny kitchen.

'It's our home and we're fine,' she said, turning on the tap to fill a kettle. Murky grey Moscow water sputtered into it. Yashin's mother struck a match and lit a gas ring burner with trembling hands, clanked the kettle onto it. 'His no-good prick of a father's in jail for stealing from the canning factory. I can't work 'cos of my…nerves. We're on the list for something better, but for now this has to do.' She hobbled two steps to the kitchen table, melodramatically flung herself into a chair. Her eye squinted like someone had stuck a hot needle in her bony arse. 'So go fuck yourself with your superior attitude.'

'Watch your tongue,' I snapped. 'I wasn't talking about the size of the flat. It's the squalor, woman. Once we're done here I'll be informing the child protection authorities about your neglect. Your boy, how old is he?'

'I'm sixteen, nearly seventeen,' Yuri interjected. 'I can speak for myself. That old bitch can go and fuck herself for all I care.'

'You ungrateful brat!' Vera grabbed a tea-stained mug and flung it at her son. He raised a hand, deftly caught it and hurled it back with double the force. She stood stock still, reflexes non-existent. The spinning mug collected her on the right shoulder, ricocheted into the sink and shattered.

'Aargghh!' she clutched at her arm, not letting go of her reeking Belomorkanal cigarette with the other hand. 'Arrest the little prick, why don't ya? I've done my best to raise him properly and look what he does. Attacks his own mamma.'

Yashin stood, puffed out his chest, jabbed a finger at his mother. 'She's the one needs arresting. Bloody child abuse.'

'All of you, just shut up.' Yegor banged a fist on the table. 'We don't want to be here, and you don't want us to be here, correct?'

Belikov, head bent, remained silent. Yashin and his mother nodded, the scowls never leaving their faces.

'Good,' I took over from Yegor. 'Vera Stepanovna. Take a walk for half an hour, OK? You boys sit still while my colleague and I inspect the apartment.'

Vera nodded, headed for the entrance on unsteady legs. I heard her grunting and bumping into the wall as she struggled to put on her boots. The door slammed and she was gone.

A quick search of the small sitting room and kitchen revealed nothing but garbage and chaos.

'Yegor, check the mother's bedroom. I'll wait here with these clowns.'

Yashin half stood to protest, I shoved him back down. 'On second thoughts, go with the nice officer while I have a chat to your mate.' I grabbed Yashin by the ear, dragged him towards the door to the solitary bedroom. 'Make sure my partner doesn't steal any valuable antiques or anything.'

'Fuck off,' Yashin said. He winced as I tightened the grip on his lobe. 'This is a complete waste of time.'

'Want me to charge you with hooliganism for today's exploits at the market?' Hooliganism is the perfect charge to nail a person for any antisocial act. I use it a lot.

Yashin shook his shaved head.

'That's a good boy. You're facing serious prison time for that knife business. Cooperate, and I might be prepared to look the other way. This time.'

I noticed minuscule pale-peach follicles struggling for life on the kid's skull as he meekly followed Yegor into the bedroom. Must be a redhead when in full bloom. Dim light from the naked overhead globe briefly reflected off the back of Yashin's pate into the kitchen window. I briefly caught my image in the grimy glass, wondered how my life had brought me to this juncture. Pathetic.

I turned to Belikov. 'You strike me as an intelligent young man,' I lied. The kid looked like he couldn't tie his shoelaces without assistance. 'Why are you mixed up with this gang of losers?' He glanced up at me for a second, top lip quivering, then cast his eyes towards his lap. 'Not so tough now, are you?'

No response.

'Answer the fucking question!' I felt the nodules in my throat strain.

Belikov raised his head, shrugged. 'Dunno. Just fell in with them hanging around the neighbourhood.'

'Who's in charge? Yashin? What about the two who fled the scene?'

He shook his head. 'No one's in charge.'

'Are you part of a larger political movement?'

Narrowed eyes stared back at me. 'Shit no. We don't care about politics.'

I didn't know whether to believe him or not. 'What about gang wars? Are you involved in them?'

'We stay away from gangs from other housing estates. Keep to ourselves.'

'Why the hell have you been terrorising people at the market? What have they done to you?'

He folded wiry arms across his chest, stuck out his chin. The moron was trying to be the tough guy again.

'If you don't answer my questions, I'll take you back to our Georgian friends. They're not kindly disposed to degenerates who frighten law-abiding citizens trying to make an honest living. They'll kick the living shit out of you while Yegor and I hold you down. Maybe cut you up with a *kinzhal*. Doesn't that sound like fun? Then we'll take you into the forest and hang you from a tree. Slice your dick off and feed it to the crows. How does that sound?'

'What the...'

From my chair I reached across to the kitchen bench, grabbed a meat tenderiser, rotten pieces of flesh stuck between its little pyramid spikes, smashed it down on the table. 'Next blow is to your fucking head. Understand?'

Yegor's voice shouted something unintelligible from the bedroom. Then Yashin uttered a profanity. A sickening thwack and a yelp of pain.

'Everything all right in there?' I said.

93

'Yes, Comrade Captain.' Yegor replied faintly. 'We were just having a little disagreement. Be out in a second.'

'See? You and your stupid friend are no match for us. Spill your guts or we'll skip the part about taking you to Irakli's clan. We might just finish you off here tonight.'

He nodded. 'All right. I get it. What was it you wanted to know again?'

I sighed. He really was thick. 'Why the attacks at the market?'

Before he could respond, Yegor frog-marched Yashin back to the kitchen, thrust him into a chair. Yegor gently placed a book on the table. 'I found some interesting reading material, comrade.'

Indeed. *Mein Kampf* in Russian. A hard item to get hold of. Possession of it was probably worth a long stretch in a Siberian prison camp with hard labour.

The lad's quivering bottom lip was swollen and bloody. 'It's not mine. Someone loaned it to me.'

'Who?'

The kid stared at his feet.

'I said who!'

'A guy I met at a party. Don't know his name.'

'What party? Where? Yegor, take notes. This could be important.'

'It was some bodybuilder dude from Lyubertsy.' Yashin's words tumbled out now. 'He just gave me the damn book, told me I looked like the type of guy who could learn a thing or two from it.'

'And have you?' said Yegor.

'Of course not.'

'I don't believe you.' I could feel my voice trembling. Could these boys be our killers? 'You carry out racist attacks, dress like white supremacists and keep banned extremist literature. Under your mother's bed, if you please. I suppose *she's* the Nazi.'

Yegor stopped writing for a moment. 'Let's take them to the cells, Viktor Pavlovich. These scumbags are a menace to society.'

'No. Wait a minute.' Yashin blinked hard. He fought to control his breathing. 'The guy offered us some money if we, you know, caused a

94

ruckus at the market. He even told us what to shout at them. Like it was in a movie script, you know. Sounded like something fun to do.'

Belikov nodded furiously. 'He's telling the truth. We don't hate Georgians, Armenians, any of them.'

'Then why the skinhead look?'

'It's just fashion,' said Yashin. 'We're big fans of ska music. English bands, mainly. This is the style they go for.' He pointed at his cranium. 'We just copy them.'

I sucked on the inside of my cheek. 'Are you sure you don't remember the Lyuber's name? Come clean. I promise not to charge either of you.'

Both boys were ashen faced. It wasn't an easy choice for them. Deal with the law or take your chances with a gang of violent thugs.

'OK,' Yashin agreed. 'But what if they find out we blabbed. Will you protect us?'

A burst of laughter. I think Yegor actually slapped his own thigh.

'Hell no,' I said. 'You want protection, pay for it like everyone else.'

Yashin took a deep breath. 'The guy's name was Aleksey.'

'Was the last name Rybakin?' I knew a particularly loathsome Lyuber called Aleksey Rybakin. We'd had a run in a couple of years ago. If this was the same guy, we could be onto something.

'No idea. It was just a party, you know? No last names at parties.'

'Where was it? A night club?'

'No.' Yashin shook his head. 'Aleksey's girlfriend's apartment.'

'Her name?'

'Klavdia. Everyone was calling her Klava. Don't know her last name either.'

'Address?'

'Pretty sure it was Staraya Street.'

'Just pretty sure?'

'It definitely was,' chimed in Belikov. 'Near the corner with Dorozhnaya. I remember 'cos my cousin lives in that street. It was building number nine.'

'Apartment?'

'Can't remember.'

'When was the party?'

'About three weeks ago, I think,' said Yashin. 'A Saturday night.'

I had no idea where this was taking us. They hadn't given us much, but the more information we had, the greater the chances of finding whoever killed Adekanye and Ivanov. We'd sniff around the building in Staraya Street, ask if anyone knew a couple called Aleksey and Klavdia. I wasn't sure how much more I could shake out of these two.

'Last question. Were there any Africans at the party?'

'Are you fucking kidding me?' Yashin arched his eyebrows. 'You think the Lyubers would invite black people to a party?'

I stood to leave, beckoned for Yegor to get up. 'Thanks for your cooperation. Reluctant as it was. Keep your damn noses clean.'

The boys' relief was palpable. They even managed a smile. A key turned in the lock and Yashin's face fell instantly. Can't be fun having a loser of a mother like Vera.

'I hope your information helps us find the killer,' I said.

'What killer?' Yashin stood up and down on his toes like a boxer itching to fight. 'What the hell are you talking about? I thought this was all about the shit at the markets?'

'Someone's been murdered.' I'd already let it slip, but I'd cover my tracks. 'We thought you may have been involved. Or know something about it.'

'Is that why you asked about Africans?' Belikov wasn't as stupid as I thought. 'We heard a guy went missing from the Gandhi University. Was it him?'

'I'm unable to say, I'm afraid.'

'That's a shame,' said Yashin. 'We like black people. Especially their music. Jamaica's the source of ska, did you know that?'

'No,' I admitted. I didn't even know what ska sounded like. Fuck it, why shouldn't I tell them what we knew? With all investigative assistance to us blocked, why should I play games? Maybe these boys could help. 'Have you heard anything else about the...victim?'

Belikov shook his head. 'Sorry.'

'Nothing happened at the party to indicate the Lyubers might've had a hand in it?'

Yashin scratched his head. 'The only thing odd was that everyone there was Russian except for one.'

My pulse accelerated. 'Who?'

'A Canadian guy. I remember 'cos he was wearing one of those maple leaf hockey jerseys. Spoke OK Russian, too. They called him Michel. He–'

Yegor and I exchanged a quick glance. 'Put your notebook away, comrade. Time to go.'

Chapter 12

Subway. Red line. Departing Gorky Park station. Fingers crossed I'd get a result from this fool's mission.

The man beside me was pressed so close we could have been Siamese twins. No matter which way I turned, I was in someone's face or armpit.

The recorded female voice made the announcement in a cordial yet businesslike manner. *Please be careful. The doors are closing. Next station – Kropotkinskaya.*

Thank God. Another five minutes of this insane commute and I'd be taking up Burov's offer of that psychological assessment. The patience of Muscovites who regularly use transit was legendary. Unfortunately, I didn't share it. Even Yegor's driving was preferable to crowded transportation with the unwashed masses. To save time and spread our razor-thin resources of two officers, I'd despatched Yegor to the apartment building the skinheads told us about.

I exited the train onto a packed platform, squeezed through the throngs. I jumped on the escalator and took a deep breath. Another escalator trundled down in the opposite direction, feeding a never-ending line of people into the insatiable belly of the V.I. Lenin Moscow Metropoliten, the Metro. A piece of infrastructure so effective and aesthetically wonderous it was envied the world over. I hated it.

Breaching the surface, I headed north-west along Gogolevsky. Trudged along pavements swept clean of snow. This was a part of Moscow I didn't often visit. Embassy territory, set aside for our honoured international guests, some of the new so-called cooperative restaurants and cafes. I strode along Gagarinsky, head bowed against the cold breeze, then made a right into Starokonyushenny Pereulok. You couldn't miss it – distinctive red-and-white maple leaf flag fluttered atop the entrance of a low-set two-storey frontage. Primrose yellow rendering, an abundance of windows. An area of prestige, privilege and power. A far cry from the egalitarian poverty of our district.

In true Soviet style, a sentry box stood next to the entryway. If I was going to get into the building, I first had to convince the hulking goon from the MVD's Diplomatic Corps Protection Service to let me in.

'Good afternoon, comrade.' I manufactured my best salute. He didn't return the favour. Why should he? People in civvies didn't command respect from officers in uniform. The brute continued to pick his teeth with a splintered match, stared at me like I was a piece of shit on the end of his shoe.

'What's the name of your superior?' I said, trying to hide the shaking in my voice. Check-point guards – at airports, government buildings, wherever – always engender an irrational fear.

'Papers!'

'Excuse me?' I should have expected the rude reception, but it still caught me on the hop. 'I'm not sure I like your tone, young man. I'm a senior officer of the MVD. Here's my ID card and passport.' I slid the documents under the glass partition. He flicked through them quickly, shaking his head.

'What do you want, Captain Voloshin?'

'To go inside, obviously. I need to speak to someone about a Canadian citizen. It's extremely urgent.'

'One moment.' He produced a large diary, ran a finger down the page. I studied the almost adolescent face under the grey *ushanka* fur hat. Hard lines for one so young – I pegged him at about twenty-two. His lips twisted into a rose knot. 'I can't see your name here.'

'Of course it's not there. I'm acting on brand-new information in relation to an important case.'

'Sorry.' He shrugged. I waited for him to say more. Give me an explanation.

'Please. Call someone. Tell them I have important information regarding a Canadian national.'

He pulled a pencil from the folds of his greatcoat. 'Tell me what you want to pass on. I'll see it gets into the right hands.'

'Listen.' I stamped my feet to get the blood flowing through my calves. 'I can't go telling a border guard. It's highly confidential.' Fat flakes began to fall. A snowy landscape in many parts of the city was nothing but an inconvenience. In this quiet alley, in a silent enclave of Moscow, it was breathtakingly beautiful. The young man behind the glass was impassive.

'I'm going to ask you to step away from the booth. Go away and come back with proper authorisation. You cannot be admitted into the embassy grounds without an appointment. No exceptions.'

Would arguing the point get me anywhere?

Objectively, no. Like a perverse version of Newton's third law, obstinance in this country is generally met with an equal and opposite level of stonewalling. One last-ditch effort wouldn't hurt though.

'Listen, sonny. My boss has a direct line to Viktor Chebrikov. Does that name ring a bell?'

A slight change of expression. Not quite alarm, but at least now he was taking a greater interest in what I had to say.

'Is that right?'

I nodded vigorously, a shower of snowflakes cascaded from my hat. 'Indeed, I was witness to a conversation between them just a few hours ago.'

'What about?'

How far could I go with this? 'A murder investigation that will have major repercussions for this city, the entire country. And if you don't let me inside this fucking embassy, for you.'

'Bullshit.' The man scoffed at my threats, knew they were as empty as the supermarket shelves. 'If any of that was true, you'd have already contacted the appropriate officials inside the embassy.' He jabbed a forefinger at the open book before him. 'And your name would be in this register. So, unless

I miraculously get a phone call from the ambassador or one of his aides, you're leaving. I'm going to count to twenty. If your arse is still visible from my guard post, you will be arrested.'

'For what?'

'I'll think of something.'

'Now–'

'One...'

'Call the ambassador, damn your hide.'

'Two...'

What a humiliation. Outsmarted, outbluffed by a kid with about as much experience in his job as I have cancan dancing. I'd slunk away defeated. Realistically, he was going to win that battle every time. Guys who stand watch over foreign embassies get to call the shots ahead of rank-and-file Militsiya cops looking for favours.

Back at the station, Yegor said I should have bribed the man – to either let me in or at least allow me to make a phone call to the Canadians. Dumb idea – the guy had been trained "the right way". Besides, backhanders would never be my approach. I looked up the embassy's number and made a call. I was put on hold for about two minutes before the number disconnected. I repeated the exercise three times, same result. Dead end. I asked Yegor how he'd fared at the Staraya Street apartment block. As badly as I had. Either no one was at home, or the residents hadn't heard of a couple comprising a body-builder called Aleksey and his girlfriend Klavdia. If they had, they weren't admitting it. It's no secret Lyubers don't take too kindly to tattle-tales.

I rubbed my eyes. Gritty. I glanced through cloudy eye-film at the plastic table clock on the kitchen dresser. Around it, a clutter of knick-knacks covered by mantle of dust. The numbers on the old Mayak clock wobbled like some special effect in a low-budget Mosfilm sci-fi movie. I tipped a bottle, the last few dribbles dripped into my glass. I shook it hard, but no more came out. What the hell was the time? I stood like a pensioner with rickets, staggered three steps to read the clock. 00.21. Jesus Christ. I'd been drinking slowly but steadily since I lumbered home, deflated after the day's litany of snafus. In order not to collapse into a paralytic coma, I shovelled a tiny bowl of macaroni and a slice of stale bread down my gullet. Watched the ever-objective state-sanctioned news, a couple of corny movie classics. Whatever drivel the government TV and Radio Agency 1 deemed fit for Soviet citizens to watch on a Thursday night.

None of the programs held my interest for more than a couple of minutes. I drifted in and out of sleep. Visions of wailing black people filled my mind. A crowd, three or four deep, eager fingers reaching to touch the coffin. The mourners at the front banged their fists on the lid, ululated their grief into a star-filled African night. If it wasn't those nightmarish images, Ivanov's widow screamed into my face, accusing. *You didn't protect my husband!* I deserved all of that opprobrium and more. In real life, not just my alcohol-addled imagination.

I sat back down on the couch to continue my one-man party. Two half-litre bottles of Pshenichnaya vodka on the chipped coffee table bore silent testimony to my dedication. The lemon-flavoured one lay on its side, a valiant soldier-bottle who died an honourable death. Ashtray full of crushed butts. I took a packet of Bulgarian BTs and peeked inside. Only two left. I extracted one with shaky hands and lit it. Took a shallow drag that raked the insides of my raw throat. I hacked out a phlegmy cough, wiped spittle from my lips with the back of my hand. The other cigarette would do for breakfast with a cup of black tea. Did I have sugar? Not sure. Maybe there was enough oats for a small bowl of kasha. Payday wasn't for another two weeks and I was skint. I recalled Irakli's implied offer of a financial incentive. I draped goose-fleshed forearms across thighs, shook my head. *Nah, Voloshin. Couldn't work.* The idea of taking a kickback made me feel dirty, like I should take a cold shower. How would *actually* taking one make me feel? A human wreck, like Dostoevsky's Raskolnikov after he bumped off the old woman for a few roubles. I knew I was taking the moral high ground, swimming against an irrepressible tide of corruption, but that was me. There was only one option. I'd have to hit Yegor up for a loan to tide me over. I wasn't sure I could get through the next few days without booze, and I was fresh out of vodka.

I flicked the off button of my state-of-Soviet-art Rassvet-307 TV set. Time for bed, mate. The bad guys will get away if you aren't on top of your game tomorrow. I'd drunk way too much. I should have put an end to the session three hours ago. Better yet, not even started.

I sat on the thin lumpy mattress, swung weary legs around and tugged off my socks. A quick sniff confirmed they should have been washed last week. I leaned back, put my hands behind my head, stared at a spot of mould on the ceiling.

There were important things to do tomorrow.

Nico, the French kid.

Before that, my weekly visit with Ksenia. One of the few things that kept me going. Usually under Svetlana's close supervision, but today I'd be taking her with me. On the case. Irresponsible, but I had no choice. Sick days all used up. No pay for a no show, unthinkable. Flat broke by the fifth of the month. I needed every kopeck possible at the end of November, a distant twenty-six days away.

I turned to look at the photo of my seven-year-old angel, in a silver frame on the bedside table. Huge white bows like butterflies, long plaited braids the colour of wheat. A couple of teeth missing in one of those lopsided smiles you only see on uncorrupted, optimistic children. I kissed my forefinger and touched the glass. *See you tomorrow, sweetie.*

By any objective measure, I'm a pathetic loser. An ex-wife who barely tolerates me. A child who only loves me because I'm her father and it's expected that little girls love their fathers. If I wasn't a detective, something Ksenia could brag to her little friends about, I'm not sure she'd feel the same.

But what were my troubles compared to what the families of Adekanye and Ivanov were going through?

Trifles.

Dammit, why does alcohol make me so maudlin? I'd book myself into detox, rehab, hypnosis, "coding" or whatever the hell they call it. Anything to end it.

As soon as I found out who killed the two men.

I reached over, turned off the lamp. My mind went as blank as a snowdrift and stayed that way until the alarm jolted me awake at 06:30am.

Chapter 13

Svetlana lives in one of those quirky five-storey apartment blocks known as Khrushchyovkas. Because a loophole in the construction code in the 1950s meant only buildings over five floors tall had to have lifts installed, these sprouted up around Moscow like mushrooms after the rain, as the old saying goes. This morning, I would've loved a lift, because, by a perverse twist of fate, my ex had scored a flat on the fifth floor. Worse, to get to her place I had to traverse the entire city, entailing a peak-hour subway ride with proletarian workers, many of them smellier than me. Then transfer to a dilapidated, unheated bus belching exhaust fumes that leaked inside through cracks, followed by a fifteen-minute trek to the apartment block through almost blizzard conditions.

On the positive side, my Militsiya ID allows me free transport around the city. A ride on anything only costs a few kopecks, but when you have no money, freebie commutes are a bonus. My cop credentials don't always work, though. The teenager at the kiosk outside my building won't accept my official ID as an IOU for smokes. I should give the disrespectful little shit a shakedown. Never one to waste an opportunity, though, I vowed to make today a health day. No cigarettes – apart from the rationed one I smoked at my food-free breakfast. It was a flexible plan, so exceptions were possible.

Finally at the top landing, I bent at the waist, hands on hips, sucked in big ones. A heart attack looming. My head throbbed like an angry hooligan wearing jackboots was kicking my temple. My mouth was as parched as Gorbachev's draconian dry law. I pressed the buzzer, heard its *drrrring* going off inside the flat.

I sensed her checking me out through the fisheye lens. Svetlana.

'Come in, you're late.' Dressed in her best white Egyptian cotton blouse and gabardine skirt. The outfit she wore to impress. Half a can of hairspray held thick black hair in place like a rock. No hat or hurricane could spoil that hairdo. Generous amounts of green eyeshadow, mascara. Red lipstick to round everything off nicely. No subtlety in the all-or-nothing makeup technique. I still found Svetlana incredibly attractive. The feeling wasn't mutual. She hated my guts.

'Can I have a glass of water?' I croaked. 'That's a helluva a hike up the stairwell.'

She gave a cynical laugh. 'Old Anton across the way manages. He's a WWII veteran, you know. Up and down several times a day, carrying heavy loads sometimes. I can't see why it's a problem for a young man like you, Viktor.' She turned to face me, squinted. 'Oh, yes I can.'

'I, uh...'

'You look like shit,' she said, back already turned and heading for the kitchen. 'I've got to meet my sister in twenty minutes, so be quick and we'll all be on our way.'

I trailed a metre behind her like a dog who's been told off. I took in Svetlana's scent, half closed my eyes. She reached up to a wire rack over the sink, poured me a half-glass of murky Moscow mud from the tap. 'Want an aspirin to go with that?'

I nodded, gave a smile that could only have looked pathetically sheepish.

'If I wasn't going to this stupid art show with Tanya, I wouldn't let you take Ksenia today. You've been drinking. A lot.'

No point denying it. 'I've got a tough case at the moment and it's getting to me.'

'Spare me, Viktor. It's always something getting to you.'

'Look, I'm not going to argue. I'm quite capable of looking after Ksenia today.' I put the aspirin on my tongue, flushed it down with a mouthful of tepid water. The glass shook slightly in my hands as I placed it on the kitchen table.

'Good. I'm going to be home around 7:30 tonight. I expect you to deliver Ksenia home no later than 8:00. I hope you've made some plans. I can't bear the thought of her hanging around in your godawful flat.'

'We're going to the Exhibition Centre, as it happens.'

She put a hand on her hip. 'Last time you took her there you only let her go on one amusement ride and didn't even buy her an ice-cream. Why are you so meanspirited with your own daughter? I've got half a mind to have your weekly access revoked.'

How could I tell her I was broke? Turns out I didn't have to. She grabbed her purse, pulled out a couple of hundred roubles. Held them out to me, flapped them too demonstratively for my liking. Taunting me.

'Make sure she doesn't go without...'

'Papa!' A small rag doll clutched firmly in her hand, Ksenia skipped across the floor and jumped into my arms. I'm sure she was a couple of centimetres taller than last week. My daughter was blossoming. My heart ached as I gazed into her adoring eyes.

'About time you got here,' she scolded. Fake frown and exaggerated stamp of the foot. 'Where are you taking me today?'

'Where do you think?'

'The zoo?'

'No.'

'The circus?'

'No.'

'The Exhibition Centre?'

I lifted her above my head. 'Yes!'

'My favourite! Can I go on lots of rides?'

'I'm not sure there're many operating in the winter. Skating?'

'Yay!'

'Just keep her out of trouble.' Sveta had to spoil the mood. 'You *have* got the day off today, right? Last time you said that you took her to your dirty old Militsiya station. Left her sitting there with one of your mates for hours while you dealt with a case. She cried all night after that disaster.'

I snuck a quick look at Ksenia as the ex checked herself out in the mirror.

107

Again. Ksenia gave the tiniest head shake and smile, unobserved by Svetlana. Sveta was so full of shit. Ksenia had had a ball at the station that day, playing board games with Rita. Perhaps Sveta had conveniently forgotten. I wasn't prepared to rock the boat today. Too many things going on in my mind; arguing with the ex while nursing a king-size hangover and trying to solve a murder wasn't going to help anyone.

'Don't worry. She'll be fine, won't you sweetie?'

'Yes, Mamma. Don't worry. I always have fun with papa.'

Sveta shook her head, sending a wave of perfume my way. It smelled damned good. 'I don't know,' she said. 'I'm not sure he sets the best example. Mixing with the wrong elements.'

I wasn't going to stand for that. 'Come on. It's those "elements" as you call them, that I'm arresting and putting in jail.'

'Ha! You Militsiya are just as bad. The most corrupt section of society if you ask me.'

'I didn't ask you.'

'I don't care. Everyone knows it. My friend Filip, you know him, the actor in that soap opera? Well, he recently paid a cop two-hundred roubles to avoid a speeding fine. And he wasn't even speeding!'

'That's a completely different branch. I've got nothing to do with traffic cops.'

'Doesn't matter. It's all law enforcement. The uniforms and badges might be different, but the culture's exactly the same.'

Another subject not worth debating. Because she was right. I grabbed my hat, gloves, scarf and coat. 'Enjoy your time with Tanya,' I said. Before Sveta could formulate a sarcastic riposte, Ksenia and I were rugged up, out the door and half-way down the first flight of stairs.

Chapter 14

The fluttering red flags at the Exhibition Centre were everywhere. Propaganda posters. Ideology. *Down with capitalism!* A macho Soviet worker delivering a foreign policy message: *Don't test our strength, Mr Reagan.* Another I remembered from my childhood: *The October Revolution opened the path to outer space.* Gauche and over the top, even by Moscow standards. But tomorrow was a big deal – the 70th anniversary of the Great Socialist Revolution of 1917. Up close, you could make out rips and tears in the banners, stitched holes. Patched-up, sewn-together tat. But from a distance, the imposing mass of red made you feel humble before greatness. *Look what the government has done for you.*

'Hey! Captain Voloshin. Over here.'

Nico.

I couldn't see him.

A steady stream of visitors was rolling in. Nothing like summer, still busy. Beanies and fur hats bobbed up and down, skates slung across shoulders, billowing clouds of steamy breath. I couldn't make out the young Frenchman among the mass of bodies and faces. I checked my watch. The kid was punctual, even if invisible.

I felt a tiny tug on my hand. For a moment I'd forgotten Ksenia was standing beside me.

'Someone called out your name, papa.' Her voice was sweeter than forest honey. Innocent. Why had I brought her along to this cloak-and-dagger rendezvous? Because Svetlana would have my guts for garters if *my* work got in the way of *her* fun. She's a good mother. Not a great one. Compared to me as Ksenia's dad, though, a paragon of virtue and a better proposition as the major parental carer.

'Over here!' Nico's clear voice penetrated the rumble of conversations, snatches of laughter. Why didn't he just walk up to me, for God's sake?

'Did you hear it?' asked Ksenia.

'Yes, darling.'

'Is it Yegor? His voice sounds funny.'

The lad burst through a pair of darkly clad humans clinging to each other like new lovers. Suddenly he was up close and personal. 'When I said by the fountain, I meant right next to it,' he said. 'Not over here by the ice-cream stand.' *Cheeky bastard.*

'Who's the strange man, papa?' I looked down to see Ksenia take a full-blooded lick of her vanilla cone.

Nico grinned broadly. 'I'm helping your daddy out with his work.'

I gave him the once over: stereotypical foreign male student bedecked in little red, gold and silver Soviet propaganda badges; even though you can buy them at kiosks for pennies Russian students don't tend to find anything fashionable about wearing the damn things. Ragged jeans, fluoro ski gloves, a tasselled beanie and gym boots completed the kitschy ensemble.

'Are you a detective, too?' said Ksenia brazenly. 'You don't look like one. And you talk weird.'

He laughed uneasily. 'What's the kid doing here?'

'She's my daughter. I had to bring her. Just one of those things.'

Nico cast a nervous glance around, back to me. His eyes were fluttering, pupils dilated. Playing spy was giving him a thrill. 'Actually, it's better this way. You look less like a cop with her hanging off you. Less conspicuous.'

'I'm not so sure about that. You look like a clown at a funeral.' I placed a hand firmly in the small of his back, ushered him away from the crowd. A combine harvester exposition was attracting few visitors. There was a quiet café next to it. Virtually empty. Ksenia clung tightly to my hand, her feet dragging behind, as I marched towards its entrance, mini red and yellow Soviet flags fluttering over the threshold. She squealed with delight at first as we tore along, then in horror as she dropped her ice-cream into a puddle. Her blubbering grew louder, attracting stares. 'C'mon, darling. Stop it. I'll buy you another one inside.' Thank God Svetlana had given me all that money. I bought us tea, some Napoleon cake, another ice-cream for Ksenia. Sveta hadn't asked for receipts, so two packets of BT smokes for me. Any leftover money after today would be returned to her; pride wouldn't let me keep it. We sat in a corner where I had an unobstructed view of the joint. I doubted it, but someone could be following me.

'I thought cops did it tough?' said Nico, his eyes taking in the little spread before us.

'My papa is the best cop in Moscow. That's why he gets paid so much. More than you ever will.' Ksenia spooned cake into her mouth.

'That's enough, sweetie.'

'I'm bored. Can I play outside?'

There was a playground with a roundabout in view of the café. Some kids about Ksenia's age were laughing, having a ball as they spun each other around. I pointed at it. 'I'll be keeping an eye on you. Don't go anywhere else.'

We watched her quickly take charge of the other three children on the ride. 'Unbelievable.' Nico shook his head.

'What?'

'In France you'd be more careful about letting a child out of your care.'

'What do you mean? I can see her perfectly well from here.'

'Still. Someone might abduct her. She'd be gone before you could get out the front door.'

A shiver ran down my spine. 'Well. This isn't France. Children don't get kidnapped in broad daylight in Moscow.'

'Whatever you say.'

'Just tell me what you know and we can be on our way.'

He smiled. 'I'm in no hurry. But since you asked me so nicely.' He slurped a mouthful of tea, wiped his mouth with a shirtsleeve. Took a deep breath. More tea.

'Well?'

'It's the Canadian guy. Lacroix.'

I gritted my teeth. 'Yes. We've established that. What about him specifically?'

'He's a huge hockey fan.'

'Not surprising for a Canadian.' This could turn into a complete waste of my time and energy. 'What else?'

'I've been chatting with this French kid. Laurent. I mentioned him to you before, remember?'

I nodded.

'I've got a last name for you. Guillot.'

I jotted the name down. I turned the notebook around, asked Nico to write the name in French.

'The guy's a weirdo,' Nico continued. 'Total opposite to Lacroix personality wise. But he tells me they share the same ideology. Which is bullshit.'

'Why?'

'Because Lacroix is up to his eyeballs in illegal capitalist shit and Laurent is a died-in-the-wool communist. Laurent lives in a bubble. Can't see the hypocrisy around him, thinks Lacroix's as pure as him. A complete fool.'

'Do you think I can get anything out of this French kid?'

'Absolutely. Physically, he's an insect. If you lean on him, he'll provide plenty on Lacroix.'

'Lean on him? What sort of tactics do you think the Militsiya employ?'

He shrugged. 'I dunno. You hear things. Besides, cops are the same all over the world. Pack of bastards for the most part.'

I was going to protest, but remembered how I'd dealt with the skinheads; my own approach was changing, and not necessarily for the better. Instead, I asked: 'You think you might be able to entice Laurent to go with you somewhere? I can catch him by surprise, get him to open up.'

'Why not just confront him at the dorm?'

'I've been warned off the Chekhov institute.'

Nico screwed up his face. 'Why? You're a cop. You can do anything you want.'

I laughed. 'You're naïve about a lot of things in this country, young man.'

112

'I guess.'

I snuck a look at Ksenia. Bossing the other children around. The apple of her mother's eye. I turned back to Nico. 'I had a feeling you were going to give me a lot more than this. I'm disappointed.'

He took a huge bite of his cake, savoured it. 'I haven't got to the best part yet.'

'I'm listening. It better be good or I'm leaving.'

'Lacroix has a connection with the Lyubers.'

Now we were getting somewhere. Corroboration with the skinheads' statements. 'What kind of connection?'

'Dunno.' He wiped crumbs from his lips with Gallic elegance. 'Has to be black market stuff. I heard a rumour some gang members come into town to play hockey. Scratch matches. On one of the big clubs' rinks.'

'Which gang and which club?'

He stared at the ceiling for a second before levelling his eyes. 'I don't know that for sure. I think it's something like the Foxes, or...'

'Wolves? The White Wolves?' *Please, let it be them.*

Nico held up an index finger. 'That's it.'

'You have no idea how useful that information is, Nico.' I reached across the table, patted his forearm. 'Good boy.'

The lad's face flushed pink. 'Anything to nail that Lacroix prick. As for the club, it's either CSKA or Spartak. Hang on, no. Dynamo. For sure, it's Dynamo.' Another piece of the puzzle. Only a thousand to go.

I decided to air my overarching theory, gauge how Nico would react. I lowered my voice even though we were now the only customers. 'My gut tells me Shukhov and Lacroix are behind the murders of the Nigerian and...'

'And what?'

'Never mind.' Shit. Ivanov's demise hadn't been made public, but the rumour mill would be running hot after yesterday's shootout on Leninsky Prospekt.

'No, go on. You said murders. Plural.' Nico leaned forward. 'Was it another student?'

113

The rumours hadn't reached him yet, but I wanted him on board one-hundred percent. A motivated man on the inside is invaluable. 'No. A Militsiya officer. I won't say more than that. But I've every reason to believe the two cases are intertwined. And that's why I need you to be my eyes and ears in the Chekhov Institute. Can you do that?'

Nico's eyes now sparkled like Yakut diamonds as he nodded furiously. 'Of course. Anything to help. What are you going to do next?'

'Only one thing I can think of. Take the train to Lyubertsy and start sniffing around.'

I tapped on the window, waved at Ksenia. She'd be coming to the Militsiya station with me after all. 'Keep your eyes and ears open,' I said to Nico.

I grabbed my hat and coat from the cloakroom, Ksenia from the playground, and headed for the Metro station.

Chapter 15

W here?' Burov ripped the plastic cover off a brand-new packet of Marlboro, tossed it on the table for me and Yegor to help ourselves. It's amazing how he's always got American cigarettes when I can barely afford the homegrown shite.

'Lyubertsy.' I said flatly, availing myself of the chief's shiny Zippo. He'd set the flame too high and I nearly lost an eyebrow. 'I've had a tip off Lacroix's been mixing with some of the heavies down there.'

Burov frowned. 'A tip off? Is it credible?'

'I've had two separate eyewitness accounts. First, a French student at the Chekhov's got his ear to the ground. Reckons Lacroix's thick as thieves with the Lyubers. Second, a group of youths we interviewed confirmed the Canadian attended a party on Staraya Street a few weeks ago. It was hosted by a Lyuber called Aleksey at his girlfriend Klavdia's apartment.'

'What does Aleksey have to say about this?'

'We haven't managed to speak to him yet,' I admitted.

'Maybe he doesn't exist and the youths you spoke to were leading you astray?'

'No way, sir.' Yegor tapped off a cylinder of ash. 'Those young men were telling the truth. We, ah, intimidated them quite a bit.' He leaned back in his seat, smiled with satisfaction.

'So you went there this morning, Lieutenant Adamovsky?' said Burov.

Yegor's smile faded. 'Unfortunately neighbours denied knowledge of both Aleksey and Klavdia, but I checked the residency register. A Klavdia

Tereshkova does officially reside at the address we were given.'

'So that's something,' I said hopefully.

'Could be,' Burov mused.

'Is the information enough to sanction a trip to Lyubertsy?' I said.

'Voloshin, sometimes I wonder what your IQ is.'

'What do you mean?'

'I'm not sanctioning anything. This is all off the books.'

I nodded. 'I understand, Comrade Colonel. I meant I wanted to square it away with you. Get your imprimatur, so to speak.'

A sharp rap made us all turn our heads.

'Yes?' Burov.

Rita Vasilyeva poked her head around the door. 'Comrade Colonel. This was shoved under the front door a couple of minutes ago.' She handed the chief a crumpled envelope. 'It's addressed to the station chief. That'd be you.'

Burov extracted a folded piece of grid-lined notepaper. He flattened it on the table with his fist, read aloud. *'Where's the news coverage, arsehole?* That's it?'

'Maybe there's more on the other side,' ventured Rita.

Burov turned the paper around. I could see it was covered in scrawled handwriting.

'What is it?' Yegor's eyes boggled. 'Is it from the killers?'

'Thank you, Rita. That will be all for now.' Burov gestured for her to leave.

'Aye, aye, Comrade Colonel.' She hesitated.

'Young Ksenia is waiting for you in the lunchroom.'

She gave half a smile, disingenuous. She liked playing with my kid, but she hadn't joined the Militsiya to be a babysitter. I vowed to involve Rita in more serious cases in the future – if I managed to hold onto my job amid the current shitstorm.

She pulled the door closed, her retreating footsteps echoing in the corridor.

Burov cleared his throat, read the note. *We are responsible for the death of the Nigerian student. You must ensure full coverage of this incident on state-run television, as well the newspapers* Pravda, Izvestiya *and regional press. Let it be*

known that interracial relationships will not be tolerated in a pure Soviet Union.
Failure to take action will see a white Russian woman killed who we have identified
as having an immoral relationship with a black man.

'Holy shit!' Yegor was on his feet. 'What are we going to do?'

'Nothing.' Burov's eyes fluttered, his voice remained calm.

'What?' I said. 'Surely we must do as they say.'

'We shall do nothing of the kind.'

'But why?' I said. 'Let's call their bluff and do as they request. I'm betting
they think we'll do nothing out of bloody-minded principle. Publicity could
be the very thing to flush them out.'

'Sorry. But I've told you before we got this letter, unless I get clearance
from above, we keep quiet. Besides, I'm sure it's just them taunting us. If
they're as interested in Russian purity as they say, there's no way they'd
murder one of our own. Especially a woman.'

'Are you sure about that?'

A long pause. 'No.'

Fuck. Caught between a rock and hard place.

The telephone screamed for attention on its cradle. Burov snatched the
receiver like it was the last loaf of bread for sale in Moscow. 'What, dammit?'
His face flushed, lips quivered, but he didn't interrupt the caller. He breathed
deeply, seemed to be gathering his thoughts to reply with a considered
response. A full two minutes of loud, agitated monologue was clearly audible
on the other end of the line. Burov interrupted the tirade.

'Now wait a minute. Tell me who…Fuck your mother!' He slammed the
phone back down. 'He hung up on me.'

Surely not another call from the Lubyanka?

Shaking fingers tugged three more cigarettes from a packet; the chief
tossed us one each across the table like he was feeding chickens. We sat for
a minute, smoking like chimneys, my health plan abandoned.

'They've just upped the ante, comrades.'

I waited for him to elucidate, exchanged a glance with Yegor. The
puzzlement in my partner's eyes must have reflected my own.

'Come on, Yevgeny Nikolaevich. Don't leave us in suspense. What the hell was that phone call about?'

'The bastard was threatening to detonate a bomb in the city unless the Adekanye story goes to press by tomorrow morning.'

'Holy Mother of God,' said Yegor, suddenly religious. 'Surely now we must act. A bomb going off to coincide with the Revolution Day celebrations would be horrific. What if they've planted explosives in a crowded area?'

'That's right,' I agreed. 'There could be scores, hundreds, thousands of casualties and deaths.'

'Calm down, both of you.' Burov took the piece of paper from the table, held it up by the corners. He winced as curling cigarette smoke irritated his eyes. The paper appeared to have been ripped from the middle of a notebook; ragged edges, smudged ink, black flecks. 'If the phone call I just received is from the same dickhead that sent this lame-arse threat, it's one-hundred percent bullshit.' He pointed somewhere in the middle of the text. 'It's full of bloody spelling mistakes, for one thing.'

He had a point, but I had one too. 'In my experience criminals are often ill-educated fools, not the tortured geniuses you find in Sherlock Holmes stories.'

'That's true. But if someone was going to the trouble of executing a plan like this, I'd expect a modicum of professionalism, not some poor excuse for an ultimatum a school child would be ashamed of.'

'What are you suggesting?' said Yegor.

'I'm suggesting it's someone close to the killers having a laugh at our expense.' Burov's face had resumed its normal shade of healthy pink. 'An acolyte who'd love to be in a position of power but is a peripheral player at best. I'd bet the people behind Adekanye's and Ivanov's murders know nothing of this.' Burov shook the piece of paper like he was trying to shoo a fly before slapping it on his desk.

We stared at our hands for a moment before I broke the silence. 'Are we free to travel to Lyubertsy now, Yevgeny Nikolaevich? I'd like to get cracking on my one lousy lead.'

The chief waved his hand dismissively. 'Of course. Call me as soon as you arrive. You may have to do a U-turn if the higher-ups want a word with you once they learn about the latest developments.'

'There's nothing I can tell them they don't already know.'

'Just be prepared for it.'

'Sure, boss.' As I stood to go, one thought nagged me. 'You know, I can't help thinking about the ritualistic way Adekanye was murdered. The cross carved in his chest, the castration. The killers would want the world to know about that, surely. Otherwise they would've just offed him in some boring way, maybe tossed him in the river. It seems too elaborate. Are you totally convinced this isn't a real threat, Comrade Colonel?'

Burov reached across his desk, stubbed out his smoke with more force than necessary. 'No, I'm not fucking convinced.' He reached for the telephone, started dialling.

'So you *are* calling the press?' said Yegor.

'No. Much as it pains me, I'm passing this evidence on to the CID. They'll no doubt engage the KGB. Alpha Group. They can scan the areas where crowds are going to gather. Send in sniffer dogs. Let the big boys handle this part.'

'I think that's the best idea, Comrade Colonel.' I tugged my gloves on. 'Any news on the Ivanov murder investigation?'

'No. Why would there be? It's a CID matter, remember?'

'I understand that, Comrade Colonel. I thought maybe something might've leaked.'

'Nope. No leaks. Tight as a drum.'

'You think they'll change their mind once they hear about the bomb threat?'

'No. But at least it'll spur them into ramping up security measures at the march tomorrow. I pray I'm right about this being a hoax.'

'Me too.' I grabbed my winter accoutrements and Yegor, and headed for the train station. Next stop, Lyubertsy.

Chapter 16

I'd hoped to find opposite-facing benches with a couple of empty spots, but the train was a bulging sardine can the whole journey. Moscow Region's mass transit brings the working class together in its own special way.

Much as I like Yegor, having him dozing on my shoulder with his slobber all over my lapel isn't my idea of a fun half-hour trip. I poked and prodded him a few times; he shook himself awake but was soon fast asleep again despite the painfully hard polished wooden seats. Across from us sat two teenagers in the flush of young love. Kissing, canoodling, laughing at each other's inane comments. As if Yegor and I weren't even there, like no one was there. I was tempted to tell the pair to cut it out, but what the hell. Their naïve happiness was the antithesis of the crusade I was on and, to be honest, gladdened my heart.

I rubbed a circle in the window with my hand. Weeks-old grime attached to my fingers, probably harbouring contagion; I should have left it alone. No real need for a sneak preview of what waited for us, but human curiosity defies logic. Through the glass I glimpsed streets scarred with deep potholes, patches of snow, dirty brown after the ploughs had "cleaned" up the roads. Soot stains on windowsills, tasteless graffiti on walls, polluted air thick with carcinogens, crumbling buildings. Two stray dogs, ribs exposed and hackles raised, faced off over food scraps. Hunched-over pedestrians with slow lumbering gaits. Joyless. I hadn't missed the place.

If the Soviet Union had a model district that reflected the state of perfection achieved by socialism, Lyubertsy would not be it. Physically, it's a shithole on every level. The inhabitants, on the other hand, are the salt of the Earth: hard-working people, honest, upright citizens who care for each other. Actually, let's back that up a bit. They're mostly the type of people you'd expect to be living in a shithole. Thieves, cheats, drunks and liars. At least that was the cohort I dealt with when I worked in the satellite city. Now, glancing out the window of the *electrichka* zooming its way to our destination, I held out hope things might have changed. As the train rolled into Ukhtomskaya Station, the sight of two ageing alcoholics by the ticket counter, slugging it out with fists and bottles, told me they probably hadn't. I nudged Yegor in the ribs with my elbow, hard. We'd arrived.

...

Checking in with Burov on a payphone took all of two minutes. He was thankful for the call, though there was an edge in his voice. Like he didn't think we'd get out alive.

I held out the neon sign. A red-and-white packet of genuine American Marlboro cigarettes. Guaranteed to score you a ride in a private taxi anywhere in the USSR. As far as currency goes, these cancer sticks beat the hell out of everything. Except maybe a litre of vodka.

'Much obliged.' The driver accepted my payment and shoved it inside the depths of a navy blue greatcoat. He wouldn't be best pleased when he opened the packet to discover the Russian stowaways inside. Hardly my fault; technically the man was breaking the law by giving us a ride, depriving authentic taxi drivers from making a living. Every socially aware citizen in the country knew about the insidious practice, though it was a rare event indeed if a driver was charged with an offense. It went on unchecked, and no one complained too much about it. Me included, especially since we'd been relieved of an official vehicle to get us around. The driver shoved a stick of gum in his mouth. 'Where to, fellas?'

'Marshall Zhukov Street. The red brick building at the far end. Know where it is?' I kept my voice as neutral as possible as we clambered into the car's back seats.

'Excuse me?' The man stuck a finger in his ear, wriggled it as if clearing a blockage. 'Not sure I heard you correctly.'

'Look, I know you might be afraid, so you can drop us off a few hundred metres away. We'll make the rest of the journey on foot.'

The driver, a clean-cut man I guessed to be in his late-twenties, adjusted his rear-view mirror to get a better look at me. He moved it again to check out Yegor. 'You two don't look like nut cases, so you must be cops.'

'Very perceptive,' Yegor whispered to me. 'If everyone in town is as smart as this guy, we're not gonna find out anything useful. Poking our noses in where they aren't wanted might get us killed.'

'Don't panic,' I whispered back. 'We're both armed, the Lyubers probably aren't.'

'Probably?'

'More than probably. These guys pride themselves on their prowess in bareknuckle fighting, martial arts. Knives at a pinch. They don't go around shooting at people.'

'Don't be too sure.' I must've spoken a touch too loud. The taxi driver reached into his pocket, started to deftly unwrap the Marlboros one-handed. 'There's quite a few lads here returned from Afghanistan. Shell shocked, not right in the head. Itchy trigger fingers on some of 'em.'

Yegor fished a real Marlboro from a packet he'd been keeping warm in his jacket, lit it and handed it to the driver. 'Save your fresh pack for later, comrade. Tell us more about the war vets.'

'What's to tell? Many got recruited from Lyubertsy because they're patriotic, and they love to fight. The perfect soldier, if you're after cannon fodder.'

The guy was a peacenik, and his tone told me he wasn't a big fan of the local thugs. The next thing he said proved it. 'The Lyubers are a fucking disgrace and bring nothing but shame on this city.' He wound down the window, spat into the icy morning air. 'If you guys are here to make trouble for them, I'm only too happy to take you where you want to go.'

'All right then,' I said. 'Drive on.'

Our chauffeur pulled his beanie low over his ears, took a last deep drag on his smoke, flicked it out the window. He stepped on the gas and the engine in the plucky VAZ-2101 Zhiguli shit-box buzzed like an angry wasp. As we zigzagged down the icy main road leading to the city centre, I had the impression our obliging stranger may have gone to the same driving school as Yegor. The speedometer nudged 100 kph as the man weaved in and out of lanes, honked at slower drivers and shouted obscenities at everyone and no one in particular. Yegor's mouth hung wide open, eyes shone. I gripped the door handle, knuckles white, ready to leap to safety if need be. Twenty-six minutes later we pulled up outside a dilapidated two-storey, redbrick building constructed with scant attention to detail; mortar appeared to be oozing out between the bricks like icing on a cake. The faded red letters on the wide façade told us the place used to be a small-scale textile factory. The building proper sat behind a concrete fence.

'Here we are, gentlemen. Headquarters of the White Wolves. You couldn't hope to meet a nicer bunch of hooligans in all of Russia and its brother republics.'

I remembered a nasty run in I had in 1985 with the gang's leader, Aleksey Rybakin. A frantic fistfight in a parking lot that knocked out one of my teeth and dented his pride. I'd broken his arm in the presence of one of his underlings. Me bobbing up would remind him of that embarrassment. 'You know who's giving the orders these days?'

The driver shook his head. 'Why the hell would I know that?'

'You know precisely where their den is, why not the personnel?'

'I know where the fucking hospital is, but I don't know the name of the doctor in charge, do I?'

Yegor burst out laughing. 'Viktor Pavlovich, I think you've met your match.'

I failed to see the humour. 'Will you wait here, comrade? We'll need a lift back to the train station once we're done.'

'Ha! Or to the hospital I just mentioned. Got another packet of smokes?'

I felt my pockets. 'No, sorry'. However I still had plenty of Sveta's money left over. All for a good cause. I peeled off four coral-coloured 10-rouble notes. 'That do you?'

He shook his head.

'Come on,' I said. 'That's plenty.'

'Give me another ten and I'll do it. I'm risking life and limb bringing Militsiya to this place.'

It was supposed to be the public bribing cops, not the other way around. I reluctantly handed him 50 roubles in total. 'Don't go anywhere. I've got your licence plate number.'

The steel double gates looked like they could stop a tank in its tracks. A thick padlocked chain snaked through a couple of square holes at eye level. I glanced over my shoulder to check on the driver; his head was buried in this morning's edition of *Komsomolskaya Pravda*, smoke billowed around his ears. He was going to be pissed off when he discovered the cigarettes we gave him were bogus, but the extra 50 roubles should have locked in his loyalty – for now. No other signs of life in the vicinity save for the ubiquitous cawing crows.

'What now, Comrade Captain?' Yegor said.

'We smash our way in.'

'With what?'

I scanned the area; plenty of rubble lying about. 'Those.' I hefted half a brick in my hand, Yegor grabbed a similar sized one and we set to smashing the padlock off the chain. Mine shattered on impact with the first blow and I thought we'd have to abandon the attempt. Yegor's held together, and on the third strike the shackle cracked enough to wiggle it free from the lock. I shouldered the massive steel gate and shoved. It wouldn't budge. Yegor bent his shoulder to the task and slowly the gate creaked open before banging against a metal pole. The noise was loud enough to raise the dead. We stopped, held our breath. After a minute or two it was apparent no one heard us.

We approached the door to the factory itself. Scratched paintwork, carved initials. *VV loves TZ. Anya is a slut.* A small grilled window on the left-hand door. Someone had tried to prise it off, only managing to lift up a corner of the grille.

I pressed my ear to the door, heard nothing. Knocked hard three times and waited. Another three knocks.

'No one home,' I said after a minute of shuffling feet and patting gloves together. 'Perhaps this was a complete waste of time.'

Yegor pushed past me, yanked the handle and pulled the door open. 'Maybe not.' He winked at me and I felt my face flush. *Idiot.* 'After you, Comrade Captain.'

Inside, a low-wattage bulb dangling from a cord gave off a faint light. For a second the image of Adekanye's head in the noose flashed before my eyes. Reminded my why we were here at the arse end of Moscow.

The vestibule was dark and only a degree or two warmer than on the street. No smell of stale piss like you'd find in the foyers of many apartment blocks. Instead, faint hints of fresh liniment, chalk and antiseptic. Beyond the staircase leading to the second floor ran a long corridor; at the far end a crack of light showed under a door. If memory served me correctly, that's where the Lyubers did their training. A spacious storage area converted into a gym. They'd been camped here since the start of the 1980s and no one had told them to leave.

As we approached, a *thwump, thwump, thwump* sound got louder and louder. We heard youthful male voices laughing, shouting encouragement. *Come on, Vanya. You can do it. Push. Good lad!*

I was done knocking. I pulled the last door open and we marched into a spacious training area full of young men lifting weights, sparring, laying into heavy bags, performing advanced calisthenics. The loud sound we heard was two men jumping rope. They stopped immediately, swivelled in our direction, tossed the skipping ropes aside. Iron bars clanked on concrete as men leapt from weight-lifting benches to their feet. All eyes focussed on me and Yegor.

I did a quick head count; I sensed my partner doing the same, assessing our position. Eleven of the bastards counting Rybakin. Some of the goons made the ringleader look demure. One snarling brute massaging a heavy bag was the biggest damn Lyuber I'd ever seen. Tall enough to play basketball for the national team if not for the massive muscle bulk. The rest of them, shirtless, sweaty and shredded, faced us with fiery anger plastered across their ugly mugs. Some of them I remembered: Kostya, Vadim, Igor. All of them fearsome thugs who rarely took a backward step. Tact was going to be the order of the day if we were to avoid violence and bloodshed.

'Fuck me! If it ain't old Captain Voloshin.' Rybakin, as cocky as ever, threw boxing gloves to the ground and swaggered towards us. I felt Yegor's shoulder press into mine. Protecting me. An evil grin slowly spread across Rybakin's face. 'What brings you back to Lyubertsy? Moscow too big and scary? I see you've brought a bodyguard.' He ran his eyes up and down Yegor, sneering disapproval. 'A bit undersized to be bringing to our HQ. He ain't gonna be much use if we decide to give you a flogging.'

'Calm down, Aleksey. I'm here on business, as it happens. We've got no issue with you guys.' *Yet.*

The leader of the White Wolves took two giant strides, stuck his enormous square jaw up against my nose. 'Didn't they teach you to knock in the big smoke? Here it's the accepted way of doing things.'

'We did knock.' I side-eyed Yegor, noticed him feeling for the pistol under his coat. 'Only no one bothered to answer.'

I touched Yegor's wrist; I hoped he read the signal to be wary with the gun. 'He's right,' I asserted. 'We observed protocol. Knocked on the front door.'

'But not this one, motherfucker. Not to mention the fact you must've broken the padlock to get in the front gates. We ought to tear you both to pieces.'

The other gang members closed ranks, lined up behind Rybakin. Some clenched their fists; bashing a couple of out-of-town law enforcers would bring welcome variety to their exercise regime. The temperature in the room seemed to surge; a bolt of white heat ran down the back of my neck. With both hands I gestured for all the gang members to calm down. 'Listen, fellas. We're only here to ask questions. Nothing more.'

'Why the hell should we answer any of your questions, filth?' barked a pimply kid with arms as thick as my thighs. Igor Zinoviev, three years older than our last encounter but no change to his youthful appearance.

'Because the sooner you do, the sooner we leave and you can get back to your precious training.' I glared at Rybakin. 'Fair enough?'

'Start talking. You've got five minutes. After that you can fuck off.'

I stifled a sigh of relief. I sensed Yegor relax as he softly exhaled. We might not get all the answers we wanted, but we'd get out alive. Some of the gang members frowned disappointedly, others grinned as their boss dictated the terms of engagement to the pair of dumb cops.

'What do you know about a Canadian student called Michel Lacroix?'

'Never heard of him.' Rybakin's eyes remained steady, unblinking. Arms folded across his barrel chest. Like he was trying too hard to pass a lie detector test.

'Are you sure?'

'Of course I'm sure.'

'Never met him, spoken with him?'

'Listen, Voloshin, if I ain't heard of him, the other questions are pointless, aren't they?'

'You're lying.' Yegor slipped a hand inside his coat again. I shut my eyes tight. 'We know you boys come up to Moscow to play hockey at Dynamo's rink.'

'So what?'

'Lacroix plays there too.' I said. 'We have it on good authority it's with the White Wolves.'

'Lots of wannabes come along to watch us mix it with the top players. Foreign kids among them. He might be one, but I couldn't tell you for sure.'

'We also have a statement from a group of skinheads; they saw you at a party in Moscow where you talked to Lacroix.'

'I talk to lots of people.'

'One said you gave him a copy of *Mein Kampf.*'

'I have to hand it to you, Voloshin. You have a hell of an imagination. Why the hell would I have that book in my possession? Hitler was a German. We're Russians. We don't need Fascist ideologies. They're the very cunts we beat into submission, or have you forgotten your history?'

All I was getting was denials, but I pressed on.

'Do you remember a man in a bright red sweater with a maple leaf on the front?'

'Never seen anyone like that.' He placed a forefinger to his temple, shot me a look of supreme sarcasm. 'Oh, yes I have. Wayne Gretzky!'

The room erupted in laughter. Even I'd heard of the Canadian superstar hockey player.

The exercise was proving worse than futile, but I went through the formalities and described Lacroix as best I could. The gang members shook their heads in unison.

'That description fits thousands of people. Nothing exceptional.' Rybakin kneaded his right fist with his left hand. His gaze never left me. I imagined how much he wanted to smash his fist into my face. Payback. The only thing stopping him would be his well-founded suspicion we were armed.

Why didn't I remember to bring the photograph of Lacroix that was in the file we swiped from Shukhov? If he spent time in Lyubertsy, us asking around the traps armed with a photo would have increased our chances of learning something useful. Dammit, time was ticking. We needed to get a result from somewhere, but the Lyubers were giving nothing away.

'I know you're covering something up,' I said. 'I admire your loyalty, Aleksey, but Lacroix is someone even fools like you should steer clear of.'

Rybakin sneered. 'We're quite capable of deciding who to associate with.'

Yegor gave a little cough. 'Perhaps if I could just–'

'Shut up, little man.' Rybakin growled, stabbed a finger at Yegor's sternum.

I slipped my hand inside my coat. Now both Yegor and I had our fingers on our pistols. The situation could explode if we weren't careful. I saw a cloud of chalk in my peripherals as one of the lads clapped his hands together. A mumble of voices echoed around us. Rybakin must've sensed the tension escalating behind him. He commanded their loyalty but a pack mentality can develop in a heartbeat. I've seen it before.

'I know you and Voloshin have guns under your coats.' Rybakin spoke smoothly, less aggravation now. 'Obvious as the red star on top of the Kremlin. We,' he held his hands up in a surrender motion,' however, are completely unarmed. Much as I'd take great delight in unleashing the boys onto you, I'm going to refrain.' His eyes narrowed to slits. 'Now if you'd kindly be on your way.'

I'd try one more approach before abandoning hope. 'You haven't even asked the real reason why we're here. Aren't you curious?'

A quick shake of the head. 'Nope.'

'Not even a little?'

'You filth can't take a hint, can you?' Rybakin's calm façade was crumbling again. 'Just turn around, walk away and don't come back. We've enough problems with our own cops without the likes of you giving us grief.'

'One more question. Do you have a girlfriend called Klavdia?'

'What's that got to do with anything? I shag plenty of women. You don't expect me to remember all their names, do you?' He pointed at the door. 'You've been here long enough and achieved nothing except waste everyone's time. Now go!'

I felt my nostrils expanding and contracting; my breathing slowed despite the fact my heart was pounding like a jackhammer. There was nothing more to say.

'A pointless trip, like you predicted, Comrade Captain.' Yegor stood legs apart where he calculated the doors of the train would line up when the elektrichka ground to a stop. To make sure we got a seat. Trains travelling into Moscow are more crowded at this time of the morning than ones heading the other way.

'Not entirely. You saw the looks on their faces. Especially the leader. Not only do they know who Lacroix is, they know him well.'

Yegor nodded. 'It was pretty obvious, wasn't it? Rybakin's denials were too vehement. They're mixed up in some bad shit.'

I nodded. 'Yes. The murder of Aaron Adekanye to be precise.'

'And Ivanov?'

I tugged my bottom lip, numb in the freezing air. 'Not directly. My gut tells me Shukhov's involved. I wouldn't be surprised if that whole tragic affair with Ivanov was a mistake.'

'I don't get your meaning?'

I lit a smoke, a tried-and-true method for getting public transport to arrive when you've been waiting a while. 'Why take him out? A beloved, non-controversial figure who did his job well. Makes no sense. I reckon they were either aiming for me or it was a warning that got completely fucked up. Rifle misfiring, sniper got the yips, something like that.'

'Why do you think so?'

'The rapid response in hunting the shooter. The Spetsnaz were on the spot way too fast.'

'But if the shooter was an inside man, so to speak, there'd be no one to hunt, right? Burov said as much already.'

'I see your point. I didn't mention my theory to Burov at the time because I wasn't a hundred percent sure he himself was innocent in all of this.'

A blank stare from Yegor. 'Well? Tell me about this theory of yours.'

'What's the one thing the KGB does better than any other organisation in this country?'

'Arrest and torture people.'

'That too. But I'm referring to the creation of scapegoats and fall guys and then hanging them out to dry.'

'So you're saying…what are you saying, exactly?'

The horn blast from the approaching train caused a bustle of activity on the platform; other folks were also trying to guess where the doors would open and racing for prime position. 'I'm saying whoever fucked up decided they didn't want to face the consequences and chose to make a run for it. If it was a KGB operative, that's something he'd be very good at. Probably kilometres away before the tactical response boys arrived.'

The train screeched to a halt, the doors burst open and we forced our way in through the crush. No niceties observed, we charged for a vacant pair of seats, collapsed side by side in a breathless heap. All the seats filled within seconds, and soon the aisle was jammed with unlucky commuters too slow off the mark.

'So, Yegorchik. Any ideas on how to proceed?' I stared out the window as I spoke, too deflated to look at my partner. His silence told me we'd reached a dead end. Three minutes later he spoke up.

'You tried the Canadian embassy and came up empty, right?'

'Thanks for reminding me.'

'Why not try the Nigerian diplomats?'

I shook my head. 'What makes you think I'll get inside this time?'

He paused for a moment. 'Maybe the guards there are more lax than at Western embassies.'

'I doubt it. But you're right. We've nothing else to go on.' A thought occurred to me. 'Flora.'

'Pardon?' Yegor sat bolt upright.

'The woman at the Chekhov. Maybe the Nigerians can throw some light on her. Something about her seems, I don't know, off.'

Yegor's dimples deepened as he flashed me a smile of encouragement. 'That's the spirit, Viktor Pavlovich. Thinking outside the box.'

The more I thought about it, the more the idea had potential. The Nigerians might also have information no one else had to paint a better picture of the victim. They'd surely want to know the truth about Adekanye's death, and be keen to restore faith among the students that their sponsor the Soviet Union hadn't abandoned them. That at least someone cared. Even if that someone was only me.

Chapter 17

'I've come to speak to the Ambassador about a vitally important investigation.' I tried to sound as nonchalant as possible while maintaining an air of authority. As if "no" was not only an answer I wouldn't take, but one I hadn't even contemplated. I slid my card and passport under the partition. The wide-eyed guard studied it for a moment, grabbed the phone, said a few muffled words, hung up and passed me back my ID. I was mentally rehearsing arguments when he uttered words that caught me completely by surprise.

'The Ambassador was unexpectedly called back to Lagos last week. However the Cultural Attaché will see you, Viktor Pavlovich.' A short sharp buzz and the gate clicked open. 'Up the path, Comrade Captain. Ring the bell.'

Once through the main door, a young black woman, smartly dressed in a camel-coloured pantsuit, ushered me past reception down a narrow corridor lined with portraits of Nigerian potentates in colourful hats. In a modern office, behind an expansive mahogany desk sat a corpulent African with the brightest smile I'd ever seen. Crisp white shirt under a pale blue jacket, cheery floral tie, chunky silver necklace. The air reeked of sweet cologne and rich cigar smoke. I took an instant liking to the man. He stood with difficulty, his spherical belly rubbing against the inside of his desk, and gestured for me to take a seat opposite him. The nameplate said Sir Harry Okocha.

'I'm assuming you've come to discuss the matter of our poor medical student, Mr Adekanye.' The smile faded, the gravitas of the situation taking over his natural ebullience. His heavily accented Russian was fluent; a product of our education system rewarded with a diplomatic post.

'How do you know that, Mr Okocha?'

'What else could it be? And please, call me Harry.'

I edged forward in my seat. 'You assume correctly, Harry. That's precisely why I'm here.'

He shook his head slowly. 'A tragic event that's touched everyone in the embassy, all our nationals across the USSR.'

'I can't imagine what you're all feeling.'

He nodded slowly. 'Would you like some tea, coffee? Whiskey perhaps?'

Against my better judgement I accepted the offer of liquor. I'd drunk a lake last night. On the other hand, a hair of the dog could be just the thing. Thankfully, Yegor wasn't here to give me a prudish lecture about drinking on the job. He'd been called away by Burov to help out at a mini riot at the markets. I hoped it wasn't those skinheads we'd let off with a warning. None of that mattered now, though, my focus had to be on the murder case. I sipped the whiskey, savouring its embracing warmth, instant reinvigoration.

'Please, tell me how we can help.' The attaché swallowed half the contents of his crystal tumbler in one mighty gulp. 'Anything to get the matter cleared up. I'm surprised we've had no visits from the Militsiya until now, it's all been through diplomatic channels. Even the cause of death is shrouded in mystery. The Russians are calling it death by accident. Our students claim it's a racist murder.'

'What do you think?'

'Do you know what happened in 1963?'

'Yes.'

'Then you know we are walking a tightrope. On the one hand, we must maintain close and cordial ties with the USSR, on the other, our people want justice. Personally, I'd like to know the truth and proceed from there.'

I wondered how candid I should be with the gentleman. Although I'd only just met him, I had to take a gamble.

'I'm hoping you might have some information our CID investigators consider unimportant but could prove significant.'

'Such as?' He finished his scotch, wiped his lips with the cuff of his shirt and reached for the decanter.

'How about we go somewhere else to continue our chat?' There could be bugs planted in the embassy. Rumours were running rife the US embassy was the target of a huge bugging campaign about to be busted wide open by the Americans. Nigeria was a minnow on the espionage front, but one never knew with the KGB. They liked to cast their nets wide.

'Where do you suggest?' The eager look on his face told me he'd be happy to abandon the office for an hour or two. Get out into the lead-polluted winter air.

'The Intourist Hotel. You know it?' The most rhetorical question I'd ever asked. This joint on Gorky Street near Red Square was not only a fine example of brutal neo-constructivist architecture, it was also a magnet for foreign tourists, businessmen, diplomats, black marketeers and hookers.

'Of course.' The man beamed like he'd just become a father to triplets. 'But it's not my favourite meeting place. I prefer the National Hotel.'

So did I. Classier, more discreet and safer, if that was possible in the world's number one spy city. 'Sure. Let's go.'

We nestled in a corner booth of the National Hotel's Heineken Bar, our only company a pair of construction workers at a tiny round table by a window. Their loud conversation in the unfathomable Finnish language sounded like jackhammers bouncing off steel. Surrounded by a phalanx of empty litre glasses, they wobbled in their seats after gunning lager and cognac. The Finns were valued by the city of Moscow for their work ethic, but as drinkers of hard liquor they gave the Russians a run for their money.

'I can't believe the look the doorman gave you, Detective.' Okocha gripped his glass with a giant hand. 'Is that what I should call you?'

'I answer to anything.' *Especially if I'm seeking information and you're buying the drinks.*

Okocha tossed peanuts into his mouth. 'Are you in the hotel's bad books?'

'No. Places like this don't allow Russians inside as a rule. They only let me in because I was with you.'

'Surely a flash of your badge would be enough?'

I took a sip of the crisp Heineken. I smacked my lips; this stuff beat the local brews I queue up for on the street and drink out of glass jars. The Nigerian was paying, and I was accepting his hospitality without demur. 'I'd rather not advertise the fact I'm a cop. Let them think I'm a business colleague or whatever, much safer that way.'

Okocha rubbed his chin. 'Ah, of course. Now, what can I tell you that might help your investigation?'

I told him all my work was "off the books", that I was operating solo but for the assistance of a partner who'd been called away on more "important" duties. 'The MVD and KGB want to keep this under wraps for now. I'm sure they're working on some kind of cover-up story as we speak.'

The generous man buying my beers listened intently. 'I'm no babe in the woods, Detective. I understand the reasons the Soviet authorities have for their approach. I'm appalled by it of course, but what can we do?' He sighed. 'Tell me, how are you going to discover the truth, huh? I applaud your efforts, but I'm doubtful you're going to achieve much.'

I shrugged, sipped the last of my first pint even as Okocha signalled the waitress to bring us two more. 'It doesn't hurt to try.'

We made small talk for another hour; I figured the more booze under his belt, the more likely he'd open up. Perhaps let slip a vital clue. I pushed on.

'Your students are prepared to go to war over this matter, you understand that, don't you?'

'To war?' His eyebrows knitted together. 'That's going a bit far isn't it?'

'Need I remind you of the protests in Red Square in 1963?'

He made an expansive gesture with both hands. 'But that was peaceful action. Not *war*. Against the might of the Soviet State, they are powerless.'

'Strictly speaking, yes. But I've spoken to some of your students. A rather excitable bunch at the Gandhi University. Their anger is almost palpable. They know the protests in '63 were futile. That's why I fear they may be prepared to, how should I put it, take more radical measures.'

'Such as?' A look of worry crept across Okocha's face.

'I wouldn't rule out large-scale riots on campuses across the city, random retaliatory attacks on Russians, things like that. There are even rumours of a bomb attack.' Some poetic licence on my part, however Okocha took it so seriously he drained an entire litre of beer in one swallow, dropped the bulky glass on the table with a thud.

'That must not happen! It would only lead to escalation of...of... everything!'

'You can see how delicate the situation is. A powder keg waiting to be ignited.'

A two-finger salute from Okocha and two more beers arrived at our table. I was lagging badly, but the attaché didn't care. He lit a cigarette and inhaled deeply, expelled a thick cloud of smoke. 'OK. You've got my undivided attention. What can I do?'

'First, what do you know about the victim?'

Okocha leaned back in his seat, shot his well-starched cuffs. 'Not much. He was a brilliant med student from Lagos, poor background. The Soviet Union accepted him with open arms, arranged the best courses. From what I hear, he attended all classes and was performing well academically.'

'And on a personal level?'

He shook his head. 'I have no knowledge of his personal life.'

'What if I told you he was socialising with a white Russian woman. That the relationship was of a sexual nature.'

'What can I say, Detective. Russian women are drawn to black men. We have a reputation for...well, I'm sure you've heard the rumours.'

I shrugged. 'Not sure what you're getting at.'

The attaché made a fist, placed his elbow in his crotch and waggled his forearm back and forth. 'Now you get me?'

I chuckled. 'Oh, that.'

He grinned. 'Yes, that. But on a serious note, I'm rather shocked you would speak of his dalliance in such a manner. Surely it's of no one's concern who he associates with. Sex is not a crime last time I checked.'

'I agree entirely. However there are elements in our society who take a dim view of interracial relationships. People prepared to take radical steps to demonstrate their opposition to them. To kill for their crazy beliefs.'

'As I said, his personal life was his own business. We at the embassy have no information other than his basic details. I mean, why would we for goodness sake?'

Why indeed. Soviet embassies around the globe track the movements of our nationals, but that isn't necessarily replicated by other countries. My gut told me only us and other totalitarian states engaged in such nonsense.

'I can tell you something about poor Aaron's parents.' Okocha frowned. 'They are absolutely frantic. We've only been able to give them the barest of details.'

'Such as?'

'The fact that he's dead and no one knows why.'

'Have they asked for the body to be repatriated to Nigeria?'

He nodded. 'They're demanding it.'

I drew in a deep breath. 'Are you aware the…ah…body has gone missing?' Thank God he didn't know I was responsible for that fuck up. At least I hoped he didn't.

'Yes. It's an utter tragedy. And something I can't fathom in a country where things are so tightly controlled.'

'Sometimes we're good at giving that impression.' My skin prickled. 'It's not always the case. Like that German kid Mattias Rust landing a light plane in Red Square a few months ago. Him sneaking under the radar highlighted the gaping holes in our impenetrable fortress.'

'Yes.' He chuckled gently. 'I get your point.'

'So, what have you said to Aaron's parents?'

Okocha coughed into his fist, readdressed his beer and took another healthy slug. 'We've been made an offer by your Ministry of Foreign Affairs. An empty coffin is to be flown back to Nigeria. The Soviet government will arrange for a funeral, pay the family some blood money and our country will receive a boost in aid. Military equipment, too. Problem solved.'

My mind started spinning. How easy to cover up a mistake with bribery. Russia's unimaginative go-to option in times of trouble.

'Are you OK with that?'

'Of course not. I want to know the truth. If you can find out what happened, I can tell Aaron's parents. Even if it's off the record, it's at least something, right?' He stared contemplatively at the high-set window under which the Finnish workers sat slumped and snoring.

I was disappointed with the diplomat's responses. I'd hoped for more. Perhaps he could help with my other question.

'Tell me what you know about a certain female student at the Gandhi, Flora Madenge. She's got control over a number of the students. Her cooperation could help quell any disruptive action, which would give me more time to dig for evidence.'

'Excuse me, what was the name?'

'Flora Madenge. Her father's a high-ranking government official in Nigeria.'

The attaché shot me a look of bewilderment. 'Never heard of her. Or him.'

'That's not possible. I've seen the woman's luxurious room at the dormitory. You can only acquire that through privilege and influence. You *must* know who they are. Nigeria's a big country with a big population. Perhaps they're flying under *your* radar, to reuse a recent phrase. I'd request you make some enquiries into Mr Madenge and his family. But do it quickly, time's not on our side.'

'I'm telling you, Detective, there's no such man in the government or its agencies. If there was, and his daughter was studying here in Moscow, I would know of them.'

'But–'

'Do not doubt me on this matter, Detective. There are twelve children of the Nigerian elite at Moscow institutions, and I know the names of all of them.'

'So who the hell is this woman?'

'Probably an opportunistic criminal, if what you tell me about her is true. If you uncover the truth, be sure to inform me and I will arrange to have her expelled from the university and sent home in disgrace.'

'Let's not be hasty about that. At least until the matter's cleared up.'

His indignant scowl told me Flora's future in Moscow could be short and unpleasant, with an even worse fate awaiting her at home.

'OK,' he relented. 'If you can use her to get to the truth behind Adekanye's death, by all means.'

I looked at my watch. 15:30. To achieve a functioning level of sobriety, I ordered a triple Turkish coffee, followed it with a quickly smoked Marlboro chaser. I thanked the attaché for his valuable time and headed to the nearby Marx Prospekt Metro station.

Chapter 18

I decided to call the station before hopping on the Metro. Let Burov know what I was planning. If I disappeared, he'd know where to start looking. Two kopecks clunked into the payphone. A couple of long beeps and his gravelly voice answered.

'I'm giving you a heads up, Comrade Colonel. I know you warned me off the institutes, but I've gotta go to the Gandhi University.'

'Don't do it, Voloshin.'

'I want to talk to a person who might have some dirt on the perpetrator.'

'When are you planning on making this visit?'

'Immediately.'

'Too risky and I forbid it.'

'Come on, Comrade Colonel. It's too important.'

'Listen, Voloshin.' A throaty grumble of annoyance. 'There's no need to rush. We've received information from the Ministry for Foreign Affairs. A story's to be released to the press tomorrow morning. Hopefully in time to stop any disruptions by the African students. Which means you'll have more time to conduct your little clandestine operations.'

I hated Burov when he was condescending. 'What's the official story?'

'Adekanye died of an asthma attack.'

'For fuck's sake. There's no body, how can they even...?' I looked to the leaden sky, trying to divine an answer.

'It's plausible at least. A story like this can buy time to–'

'Buy time? This is a sledgehammer destroying the case, ending it for good.

140

There is no *time* to *buy*.'

'I'm sorry, Viktor Pavlovich. It's been decided and there's nothing to be done.'

My heartrate went into overdrive. 'What about the phone call you received? The bomb threat? This is exactly the kind of story to piss the killers off. They want credit, not have their crime swept under the carpet.'

'Intelligence have analysed the letter and concluded it's a hoax. Security will be beefed up at the parade on the off chance, well...you know.'

Sirens wailed and traffic parted like magic as two motorcycles flew past. Hot on their heels came a long black ZIL 41047 limousine. No doubt carrying a VIP, a member of the Politburo, maybe the General Secretary of the Party himself.

'What if it's real? The organisers need to cancel the parade.'

'That's never going to happen, and you know it.'

I took two deep breaths. 'I can't leave it at that, Comrade Colonel. I've learned something vitally important. I'm not sure how yet, but I think it could help bust open the case. And that's why I'm on my way to the Gandhi University whether you approve or not.'

A frustrated sigh. 'Before you do that, drop by the station.'

'That's going to waste time. I have to speak to the Nigerian student urgently.'

'If it's that bossy female you told me about, it might be your lucky day.'

'Come again?'

'She's here.'

Chapter 19

'Put her on the phone please, Comrade Colonel.'

'Sure.'

'Wait, wait, wait!'

'What's wrong?'

'First can you ask Rita to do me a favour?'

'What?' The irritation in his voice made my skin prickle.

'Ask her to take Ksenia to my ex-wife's place at the end of her shift if I don't get there first. I've got no idea how the rest of today is going to pan out.'

'You're going to owe her one, Voloshin.'

'I know, don't rub it in.' I'd be indebted to Rita *and* have to answer to Sveta later. Not a prospect that filled me with joy,

'Is that all?'

'Pardon?'

'Are you ready to speak to the African woman now?'

'Oh, yes. Of course.'

'One moment.'

A lumbering blue and white trolleybus whooshed along Marx Prospekt. A shower of orange and yellow sparks flew from the point of contact between the powerlines and connector poles, a cheery patch of colour against the dull grey sky. I love this spot, the epicentre of my city, its bustling historic heart. Waiting for Flora to come on the line, I scanned the red Kremlin walls stretching down to the Moskva River, the columns of the Lenin State library, kiosks selling newspapers and magazines. State sanctioned, of course. Russians love to read whatever they can get their hands on. Take the politics out of it, and our education system is the best in the world, literacy rates the highest. At least that's what we're told.

'Captain Voloshin.' Her voice rang strong and confident.

'What can I do for you?' I endeavoured to convey nonchalance.

'Probably not much. For some weird reason you're the only person in authority I feel comfortable talking to.'

'I'm flattered to hear that, but there's nothing I can do unless you've got new information that will–'

'Ha! I'm the one who's just received "new" information. Your boss asked me – no, ordered me to tell everyone Aaron died of asthma. The story's going to press tomorrow morning. It's a lie! He never took medicine for that condition. He was a fit, healthy young man in his prime. Why is the Militsiya refusing to investigate properly? It's a damned coverup. You should be ashamed, all of you!'

'We're constrained in what we can do, Flora. You're no fool. Surely you have some idea of the way things work in this country. Rules, regulations, laws.'

Shallow breathing, a suspicious crackle and clicking echoed down the line.

'Our students are becoming angrier as time passes.'

'I understand.' I didn't, of course. How could I? 'But letting that anger turn into violence would be a huge mistake. Do you get that?'

'Wasn't your precious Russian Revolution achieved through violent struggle? Talk about hypocrisy!'

'Come on, that's not a fair comparison.'

'No? I think it's entirely appropriate. Anyway, your boss believes you're best equipped to calm things down, convince our people not to worry about future racist attacks.' She dropped her voice to a husky whisper. 'Come to the station and tell me the truth about what's going on.'

'Not happening,' I whispered back. Talking to Flora away from the Militsiya station would take the pressure off her. 'Meet me at the Tchaikovsky

143

Café on Herzen Street near Manezhnaya Square. You know it?'

'I'm sure I'll find it.'

I glanced at my watch. It would take at least half an hour for Flora to get to the rendezvous. I tracked back along the slushy sidewalk to the National Hotel, winked at the doorman who let me in without a word. Another drink couldn't hurt.

With her shiny dark skin peeking through the fur lining of her parka hood, Flora was the focus of everyone's attention. She waited for me at an elevated round table, no chairs anywhere. This was one of those cafés where you have to eat standing up. It keeps things ticking along, stops people loitering. Customers stepped around her with exaggerated wide steps like she was diseased, gave her disapproving looks. This was a place for locals, not foreigners. Especially not black ones. I realised it wasn't just skinheads and Lyubers who harboured racist attitudes. I felt myself flush with shame.

'Do you have your passport?' I squeezed between a grumpy faced babushka, a string bag in each hand, and an old man wearing a jacket covered in war medals.

'Of course. Why?'

'I need you to get us into the Intourist Hotel around the corner. This place was a bad choice. Don't know why I suggested it.' The joint was dirt cheap, but I wasn't admitting my reasoning to her. The hostility of strangers towards Flora proved enough to make me change my mind. I didn't want to front at the National again with a new companion so soon after having visited with Okocha, and then again on my own. That *would* raise eyebrows.

Two minutes later we were sitting in salubrious surroundings among well-dressed foreigners and Russian elites, people less likely to sneer at Flora because of her skin colour, the ground floor bar of the iconic Intourist Hotel. I sipped a warming amber scotch, Flora blew on the surface of a steaming double espresso. The combination of black woman and white man was a rarity in Moscow and her passport wasn't required; the doorman admitted us with a nod.

'I take it you didn't drop into the station simply to complain to Burov. Do you have information to pass on that can help me find who killed Aaron?'

Flora reached into a Gucci handbag, pulled out a gold cigarette case. 'No. I came to deliver a warning. But I wanted to do it through you, not that dickhead boss of yours.'

I felt my eyebrow raising. The impertinence was breathtaking. 'What warning?'

'You're going to have more than us from the Gandhi to worry about. Students across the city plan to disrupt the celebrations tomorrow. Not just Nigerians, either. From all over the Third World, even a few sympathisers from the USA, Great Britain, Germany, everywhere. I wouldn't be surprised to find one or two sympathetic Russians in the crowd.'

'Did you tell Colonel Burov this?'

She laughed and sparked up a Kool cigarette, leaving a circle of pale pink lipstick on the filter. 'Of course. That bogus asthma story won't wash. I predict a big turnout. He seems to think the state is big enough to handle us.' Her eyes blazed. 'Let's see.'

I studied her face, arrogance stamped all over it. I held her gaze, waited for her to flinch. She didn't. It was turning into a staring competition, neither of us wanted to look away first. Time to call her out using what I'd just discovered.

I leaned back in the soft lounge, stretched an arm along its velveteen top cushion. 'Do you know a gentleman called Harry Okocha?'

'Should I?'

I shook my head. 'No. He should know who you are, though, but he doesn't.'

'Stop speaking in riddles. What are you on about?'

I explained who Okocha was, that the name Flora Madenge was entirely unknown to him. 'The claims you made about your father are pure fabrication.'

She looked out the plate glass windows, observed the never-ending stream of miserable humanity trudging past the hotel's front door.

'That diplomat is a liar. I don't know why he'd say such a thing. My father is–'

145

'Stop bullshitting me, Flora. Your father is nobody important. And neither are you.' She recoiled at my words. I rested my hands on my knees, leaned forward. 'I've spent my entire career dealing with liars.'

A tear rolled down her cheek. I had to give her credit, she was damned good. 'So what if papa is a simple man. Is it wrong for a daughter to place her father on a pedestal?'

'Of course not.' I finished the fine whiskey and immediately craved another. 'My daughter does the same. Thinks I'm a big shot when I'm not. But you're a grown woman, not a little girl. It's time you came clean with me. Where the hell did you get all that luxury gear? And how did you manage to get a room all to yourself?'

Another tear followed the first, then a flood. Her body shuddered. If this was more acting, it was worthy of an award. So much so I almost wanted to give her a reassuring hug. She dabbed away tears with a lace handkerchief. 'If I tell you something, will you promise to protect me?'

'From what?'

'From the people who killed Aaron.'

'What motive could there be to harm you? You don't have a Russian boyfriend to piss off the racists. Do you?'

Her eyes focused on her lap. 'No I don't. And that's not why Aaron was killed, anyway.'

'What do you mean?'

'It's not about racism, at least not directly. Even if we do face prejudice all the time, cop abuse on the street from complete strangers.' She fiddled with the cigarette case, turned it over and over in her hands. 'This is something else.'

'Is it spying, like your friend Daniel said? Are the Americans mixed up in this?' My head was spinning with possible scenarios.

She shook her head. 'Aaron was working with a Canadian black-marketeer called Lacroix, the guy Daniel told you about yesterday.'

'Yes. I've got my eye on Lacroix.' *I would have if I could find him.*

'Aaron was stupid. He got too ambitious. Branched out on his own, started exchanging currency across town where Lacroix had already set up shop.

Aaron was undercutting Lacroix, trading dollars and deutschmarks at more competitive rates.'

'Surely a severe beating would've been enough to warn him off. Why kill him?'

'Aaron refused to back down, even when they threatened him. He told me he thought it was all a bluff.'

'Why?'

'Because he and Lacroix were originally partners. Friends.' Nico told me he'd seen Lacroix talking to a couple of black men. One of them might have been Adekanye. 'They even shared the same girl. Olga.'

'Holy shit, Flora. Why didn't you tell me this before?'

'Because...because I'm doing it too.' She stared at her coffee.

'What are you doing, exactly?' I already knew the answer.

'I have to go. I shouldn't have said anything. Shouldn't have come here.' She wiped her eyes again, smeared mascara.

'Yes, you should have. You're doing the right thing. Tell me everything. Don't hold back. I can only help you if I'm armed with the truth.'

She looked up slowly. 'I've been buying goods and selling them for big profits on the black market. Vodka, gems, caviar, religious icons, you name it. The boys you met at the dorm, they're loyal foot soldiers working for me.'

'Tell me why I shouldn't arrest you right now.' God knew I should. It would save my failing career, maybe earn me a promotion. Why should I care about Adekanye? Then I imagined what a black woman's future in a Russian prison would be like. Absolute hell. No, I couldn't do it.

'If you bring a murder charge against Lacroix, I'll make an official statement. Testify, whatever it takes. Even if he didn't do the actual killing, he's behind it.'

'What about your own little empire? Are you willing to give that up?'

She tugged at the sleeve of her sweater, which I guessed was made of cashmere or some other expensive material. 'Can you promise me immunity from prosecution?'

I told her about the attaché's threat to have her deported and sent home in disgrace if there was evidence of criminality on her part. 'Only if you get rid of all your trinkets and stop breaking the law.'

'I've got people depending on me for supply. They're going to be upset if I can't deliver.'

'Your sudden absence from the scene will be filled by someone else. The supply and demand mechanism works everywhere, even here in the communist Soviet Union. If you aren't willing to make these changes, I can't promise you anything.'

'All right, all right, I'll do it.'

'And request a room with some other girls. You can't maintain this kind of privilege and be taken seriously as a witness. You'll only wind up in trouble.'

'I paid in advance for that room.'

'Too bad. Bunking in with others will give you a better perspective on the realities of Soviet life.'

She held up her fancy cigarette case and waved it about. 'Can I at least keep this?'

'Sure. It can remind you of how stupid you've been.'

Once we'd collected our coats and hats from the cloakroom, she held out her hand. I shook it and smiled at her. 'You know you're doing the right thing, don't you?'

A weak smile creased her lips. 'Yes. The satisfaction of nailing Lacroix will almost make up for the loss.'

There was something I didn't understand. 'How come Lacroix leaves you alone?'

'He's got some warped sense of "honour among thieves". If you don't encroach on his territory, he's not bothered with competitors.'

I rode the Metro's red line with Flora until her stop. She silently left the carriage and disappeared into the crowd, shoulders back, head up proudly.

Doing a deal with Flora was never going to work. Her testimony would be smashed by any legal team working for Lacroix. That's if I could even get a charge to stick, which I doubted. Those backing him, influential people like Shukhov, would vilify her character, shine a spotlight on her own illegal activities. Bringing the Canadian student to justice would take another approach. If I had to bypass official channels, so be it.

Flora going straight was a good thing in its own right; I didn't regret asking her to make the sacrifice. Could I be confident she'd stick to her commitment once Lacroix was dealt with? Probably not. There was too much temptation to game the system if you were entrepreneurially inclined like Flora clearly was.

It was nearing 6:00pm. With no other plans for the evening, I decided to check out Nico's tip about Lyubers playing hockey scratch matches at Dynamo's home rink. Perhaps I could shake some information out of a hockey player or two. If I was lucky, Lacroix might even be there. I exited the train and crossed the platform to catch another going back towards Sportivnaya Station. I alighted to a crisp evening with snow flurries, strolled through the streets to the stadium. As I got closer, more and more people were keeping me company. Hundreds, thousands of people wearing club colours. There was a big match on tonight.

Good luck finding Lacroix or any of the Wolves tonight, Voloshin!

Chapter 20

Lenin Stadium is a monolithic edifice befitting a totalitarian state. Nestled on a bend of the Moskva River, it's Moscow's Colosseum, a concrete, steel and glass venue for our version of bread and circuses. A place where the proletariat can forget the drudgery of their day for the time it takes to watch a game of football or hockey.

Tonight the fun was taking place at Malaya Arena, built in 1956 and upgraded in 1980 for the summer Olympics. The main and only attraction, a battle between two giant hockey clubs: Dynamo versus CSKA. The KGB's team against the Army's team. You don't have to work for either of these organisations or live in a particular location to root for them. Not at all; simply pick a colour you like and you're in. Blue and white for the spies; red for the soldiers. My affiliation belongs to neither of these teams. My uncle was a pilot in the Great Patriotic War, so my allegiance lies with a lesser-supported outfit called Soviet Wings. They haven't won many titles over the years, but my interest in hockey is practically non-existent, so I don't give a toss if they win or lose.

As the human tide continued to sweep me along, I gave myself a mental head slap. How had I not considered there'd be a game tonight? It was a Friday in November, for Christ's sake. Looking for members of the White Wolves here would be a waste of time. The old Russian saying sprang to mind – *go look for the wind in a field*. Finding Lacroix at the packed stadium would be a miracle. That's if he was even here.

The crowd grew like a river swollen by flooded tributaries; people melded into the throng from a maze of alleys criss-crossing the expansive parkland around the stadium. Thicker and thicker it grew, flowing steadily until slowdown points funnelled people to an inner area where fans split into orderly queues to the entrance gates. Lines of armed cops carefully monitored the sea of faces passing by. Moscow sports fans are polite by international standards, and fighting is usually on a small scale. Our hooligans are yet to scale the heights of barbarity dished out in Britain and other countries, but more and more knives and other weapons are smuggled into our venues by troublemakers. From what I could see and hear tonight, the mood between rival fans reflected grudging respect more than hostility. Rival supporters tried to outshout each other with repetitive tribal chants: goading, teasing, mocking. The volume of noise coming from fans rattled my bones, but my gut told me there'd be no violence tonight. As we marched along, I scanned the walls of uniformed Militsiya lining the alleys; there were enough resources to deal with any trouble.

A burst of laughter split the hubbub after a CSKA fan unleashed a witty barb about the Dynamo players. Something about them dribbling before they shoot. A tall skinny man in a Dynamo scarf walking next to me tilted his head back and laughed along with the opposition fans.

'They're having a crack at your lads,' I said to him. 'What's so funny about that?'

'I dunno. It just is. Hockey fans respect a sharp wit.'

'You know if it's a sell out tonight?' Maybe I could snaffle a ticket at the entrance.

The man looked at me like I was the school dunce. 'Are you kidding? It's been sold out for weeks.'

'I should have thought ahead.'

The guy rolled his eyes at me. 'Yeah, you should have.'

We kept walking like soldiers heading into battle. The bitter evening air was thick with all kinds of stinking cigarette brands and vodka breath, and all I wanted to do now was get away. I searched for a gap in the mass of bodies. Time to split from the herd and head to the subway, back to my flat. This had been a dumb idea all along. In my apartment I could at least think in peace and quiet, have a drink and try to figure out a way forward. On the way home I'd fetch Ksenia from the police station, drop her off at Sveta's in the nick of time and avoid a tongue lashing. I got my elbows ready for the old ice-breaker manoeuvre when the Dynamo fan beside me grabbed my elbow. He reached into the folds of a jacket, held out a ticket and shoved it under my nose.

'What's this?'

'My friend got sick, so I've got a spare stub.'

Perhaps I'd stick around after all. 'That's awfully kind of you, I'm most–'

'A hundred roubles.'

'Sorry?'

'I can't give it you for free now, can I?'

'Look, I'll give you fifty.' I was already flicking through my wallet to see how much I had left from Sveta's entertain-the-kid fund. 'Since that's what I suspect it cost.'

He returned the ticket to his pocket. 'Not to worry, I'm sure I'll find someone at the door willing to pay for a prime seat like this.'

'You'll be lucky,' I scoffed. Was everyone in this godforsaken country an economic opportunist?

He wrinkled his eyes. 'There are always hopefuls at the gate begging for a ticket. Have you even been to a hockey game before?' He eyeballed my drab street attire, taking in the complete absence of club colours.

'Not since I was a kid,' I lied. I'd only watched it on TV, never attended a live match.

He fished out the ticket again and handed it to me. 'Fifty it is. You're making me sad, comrade. A grown man with no knowledge of hockey going to a sold-out match on a whim.'

'I like new experiences.' I checked the price. A hundred roubles. The guy had been honest after all. I added an extra fifty to the wad of bills and paid him full price.

'You're funnier than that wise-arse CSKA fan.' The pom-pom on his beanie wobbled as he chuckled. 'You can sit next to me and tell me what you're playing at during the breaks.'

'At half time, you mean?'

'You're joking, aren't you?'

'Huh?'

'The game's played in three periods, not halves.'

Now I wasn't sure who was the biggest idiot, him or me. Surely no game is divided into thirds. I shook my head. 'OK, I agree. Maybe you can help me out too.'

The clock ticked down on the first period. And yes, there were three of them. I questioned the sanity of the rule makers. I looked up at the game clock. Two minutes to go and still no score. The atmosphere was electric. Despite misgivings about the aesthetic merits of the sport, I found myself on the edge of my seat. Out of some innate sense of solidarity, I found myself siding with my newfound friend, Arkady, yelling encouragement to the Dynamo players and hurling insults at the opposition.

'You see that man with the puck?' asked Arkady. He took a big bite out of a sandwich he'd bought at the cafeteria downstairs. 'A superstar.' Half-chewed egg and rye bread crumbs sprayed, forcing me to shield my face with my hand. The manners of sports fans left much to be desired.

'Yes, what about him?' By the time I spoke, the player in question had deftly flicked the puck to a teammate who lined up the net, took a fearsome slapshot which rattled the goal and bounced back into play. The crowd let out a gasp of combined frustration and relief, depending which side of the fence you sat on.

'He could be a star in the NHL. Better than any of the Americans and Canadians.'

'That's a big call.' I smiled at him. 'Speaking of Canadians, I'm looking for one.'

A puzzled frown. 'One in general, or a particular person?'

I pulled out my wallet, extracted the Xerox photocopy of Lacroix I'd made at the station. 'This guy.'

Arkady studied the picture. His face was a study of concentration for a few seconds, then a nod. 'Looks vaguely familiar.' Then a shake of the head.

'But I couldn't tell you who he is.'

A roar rose from the crowd as a fight erupted in centre ice. Arkady, me and the entire crowd stood to get a better view. Nearly all the players had poured onto the rink and were throwing wild haymakers, jabs, hooks and crosses. Trying to lift jerseys over each other's heads like desperate lovers. To my surprise, they didn't attack each other with their sticks. Must be some kind of code of honour. Respect. After a minute tempers had cooled and two players from each team were put in the penalty box.

'Look again,' I said when the crowd resumed their seats. 'Have you seen him before?'

'Yes, I think so.' He scratched his head. 'I can't remember where or when.'

'Concentrate, please.' I jabbed the picture with my index finger. 'It's imperative I find him.'

Arkady gave me the side eye. 'Why?'

'You wanted to know what I was "playing at"? I'm a detective. This man, a Canadian citizen who frequents this arena, is central to Militsiya inquiries into a serious crime.'

Arkady's eyes lit up. With excitement or recognition of Lacroix? 'Ah ha! So that explains it. But why didn't you use your ID to get into the arena? Dropping by on the off chance you'd score a ticket sounds a bit, I don't know, amateurish.'

'Listen, there's a hundred reasons I have to keep a low profile, but I'm not willing to divulge why.'

'I haven't got time to chat either. The game's restarting. Wait till the break, can you?'

The first period ended in a frenzied attack on the Dynamo goal. With seconds left, the CSKA right winger pushed the puck between the goalkeeper's legs to take a 1:0 lead over Dynamo. The roar of the crowd when the goal registered shook the arena to its foundations.

The start of the break saw patrons flocking to toilets, refreshment outlets, smoking areas. If Arkady couldn't help me now, I was leaving. Much as I was enjoying the game, it wouldn't be worth facing the wrath of Sveta unless I got a good lead to compensate. Arkady stood to join the line of exiting fans and crabbed his way towards the aisle leading downstairs. I followed, cursing myself for wasting so much time on this hunch. Arkady stopped in his tracks, turned to face me. 'I remember the guy in the picture now.'

'You do?'

'Yes. He sometimes sits directly behind the Dynamo player benches. Wears this gaudy red jumper with a big white leaf on the front. Whaddaya call it?'

'Maple.'

'That's it.'

'Is he there now?' I'd been scanning the crowd since the moment we arrived.

He shrugged. 'No idea. Sometimes I get a seat opposite the benches. Tonight they're on the same side as us, directly underneath.'

I ditched Arkady like a worn-out sock, clambered over the seats. 'Sorry,' I repeated, squeezing my way through bodies. Voices told me to watch the hell where I was going. One man shoved me hard in the side. 'Look out, fuck your mother!' I turned, gave him my best psycho eyes and he backed away. I reached the concrete barrier and peered over the side.

And there he was, leaning against the perspex barrier. Lacroix. Laughing and joking with two men in blue tracksuits with the famous three-stripe piping. The players had disappeared into the bowels of the arena, presumably for a pep talk, rub down, setting of broken bones into plaster or whatever the hell it is they do in the break.

'Oi! You. Stay there and don't move!'

Lacroix's head did a quarter turn, not a trace of worry registering on his face.

'Are you Michel Lacroix?' I shouted above the engine of the Zamboni machine used to smooth out the ice after each period.

'Who wants to know?' Brazen, challenging. I hated him on sight.

I flashed my ID at him. 'Captain Viktor Voloshin, Militsiya. Stay where you are!'

'Sure.' He gave me a friendly wave. Cheeky bastard.

By the time I'd fought my way through the crowd, negotiated the maze of corridors leading to the players' rooms and reached the Dynamo bench,

Lacroix was gone. Luckily the track-suited staffers remained, I figured to tidy up gear and get the bench ready for the next period of play.

'Where did that young man go?' I demanded.

One of the men, a squat fellow with a bushy black moustache, gawped at me. 'What man?'

'You know precisely who I mean,' I hissed through gritted teeth. 'The fucking Canadian. Tell me now or I'm going to make life a misery for both of you shitheads.'

'Sorry, comrade,' said the second one, a head taller than his mate and sporting massive, broad shoulders. He was carefully attaching rubber guards to the glinting blades of a pair of skates the size of canoes, avoiding eye contact with me. 'The gentleman you're referring to had another appointment. He had to leave in a real hurry.'

'I'll ask the question again. Where...did...he...go?' I showed my ID again for emphasis. 'Perhaps you'd like to accompany me to the station to answer my questions? I'll have no hesitation arresting both of you for obstructing justice.'

'All right, already.' The first staffer had the look of a former hockey brawler who'd lost more fights than he'd won. Teeth missing, nose pointing roughly in the direction of Saint Petersburg. For a tough guy, he still feared the law. 'He said he was going to a meeting with a guy called Aleksey.'

'Don't tell him anymore, Pyotr. It's none of our business. The filth's bluffing. Michel's done nothing wrong. Just likes to hang out with the players.'

'Thank you, Pyotr.' I turned to his mate. 'And thank *you* for confirming the suspect's name.'

'Suspect?' The smaller guy's eyebrows pole-vaulted up his forehead. 'What's he done?'

It was pointless talking any more to these stooges. If Lacroix was meeting up with Aleksey, it could be anywhere. Most likely back in Lyubertsy, as far away from me as possible. If Burov didn't have any duties lined up for Yegor tomorrow, I'd take him with me to the White Wolves HQ tomorrow morning. Nevertheless I handed over a couple of business cards, thanked the staffers for their time and made for the exits.

I phoned Burov from the Sportivnaya Metro station. As I suspected, Rita and Ksenia were already on their way to Sveta's. If I hurried, I just might be able to catch them before Her Majesty got home. I barged my way to the front of the line of commuters, pressed my badge up to the controller's window for an instant, and flew down the escalator, three steps at a time.

Chapter 21

I exited the subway station, took a tram three blocks and jumped out. I hit the pavement running and launched into a full sprint. Head down, arms pumping like pistons, legs in overdrive, ever alert for patches of black ice. Svetlana in a good mood struck fear in my heart. If I was late with the child *again*, there'd be hell to pay. Worse still would be Ksenia getting there before me.

Snow tumbled in a white curtain as I rounded the last corner before Sveta's apartment building. I was drenched in perspiration under my clothes, hat, boots. Only my fingers were dry inside waterproof gloves. Working up a sweat in the freezing cold can be lethal if you don't have a fresh change of clothes handy. Last winter I'd suffered the worst fever of my life after tracking bootleggers through Losiny Ostrov National Park. Once the op was over, our unit had to endure hours shivering in the bitter cold waiting for transport vehicles to arrive. A handful of officers were bed-ridden for months. That particular gang of crooks had been armed with AK-47s, machetes and stun grenades. Sveta with a cast-iron frypan loomed as an equally frightening prospect.

I checked my watch. 7:45p.m. I was too late. Her deadline was 8:00pm; by now Rita would have delivered Ksenia and my fate would be decided.

I was rehearsing a series of fantastic excuses in my mind when, through the snowfall, I made out two silhouettes a hundred metres or so ahead. They held hands, the little one skipping merrily. It had to be Rita and Ksenia. I galloped as fast as I could in the soft snow, sliding left and right, altering my centre of gravity every couple of strides to avoid a catastrophic fall. I had to dig deeper, run faster. *Move, Voloshin!* Ripping pain in my thighs accompanied every laborious stride. *Head them off before they take to the stairs.* If they appeared at Sveta's door without me... I stopped for a split second, cupped my hands to my mouth, called out: 'Kseniaaa!' No breath in reserve, the wind in my face, it came out as a hoarse whisper I could barely hear myself.

The pair turned at right angles under a swaying streetlight. The entrance to Sveta's apartment block. I called again. Another whisper lost in the groaning wind. I pushed on, only twenty metres away now. Rita shouldered open the heavy door leading to the building's vestibule. Ksenia dropped something on the ground, a rag doll. She glimpsed me out of the corner of her eye as she stooped to pick it up.

'Papa! Rita, look.' She pointed a finger at me. 'Where have you been all day?'

I had no breath left to answer; my run slowed to a walk, then a stagger. I grabbed her hand and we stumbled into the foyer out of the cold. Already with one hand on the rail of the stairway, Rita watched the spectacle, hands on hips. 'Training for the Olympics, are we? You'd better hurry, they're only seven months away. South Korea this time, I believe.'

'Very funny, Sergeant Vasiliyeva.'

Ksenia laughed hysterically at the joke. My daughter in a good mood was encouraging; she'd be more inclined to think hatching a conspiratorial story to save her father would be a fun game and not an evil plan to mislead to her mother.

'Thank the kind officer for looking after you, Ksenia.'

'Thanks, Rita.' Ksenia gave a low bow combined with a curtsey.

I quickly learned from Rita they'd spent most of the day playing card games, drawing pictures and drinking tea. On the way to Sveta's they'd stopped for cabbage pies at a café. The only time Rita didn't have eyes on her charge was when she'd been called out briefly to assist Yegor with a minor domestic dispute. I apologised profusely to my daughter for my absence.

'It's OK, though, papa. I got to tag along when you interviewed the foreign

159

suspect at the Exhibition Centre. Besides, I like hanging out at the station with all the cops.'

'He wasn't a ... never mind. Are you sure you've had a nice day?'

'Yes.'

I mustered a weak smile. 'Are you sure?'

'Uh huh. There's always something interesting happening.'

'Burov's patience is wearing thin with you, Comrade Colonel,' Rita said softly, eyebrows lowered, as Ksenia fussed about returning the doll to her rucksack. 'He asked me to tell you he's no longer prepared to take an officer off duty to cover for you.'

I shrugged, spread my hands wide. 'What else can I do?'

'Isn't it obvious? Don't agree to have custody of her when you're working.'

'But I've got no more sick days left,' I protested.

'Take her on your days off, then.'

'I'm on a rotating shift, I can't–.'

'Sorry, Viktor Pavlovich. You're my superior and all, but these are personal issues you need to resolve yourself. I'm only passing on what the Colonel said. How you sort out your family arrangements is entirely up to you.'

I nodded. 'Yes, you're right. You're lucky you don't have an ex like Sveta to deal with.'

'No. But you do.'

Rita bent down, gave Ksenia a peck on the cheek. 'Look after your father, won't you, dear?'

Ksenia smiled. 'Of course.' The smile morphed into a frown. 'If only he wasn't so busy all the time.'

Rita slipped out the door and into the night. Her husband Timur, a protective and jealous Tatar, would be wondering why she was late. I vowed to heed Rita's advice and sort out my problems. As soon as I'd put the Adekanye case to bed. I'd give myself another forty-eight hours to find an answer for Harry Okocha, the students, Aaron's family, everyone affected by the atrocity. After that, I'd let it go.

I bent down on one knee, threw my arms around my precious child. So prepared to forgive me anything, I was going to take advantage of her good nature again. Ask her to lie for me.

I rang the buzzer. No crack of light under the door. I banged with the heel of my fist and pressed the buzzer again. I flicked my cuff; the dial on my watch showed 8:05p.m. I wanted to do a Cossack dance. Finally, something going my way. Svetlana was late, not me.

'Here papa.' Ksenia held a bronze key in her fluffy mitten.

I opened the door and flicked on the light. Inside, immaculate as usual. If Sveta saw the current state of my flat she'd refuse to let me see Ksenia ever again.

'Looks like I won't have to tell mamma anything.' She gave me an exaggerated wink.

'Just that you love her, okay?'

Ksenia nodded as she pulled a notebook from her rucksack. 'Look at this papa.' She turned the book around; a coloured pencil drawing of a stick-figure man at the wheel of a Militsiya van, lights blazing.

'Is that Yegor driving?'

'No, silly. It's you!'

I hugged her tight, picked her up and plopped her on a chair, went to make coffee. Somehow, Sveta always had coffee even when there was none in the stores.

'I'm going to draw a picture of Yegor catching a robber. Can you give it to him later?'

'Of course. I'm sure he'll love it.'

I realised the sweat was cooling under my clothes.

'Be back in a minute.'

Ksenia grunted, obsessed with her new drawing project. I went to the bathroom, stripped and dabbed my body all over with a towel. Not as good as dry clothes, but as good as it was going to get. A hot shower would be nice, but not worth the grief. I heard the kettle give a high pitched whistle. In the mirror, I saw the bathroom door handle turn slowly. Shit.

'Ksenia! I'm–'

'You're completely naked, Viktor.' Svetlana stood there grinning at me. I covered my manhood with a towel, felt my face flush hot. She spun around and closed the door, propped a chair under the handle.

'What the hell are you doing?' I mumbled as she deftly unbuttoned her blouse.

'The art exhibition was so boring, I can't begin to tell you. Now I want some excitement.'

'But Ksenia's only metres away.'

'No she's not. I sent her to visit her friend Masha two floors down. Now, drop the towel and show me what you've got.' Sveta tossed her skirt and underwear onto the floor, joining the pile started by my clothes and her blouse. 'We have to be quick, though.'

'Why?'

She leapt at me like a cat, grabbed me around the shoulders, wrapped her legs around my waist. 'Because I'm not sure Masha's at home.'

Chapter 22

Sex with the ex. A bad idea that seemed like a good idea at the time. I swore to never go there again. Unless she's wearing that heady perfume. Or she strips in front of me and asks nicely. Like my father always says, life has no rule book.

Riding the Metro, I couldn't hold back a wry smile. She'd got me at a weak moment and I'd crumpled. The decision will no doubt come back to haunt me. Sveta will somehow twist it around, turn it back on me; as if I'd lurked in the bathroom waiting to take advantage of her. In an unusual act of generosity, though, she let me take a hot shower after we'd finished. Another plus, she hadn't asked me for change after my day entertaining Ksenia with Sveta's money. Either she forgot, or it was a reward for providing her with a satisfactory performance.

A hundred metres from Sveta's flat I'd made some quick enquiries at a street kiosk. Under the counter, deficit goods were available at a premium. A quick peek in my wallet revealed I could easily afford a packet of Kosmos cigarettes, a couple of bottles of random rotgut, and there'd be a bit left over for expenses incurred tomorrow in the hunt for Lacroix. The smokes and the booze were my father's favourite brands respectively. In other words, he was particular about cigarettes but would drink the piss out of a peasant's pot if there was a trace of alcohol in it. Purchase made, including a packet of sunflower seeds, I made a beeline for Papa's flat in the city centre. My mood should have been high after the frantic romp with Sveta. It wasn't. I felt like an empty shell. Used up as a man, useless as a cop. If it wasn't for Ksenia…

My next appointment wouldn't necessarily boost my mood, but it was an obligatory one. The traditional visit to Papa on Revolution Day eve. His birthday.

The door of the train hissed open. Dzerzhinskaya station, named after the infamous founder of the KGB and architect of the Red Terror, "Iron" Felix Dzerzhinsky. The Bolshevik bastard responsible for the torture and death of hundreds of thousands of enemies of the state. My father, a true friend of the state and therefore left alone by authorities, lived in a dingy one-room apartment in Kirov Street, not far from the Lubyanka. In an ironic twist of fate, a massive children's store, Detsky Mir, stands opposite the KGB Headquarters. Innocence and evil juxtaposed.

Masses of red flags and posters adorned practically every building in the city centre. Traffic was sparse at this time of night with many roads either blocked off or restricted to VIP vehicles. Only me and representatives of the USSR's myriad security agencies had the questionable good fortune of being outdoors in tonight's wintery weather. I turned into Kirov Street and hopped on a lonely northbound bus that stopped fifteen metres from the entrance to papa's block. As I grabbed the old wooden doorhandle of the building's entrance, a loud crack echoed in the brisk night air. An instinctive glance to the left – a body-length away shards of ice lay scattered in a fan shape. The metre-long icicle that smashed to the ground would have killed me had I been standing under it. This must be my lucky day.

'You're late, son.' Papa ushered me inside, took my hat and coat and hung them up for me. Like I was too helpless to do it for myself. Clad in a dirty white singlet full of holes, he hobbled a couple of metres into the tiny living area, eased himself into a floral armchair. He'd sat in it night after night for twenty years or more. Dust lay thick on every surface. The place stank of sweat, a thousand cups of black tea and old book-binding glue. 'Come and give me a hug.' Despite his gruff, perpetually angry appearance, my father, WWII legend Pavel Stanislavovich Voloshin, has a soft spot for me. My siblings, sister Sonia the clarinettist and brother Eduard the ballet dancer,

164

are second-rate offspring compared to me, the heroic cop. He loves them too, but I'm the apple of his eye, diametrically opposing political views aside. Father never remarried after Mamma died. If he had girlfriends when we were growing up, he was damn discrete about it.

'Sorry, Papa.' I handed him the packet of Kosmos and his eyes lit up like a New Year's fireworks display. 'Sorry that's all I've brought you. I've been snowed under with work. Haven't had a chance to get you a proper present.'

'It's fine, Vitya. I know you've got important things to do.' Always forgiving me. I've had an entire year since his last birthday to organise a gift. Damn, I couldn't even remember what I bought him last year, if I got him anything at all. He reached into the pocket of the baggy trousers he'd owned as long as the armchair, pulled out a box of matches. Those pants used to be tight on him. His hands shook, the box fell to the floor, all the matches tumbled out. 'Ha ha! Must be a sign to give up.'

'It's a bit late for that, old man.' He was 79 years old today and could probably squeeze out more press-ups than me if there was a bottle of vodka up for grabs. The iron constitution matched his stubbornness. 'If the tobacco hasn't killed you by now it never will.'

'You're right there. Never a day sick in my life,' he stated with a racking cough that debunked the claim. He pointed at a large framed photo on the wall: Papa in army uniform taken on 1 September 1943, smiling and squinting in bright sunshine. He drove a tank in the Battle of Kursk. 'If I survived that hell on Earth, a ciggie now and again isn't going to hurt, is it?'

Papa never got into the nitty-gritty of his involvement in the war, but he didn't have to. Our Soviet education rammed the story down our throats and continues to do so. It was as if the USSR singlehandedly defeated the Nazis. My father took part in a pivotal battle and survived when nearly a quarter of a million didn't make it. Those ribbons and medals he wore with pride whenever he left the house, he damn well earned them.

'No, Papa. And neither will a little drink.' I pulled a bottle of cheap Georgian port wine from a paper bag.

'So you did get me a wonderful gift, after all!' His eyes sparkled. I lit his smoke and poured us a tumbler each of the rose-coloured wine. Vinegary and barely drinkable. I swallowed hard, fighting the urge to spit it out. Papa smacked his lips. 'Delicious!' His taste buds must've been destroyed by a lifetime of cigarettes; all he was getting was the glow of alcohol.

I dragged a rickety chair from the kitchen, much cleaner than the rest of the apartment. I settled in next to Papa; to my right mountains of books and magazines formed a kind of internal wall. On the TV – grainy images, interviews with old war veterans, typical pre Revolution Day programming. I gestured towards the set. 'Any of your old buddies interviewed this year?'

'They're all dead. Nikita the sniper was the last one to die. Only me left out of my battalion.' He waved dismissively at the television screen. 'These goats probably served in offices far from the front. Cooks or inventory clerks. None of 'em look like proper soldiers to me.' He swallowed another mouthful of wine, his Adam's apple rose and fell in his sinewy neck. More liver spots had appeared on his skin, especially his hands.

'Looking forward to the parade tomorrow?'

'Of course. Never miss it.' He pointed at his wardrobe with a gnarled finger. His best suit hung from a coat hanger wedged in the door, medals fighting for a place on the breast of his jacket. 'Who knows when it's going to be the last?'

'Come on, Pap. You've got many years left in you.' The way my life was panning out, he'd be burying me before he turned up his toes.

'I'm not talking about myself, son. I mean for the country. The way this moron with the stained skull's going, the USSR will soon cease to exist, mark my words. People are taking these freedoms too far. Wrecking everything we've worked for since 1917! Creeping capitalism. They're even selling Coca Cola.'

'Know where I can get some? I haven't seen much of anything for sale lately. Your so-called ideal society's failing badly when it comes to providing for the people.'

'It's the Americans.'

'Pardon?'

'They're manipulating the world's economy. Taking care of the rich in the West. Keeping us down in the shit.'

166

'Oh, I see. But when *we* achieve something great, that's all down to us, is it?'

He crushed a smoke out like he was forcing a nail through the ashtray into the coffee table. 'That's not the same thing, and you know it.'

I let him contemplate the contradiction of his statements for a moment. His brows furrowed as he sipped wine, probably searching for the argument that could not be countered, the killer punch. He blinked hard, the answer eluding him. I wanted to know more about his prediction of the demise of the USSR. 'What evidence do you have Gorbachev's ruining the country?' I said. 'The way I see it, he's not giving much away at all. We're going to be locked up in this socialist workers' paradise forever.'

'Back in my day your seditious attitudes would have landed you in prison, son.' A cloud of cigarette smoke enveloped his close-cropped grey head as he spoke. 'Or worse.'

'I can't understand why you've always supported a regime that fears its citizens so much it has to silence opposition.'

'Because it's been necessary.' His lips and eyebrows danced as he warmed to his pet theme. 'Regrettable, but necessary.'

'Come off it, old man.'

'I mean it. Resistance had to be crushed to allow socialism to take root, for people to understand the system was perfect. Dissenting voices led people from the true path. Had they been left to spread their nonsense, they could have derailed the whole process. Taken us back to the tyranny of the Tsar.'

'Swapping one form of tyranny for another is not progress.'

'Millions would argue differently. Including the massive crowds you'll see out in the streets supporting the CPSU tomorrow.'

'You don't think some of those people are coerced into taking part?'

'Nonsense. You'll only see proud, smiling faces in the parade.'

I poured him another drink. He repeated the same thing year after year, and on every other rare occasion I visited. I let him rave on because he was my father and I loved him, even when he was spouting rolled-gold bullshit. Besides, it made him happy to educate me.

'You may be right about that,' I conceded.

We sat in silence for a few moments, puffing away and watching the TV. Papa's face grew redder as the first bottle emptied and the line in the second one headed south. His blood pressure had been elevated in the last few years, so I had to be careful with the dosage. I didn't want him having a stroke on his birthday. Not only that, if he got completely drunk and missed the parade tomorrow, he'd blame me for not taking care of him. I poured small portions for him, larger ones for me. *Sit with him for another hour or so and put him to bed.*

The glow of the TV and the alcohol were combining to send the old boy to sleep. His eyes drooped and closed, his head bobbled forward. I contemplated picking him up and carrying him to bed; instead I grabbed a blanket, lay it over his knees as he snored away. I was wobbly myself after drinking the bulk of the booze, plus what I'd already put away over the course of the day. He'd join the parade, like always. A slight hangover never prevented his attendance before, nor would it tomorrow.

As I edged past papa's chair, I bent forward and kissed his forehead. I imagined Aaron Adekanye's grieving father somewhere in Nigeria, his son ripped away from him. Sent to Russia to get a first-class education and return home triumphant. Now he wasn't returning home at all, not even as a corpse. I hadn't brought up the case with Papa, even though he'd no doubt be full of ideas on how to solve it. Was it because I wanted to spare him the gruesome details? No. He'd seen it all in the war. Dismembered bodies, blood and guts. Deprivation and cruelty beyond imagination.

No.

I didn't tell him because I was afraid my loving heroic father would turn out to be a racist.

Chapter 23

Warmed on the inside by the bottle and a half of Georgian plonk, I debated whether to grab another on the way home. Something stronger. More Russian. Vodka. The affirmative side of the argument won the debate.

The lights of the night kiosk glowed brightly at the wide intersection near my apartment. I accidentally knocked my boots together as I approached, stumbled a few steps. I fell into the kiosk counter with a thud, fished out my well-worn wallet, thinner and lighter than this morning. I quickly thumbed through the banknotes, 125 roubles left. Relatively speaking, that's a lot of money. When it comes to purchasing deficit goods like hard liquor, it isn't.

'Good evening!' I called out to the attendant in the cheeriest and soberest voice I could summon.

'What do you want, uncle?' It was the same surly youth who'd been giving me the shits for months. His face turned into a sneer. 'Oh, it's you, Mr Militsiya Man. Are you here to give me a hard time?'

Butter him up, Voloshin. Don't cause a scene. 'Not at all. I want to wish you a happy Revolution Day for tomorrow. And purchase a bottle of vodka to honour the Motherland.'

The lad waved at the goods laid out before him on the counter. 'What are you talking about, comrade? All I have is some mineral water, chewing gum and cigarettes. No licence for alcohol.'

A sharp gust of wind bore into my earhole. I should tie the flaps of my hat down when it's bitterly cold and there's a breeze up, but I always forget.

'Look, I'm just after a bottle of good old wheat vodka, not to cause you any trouble.'

He laughed. 'What trouble? There're some pretty tough guys taking care of this little business. Protecting it. You Militsiya think you're in charge of the streets, but you're not. Things are changing.'

'Is that right?' His tone infuriated me. I fought an overwhelming urge to pull out my pistol and plant a bullet right between his eyes. But I wanted that bottle even more. 'We can chat about the power balance in Moscow some other time.' I showed him a rare 100 rouble note. Rare for me, that is. 'Just sell me a bottle of vodka like a good boy and I'll be on my way.'

His head disappeared under the counter. His dopey visage reappeared brandishing a bottle of something I hadn't seen for a while. Lemon flavoured Stolichnaya. 'This is the best I've got. Normally costs a ton, but since you're being so friendly, I'll make it 80 roubles.'

'That's a rip off.'

He gripped the neck of the bottle, stashed it under the counter. 'If that's how you feel, try somewhere else.'

'Look,' I said through clenched teeth. 'I've had a tough day.' I tugged the Makarov from its holster, went to raise it and point it at the lad, but the weapon slipped from my grasp, clattered on the pavement. Sarcastic laughter grated my ears. I scrabbled around in the slush on the ground, regathered the gun.

'Drop your wallet, pisshead?'

'No.' I stood, stuck the pistol in the youth's face. 'This.' All traces of arrogance disappeared as he stared down the barrel. His eyes widened like soup bowls as he raised his arms in surrender. No doubt my own shaking hand added to his terror.

'You're right about one thing. I *am* a pisshead. I've got just enough booze in my system to make rash decisions.'

Tears were pouring down his cheeks, but I had no sympathy for the little bastard.

'I've decided your price is too high.' I made a come-on gesture. 'Hand it over.'

'What?'

'I'm confiscating it.'

'No way!' His eyes darted left and right, like he was about to have an epileptic fit. 'The boss will kill me. I have to account for all the money in the till.'

'Is that right? You should have thought about that before you got all cocky.'

'Listen.' His voice quavered. 'I'm begging you. Take it for 50 roubles, and I'll make up the rest. Just don't shoot me.'

'Sorry. I'm taking it as evidence of illicit trading in alcohol.' I stuck my hand through the small hole in the glass partition, snaked it to the left and grabbed the necks of two bottles of mineral water. I yanked them out of the hole, dashed them to the pavement. The kid's hand shot to his mouth. Stock he'd have to account for. 'You've been giving me cheek for too long, and I'm fucking over it. Understand?'

He nodded frantically. 'But–'

'Shut up, you weasel! Hand me over the bottle, fuck your mother. I know there're more under the counter. You're lucky I don't take them all.'

He placed the bottle on the counter and I handed him 100 roubles. His eyebrows knitted in confusion. 'But...?'

'It's simple. Treat people with civility and you'll get it back. Understood?'

'Uh huh.'

'The extra should cover the loss of the mineral water.'

'More than cover it.'

'In that case, give me a packet of Kosmos smokes as well.'

My purchased goods in a gaudy plastic bag, I turned to head for home. I felt eyes burning a hole in the back of my head and turned to see if the youth had completely lost his shit. He looked like he'd seen a ghost, eyes wide and staring 'What the hell's the matter with you?' I said.

'Th-thanks for not shooting me.' The lad's lips drooped at the edges, like he was about to start blubbering.

I sighed then put on the tough guy face to reinforce the lesson. 'I had to deal with some nasty skinheads yesterday, son, and I've been itching to take out my frustrations on someone. You're lucky I'm in a good mood tonight.'

The government TV channels, ever reliable and predictable, broadcast breathless reports from around the nation. Happy revolutionaries, wall to wall. Our dear brother republics preparing to share the joy of Revolution Day. Folks in their national costumes danced, laughed, sang songs of praise to the gods of Lenin and Marx, denounced the evil West. Lauded Gorbachev and his genius policies of Perestroika and Glasnost. On display all the myriad ethnicities and nationalities of our country, as big as a continent and spanning eleven time zones. Words of love and gratitude to the CPSU on red and white banners and propaganda posters. Interviews with sycophantic party hacks governing these fiefdoms, pledging eternal allegiance to the ideals of socialism.

And from overseas. Eastern bloc countries marching as one with their Big Brother, singing in harmony from the same song sheet.

No mention of the lack of food in the stores. Of the miserable living conditions endured by millions of the USSR's inhabitants.

No mention of murdered African student Aaron Adekanye, nor of slain forensics officer Ivanov.

But why would there be? Nothing spoils a 70th anniversary party like bad news.

It all made me sick to my stomach. And to think, tomorrow is going to be even worse.

I turned off the TV and flicked on the radio to listen to the Mayak station. Alla Pugacheva. The darling, approved pop star of our times. Tresses of hair cemented into place, fluffy white boa, she crooned a song about a million roses. Not my favourite music style, but it beat the hell out of inane propaganda.

To toast the incredible raspy vocal talent of Comrade Pugacheva, I drained a glass and smacked my lips. 'To Alla, bless her soul!'

The cracked and stained toilet bowl swayed. Or was it me? I palmed the wall with one hand, aimed my trajectory at the middle of the water. Pretty sure most of it landed where I intended it to go. If I remembered, I'd double check in the morning in case I sprayed wide and hit the floor. Too hard to tell in this state of inebriation. I tried to recall how much alcohol I'd consumed today. A handful of pints with Harry Okocha, whiskey with Flora, wine with my father, vodka at home alone. A cosmopolitan combination befitting the International Revolution. All that was missing was a cocktail. A fucking Molotov cocktail.

I collapsed in my armchair, tipped the remaining lemon vodka into a shot glass. Barely filled a third of it, not enough to get a sparrow drunk. I turned the TV back on, curious to see if there'd been any change in programming. No such luck. I dropped back into my chair, tossed back the spirit. I let out a noxious burp, grabbed the bottle just as a reporter sporting a towering industrial perm was describing the incredible economic performance of the USSR over the year of 1987.

'People are fucking starving!' I roared and hurled the bottle. It bounced off the screen like a rubber ball off a brick wall, landed a couple of centimetres from my slippers. A tiny crack zig-zagged across the set, but otherwise the show went on. I dipped the TV volume a touch, and the blueish images flickered to the accompaniment of patriotic radio. It's a hard heart that doesn't react to the Red Army Choir belting out *Katyusha*. Tears welled in my eyes. I knew it was maudlin nonsense magnified by the vodka. For many Russians like my father, the folk-inspired military song fills their hearts with pride. Sometimes it works its magic on me in the same way. Tonight, though, I was weeping for Aaron Adekanye.

The next day was a huge occasion for my country, the land I loved despite its flaws, its monotone system that stifled creativity and demanded conformity. I would not celebrate, would not sing, would not applaud. I'd have the hangover from hell, but the investigation into a murder would continue. The murder no one could talk about.

Chapter 24

The screaming alarm clock jolted me awake. A dreamless anaesthetic sleep interrupted by what sounded like an air raid siren. 'Shut the hell up, you son of a bitch!' Yelling at the inanimate object had no effect. It continued its pitiless vibrating tirade. 'Shut up I said!' *For fuck's sake, why won't it stop?*

The morning of the 7th of November 1987 wouldn't be the same waking nightmare for everyone as it was for me. All over the USSR, diehard believers would be greeting the morning with a huge smile, ready to commemorate this auspicious day in our history. The 70th anniversary of the 1917 Bolshevik Revolution. The only thing to beat Revolution Day for generating patriotism is the massive Victory Parade that marks the end of World War II. We don't call it "The Great Patriotic War" for nothing. You have to wait till the warmth of early May for that grandiose display of military might. Victory Day is designed to shore up support for the fighting forces. Today, however, is all about reinforcing the ideological message, much better achieved in the bitter cold of November.

The alarm clock buzzed relentlessly. My arm flopped in the general direction of the recalcitrant timepiece, my hand felt around in the dark. *Where's the damned off button?* I had to kill the thing before its shrill wailing killed me.

Found it, slapped it, ended it.

I stifled a sigh of relief as blessed silence descended. Without warning, field gun artillery rounds exploded in my head. One after the other. *Bang,*

bang, bang. Then a duller ache, like a sadistic nurse was pushing a long, hot needle into my ear. I clasped my hands to my head, pressed my temples. No relief.

I'd meant to buy aspirin after the last bad hangover. I'd clean forgot. Did the pharmacies even have it in stock? I doubted it. There'd be some at the station in a first aid kit; I'd force myself to get to work today, even if I had to crawl. Jesus, how I wanted to cry. To let out the anger, the frustration, the pain. No tears would come.

My state of mind hovered on the edge of depression. Not talked about among men, dismissed as cowardice. It was a condition that affected millions of our citizens. Depression was all around, invisible like the wind, yet ever present. Seeking solace in substances wasn't the answer. I had no idea what was. The MVD offered psychological help to its officers; rumour had it the treatment was worse than the cure, so I never applied for help. Word could get out I was loco. How embarrassing for colleagues to know you weren't coping. My health – physical and mental – was teetering on the edge of an abyss.

I rolled my tongue around inside my mouth, drier than an old cork. My skin felt dehydrated, looked pallid as a junkie's. I felt my heart thumping, racing like a steam train. I fought to breathe, panic was taking over.

Calm down, idiot. Deep, slow, even breaths. Rein it back.

That didn't work. My lungs rattled as my chest expanded and contracted. Probably full of fluid. I coughed hard, a ball of bitter phlegm lodged in my throat. My mouth filled with thick salty saliva. I stumbled to the bathroom, spat out the vile gunk before I vomited.

Heart again.

Pounding.

God almighty, you're going to die of a coronary before you get out the door. Stay alive for Ksenia.

I rinsed my mouth with copper-flavoured tap water, started the breathing routine again. I felt my pulse: 130. Too fast. I sat in the kitchen chair, continued the breathing routine for five minutes. Checked the pulse again. 115. Coming down, but still too fast for a resting heart rate. *You should've walked straight past the kiosk yesterday, made a pot of tea and gone to bed at a reasonable hour. Not 02:03am.* That was the number I remember seeing on the kitchen clock when my body shut down, exhausted and poisoned. After 15 minutes in the chair my pulse slowed to 95 beats per minute. Terrible, but now I could function.

I managed a quick shower, palms spread on the tiled wall for balance, legs quivering. The strains of *Katyusha* rang in my throbbing brain, taunted me for my stupidity. Hot water was a balm, but it only soothed for a few minutes. I felt protruding ribs as I dried off with a scratchy threadbare towel. I shook all over like a leaf, teeth chattered. Maybe I'd caught something, the 'flu. I chuckled to myself: the typical alcoholic's excuse. *I can handle the booze. It must be something else making me feel like shit. A stomach bug.* Never mind, press on. There's a job to do. Killers to track down and...I wasn't sure about the next bit. I'd let intuition guide me.

Dressed in my cleanest civvies; fawn slacks and an almost matching brown jacket. Trusty gabardine overcoat. Hot tea, no sugar. Cigarette followed by a second. Metro ride. All done in a foggy semi-dream.

I regained a degree of clarity on the chilly walk to work. The reality of the megapolis Moscow city smacked me in the face like a ton of bricks. Air thick with fumes of diesel, oil, petrol. The gaudy bunting of the last few days had multiplied overnight like forest fungi. Wherever you looked, red and white flags and banners, hammers and sickles, colourful posters telling me how to act and think, portraits of living and dead legends of the Marxist-Leninist pantheon, stony-faced members of the Politburo whose names nobody knew.

Roads blocked, detours, men and women in uniforms, military machines of all shapes and sizes. Old men wearing badges and ribbons, stylish ties and dry-cleaned suits underneath overcoats that had seen better days. Children in their best clothes; boys in quasi-military Pioneer regalia, girls with plaits and white ribbons. Boy and girl soldiers for the cause. And the stark counterpoint to this circus – queues of proletarians stretched around corners, patiently lining up for scarce goods the system struggled to provide. Not luxury items, but basics like bread, milk, eggs. The hypocrisy of it all

176

sickened me. I shook my head. Seventy years to get it right, and they're still fumbling for that elusive, perfect socialism. You know the one: it's almost in sight, tantalisingly within grasp. If it weren't for domestic non-believers and nasty foreign devils derailing the efforts of our all-loving, all-benevolent Central Committee, we'd be there already. Hang tight, comrades. We'll get there!

Yeah, right.

A block from the Militsiya station I heard the cheery sound of a brass orchestra playing a military march getting closer and louder. Tubas dominated the other instruments. As a pair of cymbals crashed, a thought occurred to me. The investigation into Adekanye's murder had been stopped before it even began, a clampdown that was, on the face of it, contradictory to the policy and spirit of Glasnost. But did that very same Glasnost necessarily apply to law enforcement agencies, a law unto themselves? No, the very idea was laughable. But this was the paradoxical Soviet Union, so it was perfectly reasonable to contemplate the simultaneous existence of two diametrically opposed realities. The security agencies would continue to operate covertly and no one would know what the hell they were up to. Just like before. On the other hand, the civil population's tolerance of incompetence and deceit could evaporate if Gorbachev's policies of openness continued. They'd find their voice, demand things, create conflict.

Maybe Papa was right in his prediction after all. The unthinkable might happen, the regime could totter and fall. Why not? Rome did. The Fourth Reich did. Continued deprivation around the country teamed with new freedoms might lead to a change. A counter revolution. A putsch leading backwards towards repression on a massive scale. I wouldn't want to be in charge of this country; whichever way you went could lead to disaster.

My internal speculation ended when I entered Burov's office. 'Morning, Comrade Colonel.' As usual the space was thick with smoke. Today he was puffing on a rosewood pipe. The tobacco smoke smelled delicious. God knows from whom he expropriated it.

'You look like shit, Voloshin.' Not the greeting I was expecting.

'Excuse me?'

'I said you look like shit.'

Rita stuck her head around the door. 'Comrade Colonel, you're wanted at the front desk.' She gave me a weak smile that said *oh, you poor thing, you look like shit.* I guessed she'd be thinking I got wasted after a nasty standoff with Sveta. Which would have almost qualified as a valid reason for my dishevelled appearance.

'What is it?' said Burov, tipping the spent contents of his pipe into the ashtray.

'Not sure. A young lady. She says it's very important.'

'Flora Madenge again?' I wondered out loud.

Rita gave a mini head shake. 'No. Her name's Natasha. Says her alcoholic husband's been beating her and she can't take it anymore.'

'Nothing I hate more than a wife beater.' Burov stood, pulled a jacket from the back of his chair and threw it on like a matador donning a cape. 'Any injuries?'

'Nothing visible, Comrade Colonel.'

'I'll need you to pull her aside for a preliminary physical assessment. Take some photographs – you, not Morozov – if there's any bruising, cuts and so on.'

Burov puffed out his cheeks. 'Voloshin, I've been sent an urgent request to send all available men to the parade.'

'What the hell?'

'The bomb threats.'

'You said they were assessed to be a hoax.'

'Well, there's been a change of thinking. Better safe than sorry. You'll need to go home and change back into uniform for this assignment. You're to report to Major Zinovy Livshitz, Arbat Station. You know where that is?'

'Yes, of course I know.' My heart sank. 'I humbly request to be excused from the assignment.'

'On what grounds? It's Revolution Day, for Christ's sake.'

'I'm fully aware of that. I was hoping to pursue another lead in the Adekanye case.'

Burov raised one eyebrow. 'Yes? And what lead is that?'

His desk phone jumped to life before I had a chance to formulate an invented response. He snatched the phone in annoyance. 'What now?'

A dark cloud passed over Burov's face. 'Are you sure?' A few head nods, some aggravated nail chewing. He gently placed the phone back on the cradle. He eyeballed me like a doctor about to tell me I had a day to live.

'Who was that?' I couldn't wait for a response; his crestfallen expression got my heart racing again.

'Despatch. Bad news, I'm afraid.'

'What?'

'It's Yegor. He was beaten up outside his apartment block this morning. Ambulance should be on its way.'

'So am I.' There'd be no changing into uniform now, no assisting at the parade. Burov said nothing as I raced out the door.

Chapter 25

A small crowd of six or seven people had gathered where Yegor lay; five metres to the right of the short flight of concrete steps leading to his apartment block in a relatively well-to-do part of north-eastern Moscow. Clean parks, tidy streets, low crime. The area where Yegor lay was clear save for a brimming skip bin, two dented and rusty Zhiguli sedans, and an empty children's playground. My trusty elbows got me through the tight cordon. A young woman was kneeling beside Yegor, holding his gloved right hand, which poked out of a heavy chequered blanket. He lay on his back, limbs tucked into his sides, only his battered head visible. His uplifted face was catching snowflakes the woman brushed away gently as they landed. He looked like he'd nodded off in a sleeping bag. *Please don't be dead.*

I was puffing hard after the flat-out sprint from the Metro station. My nuclear hangover was wreaking vengeance: cotton-dry mouth, rocketing pulse, dizziness. 'Jesus Christ,' I gasped. I quickly forgot my own problems. 'Look at the state of you.'

Yegor's face was a gross mess of dried, congealed blood, eyes swollen like ripe plums, a long ragged laceration in the bottom lip. His entire head appeared to be one and a half times the size of normal. The assailants had destroyed his nose, which now resembled one of those flat wild mushrooms I used to gather with Papa when I was a kid. I wondered what horrific damage lay out of sight under the blanket. I scanned the circle of concerned faces, announced my name and rank, flashed my Militsiya identification.

'Did any of you witness the attack?'

Silence and head shakes. Not a good start. I'd make enquiries in the immediate area as soon as Yegor was collected by the ambulance, phone Burov and ask for help with interviewing people. Surely not all officers had been seconded for Revolution Day duty. Still, I wasn't hopeful.

'Who got here first?'

'I did,' said the woman crouching next to me. 'I haven't left his side.' She glanced up, eyes beseeching. 'Do something. He's in a bad way.' Her hand wiped away another couple of snowflakes.

I felt inside Yegor's mouth. Some loose teeth, tongue bleeding and swollen flesh inside the cheeks. 'I can see that, madam. What's your name?'

'Marina Stepanova.'

'Thanks for waiting here with him, Marina.' I offered her a grin of gratitude that was barely a parting of the lips.

'What else could I do? He looks a lot like my brother-in-law.' She sniffed back a tear, regripped Yegor's hand. There was no need for her to do this but I didn't stop her.

'What happened exactly?'

'I don't know, I didn't see the attack.'

'No. I mean what were *you* doing when you found him?'

'Oh, sorry. I was leaving for work this morning, heading for the bus stop, when I saw him lying here, all twisted up. Blood all over the place. He was moaning and groaning for a while, then he fell silent.'

'How long ago was that?'

'I'd say roughly an hour and a half.'

I shook my head. Damned Revolution Day, sucking up all the city's resources, leaving ordinary citizens vulnerable. All across the Soviet Union, sick and injured people would die unnecessarily today. Because doctors and nurses and cops and ambulance drivers were syphoned out of the system, standing by at the festivities *just in case* something happened there. A disgrace.

'Out here in the freezing cold the whole time?' He'd been lying on the pavement, exposed to temperatures hovering between -4 and zero degrees;

gusts of icy sleet swept over us in the courtyard.

'We decided not to move him,' said a fussy middle-aged woman encased in a dark green windbreaker jacket. She clutched a string bag stuffed with black bread.' I used to be a nurse. It can be a lot worse if a person's suffered injuries and you try to–'

'He could get frostbite dammit,' I protested. Rude, I admit, considering the good citizens had been maintaining their vigil in the cold conditions.

'Ah, no he couldn't,' said green jacket. 'He's covered by a couple of woollen blankets, and there are hot-water bottles tucked inside. We changed them over for fresh ones a few minutes before you appeared.'

'OK, then.' *Ease up, Voloshin.* 'Well done everybody.'

I palpated Yegor's body through the blanket, smiled when I felt the warmth of one of the hot water bottles. 'Where the hell is the ambulance?' It was a rhetorical question, yet someone saw fit to reply.

'Hopefully not far now. We called for help right away.'

'Who placed the call?'

'I did.' An elderly man in military regalia confirmed he'd rung emergency services minutes after Marina had found Yegor. I thanked the man for doing his civic duty; his reply was a curt nod and a smile of smug self-satisfaction. One thing you can always count on in Soviet society is this: if you're lying motionless in the gutter, someone will at least check to see if you're alive. As a rule of thumb, most will take the next step and call for help. Anecdotal evidence said members of the public were becoming less inclined to help their fellows with each passing year. Scared of criminals pretending to be drunk or sick, usually late at night. These pricks waited in ambush to rob you if you made the mistake of stopping to assist. When I first heard these stories I thought they were pure invention. I was wrong; scores of offenders had been prosecuted for such incidents in south-west Moscow alone. What I saw in Yegor's courtyard gave me heart. Many people still gave a shit about their fellow man.

'Do you know the officer?' I asked the woman as I gently ran my hands up and down the top of the blanket, felt a couple of protruding bones in both lower legs. If there was internal bleeding, cracked ribs, busted organs, anything like that, doctors would diagnose it.

'To say hello, but no more than that. He lives on the third floor, I think. I don't really know about his family situation. Haven't seen him about with anyone else.'

'He's single.' I felt a wave of shame. I should know more about Yegor; we've worked together long enough. Eighteen months, often on the same shift. It was ridiculous, now I was forced to think about it. I knew he more or less supported the regime and he was a terrible but enthusiastic driver, but not much of the personal stuff. I'm always banging on about my unreasonable ex-wife, the daughter I adore, my oddball father. I knew nothing about Yegor's parents, whether he had siblings, romantic interests. It was always about me and my miserable lot. I ran a finger along Yegor's cold cheek, vowed to myself things would change once he'd made a full recovery.

Marina stared at me. 'If hooligans are going around attacking Militsiya officers in uniform, what chance do we have?' The woman's voice quavered. 'We used to feel safe here. There's lots of children in this neighbourhood. Old people. What's the world coming to?'

I ignored her question. Mainly because I didn't know the answer, but also I was preoccupied with my fallen colleague. I placed an ear to Yegor's mangled nose. He was somehow managing to breathe, tiny pink bubbles popped with each soft exhalation. I wanted to shake him awake, but knew it could exacerbate his injuries. I leaned in close. 'Yegor! Can you hear me?' No response. 'Christ, where is that damned ambulance?' I mumbled under my breath.

Marina let go of Yegor's hand, regripped it. No doubt she was exhausted. I should send her – all of them – away, but I wanted to question them after the ambulance had taken Yegor to hospital. Marina rubbed her nose with a sleeve of her jacket. 'It might take a bit longer than usual for them to get here today.'

'Yeah, I guess so. Still, it's not good enough.'

Sirens split the air.

Two young faces appeared. A man and a woman. The pair of ambulance officers lifted the blankets off Yegor, picked him up with extreme care, eased him onto a gurney. They made a quick assessment of the patient, exchanged a couple of medical terms I didn't understand, put a clean, dry blanket on him and slid him inside the vehicle. The woman jumped in after Yegor and closed the door, leaving me with the male officer.

'Well?' I said. 'How bad is he?'

'Pretty bad.' His face twitched; I guessed he was eager to get the patient to the hospital, not stand around chatting to me. I endeavoured to keep it short.

'Is he going to live?'

'Can't say. He'll need to be x-rayed at the hospital. Whoever beat him up knew what they were doing.'

'Are you sure? He's still breathing.'

'Only just. Without seeing x-rays, I'd say he's got a cracked skull, broken bones, definitely ribs. His nose...fuck, excuse me. I've never seen one like that that wasn't the result of a traffic accident. I'd say someone's taken to the poor fellow with a metal bar or a lump of wood. Fists wouldn't do this amount of damage.' He wiped his hands on his trousers. 'Man, I've never seen a uniformed cop beaten like this. Makes you wonder.'

'Wonder what?'

'How safe we are.'

The same thing Marina had said.

'If the attackers knew what they were doing, why isn't he dead?'

He shrugged. 'Maybe someone disturbed them. Look, he needs to get to the hospital. You want to come along for the ride?'

I considered the offer for a second. 'No. I want to make some inquiries in the neighbourhood. Someone must have seen something.'

'He'll be in intensive care at Hospital No. 50.'

I shook the officer's hand, thanked him for his service. He'd been rattled by what he'd seen. Cops aren't meant to get bashed in broad daylight. I grabbed the names and addresses of all present at the scene. Everyone co-operated willingly, but could offer no useful information. I canvassed Yegor's apartment building, got no joy from the residents. Except for one kindly babushka. She heard a scuffle and some yelling when she opened her window to chase crows from her balcony, but when she leaned over to see what it was, there was no one there. I asked if I could use her phone to call Burov; the chief swore blind there wasn't anyone he could send to help me with my doorknocking. I kept at it for another twenty minutes before I realised pounding on doors by myself was a mug's game.

Only two out of the forty or so residents I spoke to even knew the cop who lived in their building was called Yegor. Some vaguely recalled the surname Adamovsky from his letterbox inside the entrance way.

Back outside, I asked a few random people passing by if they'd seen or heard anything suspicious today, yesterday, this week. Again, I drew a blank.

As I lumbered in the direction of the subway station, I was filled with a crazy anger, something raw. I'd never felt it in my life. If I was pissed off about the murder of Aaron Adekanye, then this attack on Yegor raised my ire to another level altogether. This was a new type of rage, one that cried out for vengeance. I understood perfectly that this culmination of criminal acts so heinous, so gratuitously violent, would never be sorted by due legal process. No guilty party would be arrested, prosecuted and punished.

My gut told me who was behind this. It was no coincidence; it was connected to our trip to Lyubertsy. Lacroix and people protecting, even supporting him. I'd be the next target on the list, no doubt. But they wouldn't catch me napping. I'd be more prepared for whatever they were thinking of dishing out. I felt the hardness of the Makarov in my pocket. Reassuring, but perhaps insufficient. I'd need to arm myself better, because I was going to take these fuckers down.

Chapter 26

Sergeant Anatoly Pronin sat on the cold steel bench, elbows resting on his knees. He alternated between whimpering like a scolded puppy and sobbing softly. I'd never seen him display emotion like this. His anguish was almost palpable as I neared him. I coughed as I entered the squad room. The saddest pair of eyes I'd ever seen on a Moscow street cop glared up at me. You'd think the man's mother had died. He liberated a handkerchief from his pants pocket, rubbed damp patches on his cheeks.

'I didn't pick you for a sentimental fool, Tolya.'

'I'm not, generally. But when it's one of us who gets attacked then...'

Pronin's grief was even rawer than my own. A good thing – a grieving ally is an aggrieved ally. And a powerful one. Both he and Yegor had been posted at this station three years ago. I had to ask. 'What do you know about him?'

'Sorry, Comrade Captain?' He seemed defensive.

'Yegor. What do you really know about him? His personal life? I don't mix much with colleagues after work, keep to myself most of the time. I was hoping you could throw some light on his...character, I guess.'

If Pronin portrayed grief when I walked into the squad room, now I detected discomfiture. I remembered Tolya was a single man. Like Yegor. I'd never heard of him having a girlfriend, he never talked about women apart from those he worked with or encountered on the job. Like Yegor. The two of them expressed more interested in politics, literature, art exhibitions. Was it possible he and Yegor were...? No, unimaginable. If the margin of tolerance for foreigners and other races was paper thin in Russia, if what I half suspected was true, the two men were really running the gauntlet. Then again, it could be my overactive imagination getting out of control. Yes, that was it. Pronin's grief was comradely, not that of a homosexual lover.

'Um, he ah…' Pronin's stammer made me wish I'd never asked the question. 'I'm not sure, Viktor Pavlovich. I mean, he's a solitary guy. Like lots of us in the Militsiya. Comes to work, does his shift, goes home. What he does after that, on weekends, I have no idea.' Pronin was lying. He knew a lot more than he was letting on. That "private" information, though, wouldn't help me catch the culprits or avenge Yegor.

'Fair enough. What are you doing here at the station, Tolya? Burov said everyone had been deployed to the city centre. I was expecting to see you on the news tonight guarding Gorbachev's wife.'

'Good one, Comrade Captain.' Pronin forced a smile. 'Believe it or not, I was two hundred metres from Red Square when I got the call on my radio to turn back.'

'Didn't you ask why?'

'Of course I did.' His voice had a sharp edge. 'Why the hell do you think I've been crying like a baby?'

Perhaps they did have a romantic connection after all. I pushed it. 'Were you and Yegor, you know…?'

Pronin leapt to his size 46 feet, breasted me. 'What do you mean by that? Huh?'

'Nothing.' He edged closer. I could smell vodka on his breath.

He shoved me hard in the sternum, my back rattled the locker door behind me. 'No. Tell me. What the hell are you insinuating?'

I quickly turned my back to him, stuck the key in my locker, opened the door. Not to take out or replace anything, but to avoid looking him in the eye. I'd overstepped the mark, with no grounds to do so other than a salacious hunch. Pronin was having none of it; he grabbed me by the shoulders and spun me back around with a strength that surprised me. His nostrils flared like a horse at the end of a race, eyes darted left and right. In my peripherals I saw his ham-sized fists bunching. He was never scared of a verbal stoush with me, I wouldn't rule out a physical one.

'Stop, Tolya. I'm warning you. Don't touch me. You're upset, I get it.'

He let go of my lapels, dropped his hands, cast his gaze to the scuffed parquetry floor. 'Sorry. I don't know what came over me. It won't happen again.'

If Yegor wasn't lying in a hospital bed clinging to life I would have bawled out Pronin like a first-year cadet. 'What you do in your personal life is your business, Sergeant. I make no judgement.'

'But I don't–' he was on the point of shouting again.

'Shush. Drop it. I was just wondering if there's anything in Yegor's background that may have been a motive for what happened to him.'

Pronin resumed his seat on the bench, twirled his hat in his hands. We both took some deep breaths, let the tense moment pass. He was first to speak. 'Do you believe there actually *was* a motive? He couldn't possibly have enemies. I'd say it was a random attack. Yegor was the unlucky cop on the receiving end.'

I took a seat next to Tolya and we both stared at the floor. 'I'm pretty sure I know who did it,' I said. 'Or at least who ordered the hit on Yegor.'

'*Ordered the hit?* You make it sound like the Mafia.'

'A hit is exactly what it was. A warning. *Stop poking your nose in where it's not wanted.* That was the message.'

'You mean the Adekanye murder? Weren't you ordered to back off? I heard a rumour the CID are close to making an arrest, so why would you be the target?'

'Bullshit. Burov would've told me. He's said nothing about any arrests.'

'Maybe it's baseless speculation. You know how that stuff gets tossed around, especially when things are shrouded in secrecy. Best breeding ground for rumours.'

'I understand that, but can you tell me who said an arrest was imminent?'

'Kirill Gregoriev. Please don't tell him I told you it was him. Kirill reckoned the CID had linked Ivanov's killing to Adekanye's and there'd be an arrest in the next two or three days.'

'Who do they like for the crime?'

Pronin's lips formed a tight knot. 'That part he didn't know.'

'That's because the little shit made it all up.' I would've loved to press Kirill for his side of this story, in case what he claimed did have foundation, but right now he'd be standing shoulder to shoulder with other officers in a cordon somewhere. 'Nothing better to do than make up gossip.'

'But Yegor...he was heading to the parade. Why would they go after him instead of you?'

'Perhaps they saw him as an easier target. Don't know why; you should have seen how he handled himself the last couple of days. A joy to behold. But a cowardly surprise attack – no one can ever defend themselves against that.'

Pronin gave a nod of agreement.

'As for being pulled off the case, I ignored that order. Burov's been turning a blind eye, but the higher-ups will get whiff of my disobedience sooner or later. I'll probably get sacked for not toeing the line. Or end up like Yegor.'

'Holy shit.'

'They don't scare me.' *I was terrified.* 'I'm ready for whatever they can dish out.'

'I wish I had your attitude, Viktor Pavlovich.'

'I'm glad you don't. You're young. My advice – stay out of trouble and you'll have a long and distinguished career. Don't rock the boat. Or if you've got too much of a conscience, get out of the force now, find another job.'

'No.' He shook his head. 'If I have to cross the line to get things done, so be it.'

I patted him on the shoulder. 'Good man.'

'I've got a feeling I'm going to be crossing that line soon.' Pronin continued. He glanced up at me, his chin quivered for a second. 'I can't stand by and let whoever beat up Yegor get away with it. I don't care if it's going to cost me my job.'

'Let's see what we can achieve on the quiet, hey? If we're smart, we can avenge Yegor and neither of us will lose our jobs. We have to be extremely careful. Understand?'

Pronin nodded slowly. 'Our best chance would be to make our move today, wouldn't it?'

'Agreed. Everyone's preoccupied with the parade.'

'What's the plan then, Viktor Pavlovich?'

The lad was bright, no doubt about it. I decided to give him a touch more background before I fully enlisted him into my two-man hit squad.

'Initially I wanted to do everything by the book, I really did. Find evidence, present it to the public prosecutor, let justice take its course. When Burov told me CID would be handling it exclusively and my enquiries weren't welcome, I realised that wouldn't work. The killers will get off scot free if we don't bend the rules a fraction.' I lit a cigarette for each of us. 'I've been making private inquiries with Yegor's help, asking questions that have clearly rattled some people. Unfortunately, I failed to turn up hard evidence. Not that it would do any good.'

'Why not?'

'It's a filthy, stinking coverup, that's why not. But I know the truth. The Wolves must've set a tail on Yegor, found out where he lived and waited to ambush him.'

'The Wolves? What are you talking about?'

I clued Pronin up on our brief trip to Lyubertsy, and what else I'd been up to: sniffing around the institutes, intelligence from Nico, Flora Madenge and her entourage, getting short shrift at the Canadian embassy but better luck with the Nigerian attaché Sir Harry Okocha. The hockey match, Lacroix doing a runner before I could talk to him.

'So you reckon that Lacroix kid is responsible for the murder of Adekanye?'

'One hundred percent. For that alone payback is worth it. Add Ivanov and Yegor into the mix and–'

'I'm with you all the way, Viktor Pavlovich.' He flipped his hat again and slapped it on his head. 'You know, there's a weird element to Adekanye's killing that's been gnawing at me.'

'Really? What's that?'

'The fact Lacroix means "cross" in French and the cross that was carved into the kid's back. Was that what made you think it was the Canadian?'

'No. I would have liked Lacroix for the crime in any case.' Now wasn't the time to admit I didn't know a damned word of French.

'I can't stop thinking about the way Adekanye was mutilated. Someone capable of that doesn't deserve normal justice. And now they've gone after our Yegor...'

'Come with me.' I crooked my index finger.

Pronin followed me down the corridor to the evidence room, our bootsteps echoed in the empty space. 'Are you going to show me some secret evidence you've kept up your sleeve?' Pronin was sardonic as ever.

I laughed. 'No. Sasha Kozlov confiscated illegal weapons from a gang of thugs a while back.' I opened a sliding door to a huge steel cabinet, ran my eyes up and down the shelves. There they were. Three pairs of shiny knuckledusters. We only needed two. I'd make sure they were cleaned thoroughly before I returned them: of blood, skin and bone. With luck, the weapons would be back on the shelf before anyone realised they'd been taken. I'd hate for the original owners of these despicable devices to go free because of missing evidence. I handed a set to Pronin.

'Holy shit, Comrade Captain.' He hefted them in his hands. 'These could do a lot of damage.'

'I certainly hope so.'

I tucked the brassies into my coat pocket. Pronin held the shiny weapon centimetres from his eyes, stared at them as if he was hypnotised. A shadow crept over his face; the man appeared exhausted, he needed to sleep, rest, not embark on a dangerous mission of revenge with me. 'Are you sure you want to be a part of this, Tolya?'

'Are you kidding me, Comrade Captain? I'm with you all the way. How much ammunition do you have?'

'Not enough.'

We headed for the armaments room. There'd normally be an officer there to monitor arms supplies. Not today. We helped ourselves to three boxes of 9x18mm bullets and extra magazine clips, put them in a large canvas bag we found in the bottom of a cupboard.

'One more thing to do before we go.'

'What's that?'

'Firing range. I need to practise.'

'You'll be OK with me, Viktor Pavlovich. I got top grade for marksmanship at the academy. I'm still a good shot.' He said it without any egoism.

'Glad to hear it. I'm a little rusty myself.'

An hour of shooting at silhouettes of people on pieces of paper set 50 metres away proved one thing. An hour wasn't enough to get my eye in. Pronin hadn't been kidding about his accuracy; he pumped his bullets much closer to the centre of the targets than I did. Some of my shots were way wide of the mark. He gave me some useful tips on aiming and regulating my breathing. I'd be lucky to remember it all in the heat of battle.

'Well done.' Pronin smiled as he removed his earmuffs. 'We'll make a sniper out of you, yet Comrade Captain.'

'I'm hoping it doesn't come to that. My plan is to coax a confession out of Lacroix. With you as a witness. The brass knuckles should be enough. The hard part's going to be finding him.'

'But how's getting a confession going to work? With all due respect, if there's a coverup as you say, anything you present will be suppressed. Probably destroyed. Along with your career, and mine for abetting you.'

'Yes, but I have an idea.'

'Care to enlighten me?'

'Not yet. First we have to go back to the station. Is Burov on shift?'

'No. Only Rita manning the reception. Everyone else is doing their patriotic duty. Why?'

'A second idea.'

'You're full of them today, Viktor Pavlovich. I hope they're good ones.'

I drew a deep breath. 'So do I.'

Back in Burov's office, I opened the door to a cabinet that held his confiscated booty. Three shelves stocked with the finest foreign booze, cigarettes and sundry luxury goods. A veritable Aladdin's cave. I extracted a bottle of Rémy Martin cognac and two cartons of Camels. Better than cash for what I had in mind. As I was closing the latch, something tucked away in the back corner caught my eye. I crouched low and squinted hard. A Kodak 227X instamatic camera, a spool of film and a box of flashes bearing the delightful name "magicubes".

'Ever used anything like this before?' I said over my shoulder. Pronin's face appeared next to mine as we both gazed into the cabinet.

'No, but I've heard of them. I reckon between us we can figure it out. What's your thinking?'

'We get Lacroix to hold up a confession, take some snaps and get them developed at the big photography shop on Kalininsky Prospekt. Then we release the photos to the Western press if the MVD won't do what's right.'

Pronin grinned. 'That's a fantastic idea. We'd better not beat him up too bad, though. Won't do your cause much good.'

'Words are often enough to encourage cooperation. If we show him the brassies and our Makarovs, let him know we aren't mucking around, he'll confess to the assassination of John F. Kennedy.' *We can beat the shit out of him post confession* were the words I left unsaid.

I raked the photographic gear together, gently placed it all in the canvas bag. The damned thing was starting to get heavy. This little haul of contraband would be worth two months of my salary.

'What's the booze and smokes for?' Pronin asked. 'I thought you were a straight cop?'

'This isn't for me.'

'What then?'

'There are no vehicles in the pool. The cognac's to hire ourselves a driver.'

'And the Camels?'

I felt my cheeks flush fiery hot. 'Compensation for work-related stress and mental anguish.'

Pronin and I marched a hundred metres through slowly melting snow, turned right and stood on the side of Leninsky Prospekt. I stuck my thumb out and waited while Pronin studied the instructions for the camera. His English was almost as bad as mine, but there were diagrams he could follow. My arm grew numb; no one would stop for us. Every vehicle zoomed past like it was late for an appointment.

'Perhaps it's my uniform putting people off?' Pronin ventured.

He was right. Would I stop for pair of men – one in civvies, the other a street cop in uniform – hailing a ride? Unlikely. I pointed behind him. 'Go hide behind that tree. I'll have better luck on my own.'

'Sure. May I make a suggestion?'

'What?'

'Flash a bit of the contraband.'

Pity I hadn't taken Marlboros from Burov's stash. It was the best-known brand with maximum buying power. I could only work with what I had; I didn't want to use the cognac in case I dropped it on the pavement. With Pronin out of view, I held out a carton of Camel and waved it about like an orchestra conductor who'd reached the fast part of the symphony. Two minutes later a lemon coloured hatchback stopped in front of me with a skid. Slush flew up, struck the legs of my pants. I wanted to yell at the stupid driver but forced a smile.

Behind the wheel of the shiny, brand new VAZ-2109, known colloquially as a Devyatka, sat a thin man in his early twenties; navy blue woollen beanie, tacky gold chains around his neck. If he was able to afford a car like this at his age, he was involved in criminal activity. Or his father was a crook. Either that or a bureaucrat, which was often the same thing.

The driver wound down the window, favoured me with a courteous smile. 'Where to, uncle?'

I opened the door and leaned my back against it in case he decided to drive off. 'Chekhov Institute.'

'But that's just around the corner, man. Are you from out of town? You can walk from here in, like, five minutes max.'

'I've got a sore leg, comrade. I'd rather you drive me there.'

Ho ogled the carton of cigarettes, still in its plastic wrapper. 'I'm actually supposed to be somewhere else. How many packets out of that block are you going to give me?'

'All of them.'

'Shit, man. For that I'll drive you to Vladivostok.'

I whistled and Pronin came running. 'Just what I was hoping you'd say.'

In a flash Pronin had covered the 10 metres to the car, flipped the handle of the rear passenger door and leapt inside the vehicle. I got in and closed the door, gave the man my friendliest smile. Inside it was toasty warm and smelled like a freshly washed jumper, not a trace of malodour. No smoking occurred in this vehicle. The cassette player blasted out the schmaltzy pop of a singer called Sofia Rotaru. I only knew that because Ksenia was wild about her. The driver checked the rear view mirror, clocked the uniformed cop and his jaw dropped. He gawped at me for a second before reacquiring the power of speech.

'What's going on here? I only offered to take you. Why is there a damned *ment* in my car? I'll have to get this baby cleaned after carting rubbish around in the back seat.'

'Settle down, friend.' I turned to see Pronin demonstrating faux annoyance via a furrowed brow.

'Hey,' said Pronin. 'No need for name calling, brother.'

'You're not in any trouble,' I said in the calm voice I use to reassure Ksenia when she's anxious. 'We just need you to drive us both around for a while. Can you manage that without wetting your pants?'

'Dammit.' His jaw clenched tight for a second. 'What if I refuse? I mean, what if someone I know sees me with a fucking copper in the back seat? My reputation will be ruined.'

'What reputation is that?'

'Never mind.'

'Actually, I will mind.' I pulled the Makarov from its holster, tapped the barrel on his immaculate dashboard. 'Before we set off, show me your driver's licence and passport.'

The man's eyeballs nearly rotated inside his skull. Whatever that reputation, the sight of a weapon put it on the backburner. He meekly produced the documents with trembling hands.

'Right, Stepan Bandarchuk. Age 22 and residing in...shit, nice neighbourhood...Strogino. Tell you what. If I'm satisfied with your service, when we part company I'll give you a lovely bottle of cognac. Show it to him, will you Sergeant?'

Stepan's initial fear evaporated like late frost on a bright spring morning; his lips moistened as he watched Pronin pull the bottle from his rucksack and show the label. The young man knew its true value, because, after sighting the prize, like the Nazis in 1945 his capitulation was unconditional.

'I take back everything I said. Don't shoot me and I'm sure we'll get along fine.'

Chapter 27

'**P**ull into that driveway on the right and wait. We'll walk from here.'
'Sure, boss.' Stepan's attitude verged on the familiar. I briefly entertained the idea of punching him in the face. He expertly edged the car against a gutter painted black and white like a giant zipper.

'You'd better not disappear,' I warned. 'We've got your details in case you're thinking about doing a runner.'

I was tempted to leave Pronin with Stepan while I quickly made the rounds of the Chekhov – in case our new friend got antsy and ditched us – but two cops covering the tower block dorm would take half the time.

'I'm not going anywhere, Comrade Captain.' Stepan smirked. 'I'm starting to think this whole adventure could be a lot of fun.' Stepan ripped the plastic off the carton of cigarettes, squeezed out a pack, opened it, pulled out a smoke and lit it. But only after he'd stepped out of his pride and joy. He'd already asked us not to smoke in the Devyatka; the cocky spiv was already growing on me, so I thought it a fair request.

'Take off your hat and coat,' I instructed Pronin.

'It's bloody freezing,' he protested. 'Why?'

'They've got Militsiya insignia on them. You can borrow my jumper. I'll make do with the overcoat.'

'Losing the coat, fine,' he relented. 'The hat I'll only take off if you do the same.'

Tolya had a point, besides it was only −1°C with no breeze. I once grilled a drunk and disorderly Finnish construction worker who proudly declared men in his country only wore hats when the mercury dropped to −10°C and anyone who wore one when it was above that was a pussy. That man was full of shit, but walking a couple hundred metres in this weather hatless wouldn't kill us either.

'Agreed.' We tossed our hats into the back seat.

'Why didn't you ask me to change back at the station?' Pronin asked. 'I had a set of street clothes in my locker.'

'Sorry, didn't think about it at the time.'

'I can help you out.' Stepan, a corkscrew of tobacco smoke pouring from his mouth, jerked a thumb towards the back of the car. 'You can borrow an item or two from my private collection. Just don't damage the goods.' Dozens of jackets and other pieces of clothing with expensive fashion labels were jammed into the boot. For Pronin, we found a cashmere jumper and olive green men's windbreaker with a fluffy fur collar. The outer garment was a little roomy on Pronin's light frame, but good enough to hide the sky-blue Militsiya shirt underneath if he needed to unzip the jacket. Each of us grabbed a dark woollen beanie. All traces of our allegiance to the MVD were now hidden from view.

'Grab the camera gear.' I said. 'Keep it on you at all times.'

'Aye-aye.' Pronin reached into the back seat, took the instamatic and stuffed it in the pocket of his borrowed windbreaker. He'd already loaded a spool and quickly figured out how to mount the flash on the short drive to the institute.

Stepan nodded appreciatively. 'Awesome little devices. Maybe we can take a group photo later for my family album?' He laughed, crushed the cigarette butt under his shoe and got back in the car.

Now both nondescript civilians, Pronin and I strode into the Chekhov Institute, straight past the frightful old woman who was supposed to check the IDs of all who enter the building. Lucky for us, she was in the middle of a heated argument with two young women who weren't students of the institute but, from what I could make out, were desperate to visit a sick friend inside. Babushka was having none of it, said she could see right through them and they were sluts on the prowl. Pronin followed a step behind me into the canteen; it had just gone midday so I expected to find people to question there. Half a dozen forlorn students sat alone at tables. None of the students had white faces; I pegged them for Arabs or Turks. I'm no expert though; they could've been kids of immigrant Americans for all I knew. What was sadly obvious: none of them were Lacroix or Nico. We quickly questioned them all, to no avail. Not only did they appear shit scared when they clocked our IDs, their abysmal Russian made communication nigh on impossible.

'What next, Viktor Pavlovich? Knocking on doors?' His expression told me that was the last thing he wanted to do.

'If necessary. But I want to try something else first.'

From a discrete distance, I showed Pronin the door to Shukhov's office. I'd stuffed my pockets with four packs of Camel. A petty bribe might appeal to the rector. 'If he's in, ask to see Lacroix. Tell Shukhov you're a top coach from Dynamo. You've got a message to deliver about a training session. Share these.' I handed Pronin a pack of cigarettes. 'See if he bites.'

'What if he denies knowledge of the guy?'

'I doubt he will. Your new outfit smells of money. There's a good chance he'll believe what you tell him, might even ask for a ticket to a game. If he suspects you're not legit, bow out as gracefully as you can. Then we go door knocking. I'll wait for you in the canteen. If I'm not there, we rendezvous back at the car.'

'Roger that.'

First stroke of luck, the rector was in his office; I made myself scarce once Pronin disappeared behind Shukhov's door. I nonchalantly strolled back to the canteen and ordered a bowl of pea soup with a rock to mop up the dregs. On the off chance, I told the ladle-wielding woman serving the food I was a cop and asked if she knew of Nico. She looked at me askance. 'We're not allowed to fraternise with the students. Strictly forbidden. I couldn't tell you the name of a single one of them.' She crossed her arms with satisfaction.

I took a seat in a corner far from the entrance and waited. The soup didn't help pass the time; it was bland even with a spoonful of sour cream added and half a shaker of salt poured into it. I checked my watch; Pronin had been in with Shukhov for ten minutes and my optimism setting was on high. The sergeant had always struck me as a frustrated actor eager to perform. Perhaps this was his moment of glory. Another five minutes passed. This was looking better and better. I couldn't wait for Pronin to debrief me on what went down.

Foggy condensation covered the massive plate glass window facing the car park. I rubbed a circle in the mist and stared outside. An apartment building across the street was festooned in the mandatory Revolution Day banners. They hung limply under grey skies, lining up squarely with my opinion of the charade they represented. My attention was drawn by a murmuration of sparrows swooping past the bus stop about 50 metres away. A young man stood waiting patiently, leaning against a pole and reading a book.

Nico.

'I'm not going to sign a statement. No way.' Nico kicked a piece of snowy mud off his boot, glanced left and right as if mentally willing a bus to come and whisk him away from the annoying cop.

'I'm going to need all the evidence I can get to have this scum charged. So far, I've got nothing. Your testimony could be crucial in getting a warrant for Lacroix's arrest.'

The panic in Nico's eyes almost made me feel sorry for him. 'If I make an official statement, my time studying here is over. Do you understand that? Over. I gave you enough information already. It's up to you to act on it.'

I shook my head. 'I'm afraid without corroboration it's useless.'

'Then get corroboration from someone else.' He readjusted the straps of his rucksack. I noticed the bag was bulging fit to burst. A thought flashed through my mind: the lad's embroiled in something illegal. He was certainly keen to get away from me after previously cosying up. Was he pointing the finger at the Canadian to deflect attention from himself?

'Open your bag.'

'Excuse me?'

'What, suddenly you don't understand Russian?' I tore the bag from his shoulders, ripped the zip open. Instant regret. The stench of unwashed clothes made me wince. A pair of socks near the top of the pile gave off the pungency of old cheese.

'I'm going to the laundromat. What did you expect to find in there? Contraband?' He snatched the bag from my grip, shoved back in a pair of underpants that was poking out and zipped the bag shut.

'Can't blame me for checking.' I should have apologised, but his refusal to provide a statement riled me, especially since he'd already given us a lead. I took a few deep breaths while he slung the rucksack back over his shoulders. I understood his reticence to cooperate and pushing him would get me nowhere. 'Who do you suggest then?

'The guy I told you about before, Laurent Guillot.'

'You said your compatriot worshipped Lacroix, thought he was a fellow true believer.'

'He did. Until I told him otherwise.'

'Where is he now? At the parade?'

'You're in luck. He's in the common room watching it on TV with a bunch of commie cronies.'

'That surprises me. Types like that usually want to experience the real thing.'

'He hurt himself falling on black ice. Can't walk. Leg's in plaster so he's not going to run away.' Nico could barely hide his sarcastic pleasure. Schadenfreude they call it in fancy literature. There's even a Russian word for it. *Zloradstvo.* I explained it to Nico and he committed the term to memory. 'I've got a feeling I'll be using that one.'

'I reckon you will.' A quick mental assessment of the program: the parade started at 10:00 a.m. Most years it runs for about two hours but this year was a big anniversary edition, so it was probably still being broadcast. 'Where's the common room?'

'Fourth floor, exit the lift and head right. End of the corridor.'

'Thanks. If you change your mind about making a statement...'

'I won't.'

I shook his hand and turned to head back to the institute.

'Room 1111.'

I spun on my heel. 'Pardon?'

'Guillot's room. Just in case he's not in the common area. And mine's 844 if you'd like to come visit me once you've sorted out this whole mess. You can teach me more esoteric words.'

I touched a forefinger to the side of my head in a mini salute. 'Might just do that if I don't get exiled to Siberia for what I'm about to do.'

Chapter 28

A quick check of the canteen told me Pronin was either still getting pally with the rector or he'd gone back to Stepan's car to wait for me. At least I hoped that was the case and his cover hadn't been blown.

After conducting a futile check of Lacroix's own digs at room No. 902 and all the apartments on his floor, I followed Nico's instructions and located the common room. There were four people glued to the TV like zombies, unaware of my presence. The passing parade on the screen would have bored a normal person to death, but the indoctrinated lapped this shit up like it was the greatest entertainment ever devised.

Picking out Guillot was easy – he was the only one wearing an unseasonal pair of shorts, plaster up to the knee. Crude hammer and sickle drawings covered the white cast. He occupied an old armchair, his comrades squeezed together to his right on a scruffy couch. All four, eyes fixated on the black and white TV screen, were male and white. Pasty-faced, bookish types, heads crammed full of idealism. Not a whiff of cigarette smoke in the air, which struck me as unusual for a gathering of students. No booze in sight either; instead, glasses of black tea in traditional Russian filigree holders sat on a lowset table. Guillot and his companions wore blissful expressions; they appeared to be on the verge of drooling on the worn beige carpet.

The military stage of the grand parade must have concluded; now thousands of ordinary workers and their families slowly traversed Red Square. Columns of the faithful marched behind giant red banners bearing the names of the district of Moscow they represented – Proletarsky, Leninsky, Frunzensky, Sverdlovsky, and on and on it went. I never grasped the point of this parochialism, but there was a lot about the beauty of communism that went over my head. The masses filed past the mausoleum containing the mummified body of V.I. Lenin, or Dead Fred as I liked to call him. The joyous throngs waved dementedly at high-ranking officials in overcoats standing on the viewing platform; the glum-faced VIPs waved back with mechanical benevolence. Among the honourable dignitaries I recognised the Cuban patriarch Fidel Castro, German lapdog Erik Honecker and the Butcher of Bucharest, Romanian dictator Nicolae Ceausescu.

I coughed loudly. No reaction from the enthralled gallery. I strode to the television and switched it off, turned and held out my ID amid howls of protest.

'Hey, we were watching that,' Guillot shouted in heavily accented Russian. Then he underscored his displeasure with *merde*, which I guessed was profanity.

'Too bad. You've already seen the tanks and soldiers, so the fun part's over.'

The three other lads squirmed uneasily in their seats, glanced furtively at the door. God only knew what was racing through their minds.

'What's the problem?' said Guillot. The others clammed up after their initial outburst. Better for them if the Frenchman I'd come to see did all the talking.

'I'd like to speak to you alone, Laurent.'

All colour drained from Guillot's angular face. I moved fast to reassure him. 'You are not in any trouble, don't worry.' He shifted uneasily in his seat, snatched at a wooden crutch leaning against the arm of his chair and only succeeded in knocking it to the floor.

I pointed a stern finger at the other lads. 'You three, wait in your rooms for fifteen minutes, then you can return to see the rest of this...' I waved at the blank TV screen '...show. I'm going to ask your friend some questions.'

Alone with Guillot, I aimed to make it quick. Hopefully, he'd play ball. 'What can you tell me about Michel Lacroix?'

'Not a lot.' He stared at his fingertips, aiming for cool, but those fingers were shaking.

'I don't believe you.'

'Well it's true. I'm sorry you've wasted your time...sorry, what's your name again?'

'Captain Viktor Voloshin. Call me Viktor.' I'd never asked a potential witness to call me by my first name. He smiled faintly. A small degree of trust gained. 'Please be truthful with me, it's important.'

'It is the truth. Why would I–'

I placed my palms on each arm of his chair, stuck my face right up in his. I could smell fear, but I had to hand it to him, young Guillot was toughing it out like a captured guerrilla fighter. 'Listen, you believe in equal rights for all, correct?'

Guillot gave a sharp nod. 'Of course. It's a basic tenet of socialism.'

I flopped on the couch, spread my arms along its back. 'Do you believe the life of a black man is equal to that of a white man?'

'Absolutely. I'm a fan of Paul Robeson. Have you heard of him?' He asked the question like he was sure I'd have no idea.

'Yes.' I knew of the man. A black American famous for his magnificent singing voice, but also for his sympathies towards the Soviet Union. 'However I'm talking about a black man no one has heard of. He's not famous, but he damn well should be.'

'Why?'

'Because,' I raised my voice loud enough to make Guillot flinch. 'He was murdered by your friend, Lacroix!'

He quickly turned his head to one side, unable to meet my gaze. 'I told you, I don't know much about him.'

The wooden crutch slammed into his exposed knee, plaster dust puffed into the air. I tossed the crutch to one side and stared aghast at Guillot, who grabbed at his patella and screamed in agony. I don't know who was more shocked by what I'd just done, him or me.

'Everything all right in there?' A female voice came from behind the door. It opened and a corpulent woman in a hideous floral dress barged in.

'He was trying to stand up, twisted his injured leg horribly, didn't you

Laurent?'

Words failed him but he nodded frantically.

'See?' I said. 'All fine. Now, if you don't mind, we were having a private conversation.' I stood to my full height, gave her a brutal sneer and she disappeared.

I turned my attention back to Guillot, whispered through tight lips. 'Do you want another broken leg? Continue to talk bullshit and I'll kindly oblige.'

He held up his hands. 'All right, all right. I got it.'

I handed him his glass of stone-cold tea. He slurped at it and handed the glass back to me. He was on the ropes. Maybe to the point of signing a statement.

'Now,' I said. 'Tell me what you know.'

For the next ten minutes, Guillot talked. I jotted down notes as he went. It was the story of a man betrayed. He and Lacroix had become fast friends through their unshakable belief in the virtues of socialism, its inevitable global victory, blah, blah, blah. The friendship soured when Guillot learned, through Nico, of Lacroix's activities in the black market. Guillot then did his own digging around. Found out Lacroix was working for the KGB, recruiting students from the Gandhi University to spy on their own compatriots, report on anti-Soviet agitators, miscreants. For doing this, the KGB allowed Lacroix to run his grubby little business, with scum like Shukhov gifted contraband goods, granted favours. The hypocrisy of it all made Guillot sick to the stomach. Turns out Nico got one thing wrong. Guillot hadn't broken his leg slipping on black ice – Lacroix sent a thug in a ski mask to attack him with a tyre lever. To ensure Guillot's silence.

'Holy shit, Laurent. What the hell do you know that warrants a broken leg?'

'I jokingly told Lacroix I'd rat him out for his illegal trading unless he returned to the right path. The arsehole took me literally and this is the result.'

'Is that all?'

He shook his head. 'I've said way too much already. He'll have me killed if he finds out I've been talking to Militsiya.'

'No he won't.' I waggled my pen in front of my eyes, tried to figure out how to get him to dish the dirt on Lacroix. 'I'll make sure you're protected.'

He tilted his head back and roared with laughter. 'The Nigerian thought he was protected, too. Looked what happened to him. And me!' He pointed at his leg.

'Did Lacroix murder him, Laurent?'

'No.' The Frenchman lowered his eyes.

'Who then?'

'I can't tell you! Don't you get it? The ideals I believe in...' he pointed at the blank screen, '...all that joy at the parade we were watching. Ruined by traitors and saboteurs like Lacroix and that prick, Shukhov. They have all the power. They *will* kill me!'

Threatening the lad with the crutch wasn't going to work anymore. Nor were promises of justice.

'Listen. I'm going to make Lacroix confess. If I have to coerce him, I will. By whatever means. Your testimony would be the icing on the cake, but I won't need it to secure a conviction.'

'You've got no hope. Who are you against the might of the system?'

'Might of the system? You're completely deluded, son. What you perceive as might is like the elaborate painted backdrop of a stage play. Fake.'

'I don't get your meaning.'

'I'm here talking to you, aren't I? I was warned off, told to keep my nose out of it, threatened. But who stopped me? No one. I even whacked you, a privileged Western guest, with a wooden crutch, and there's no one here to prevent it. This is a totalitarian state, that's true. At its core the system is weak, under-resourced. They simply can't watch everyone all the time.'

Guillot shifted in his seat, digested what I'd said, probably trying to convince himself to do the right thing.

'I can use information you give me to threaten Lacroix. You don't want to stand by and do nothing while he flouts the system you so fervently believe in, do you? While he gets away with murder!'

'OK. But you heard none of this from me, agreed?'

I nodded, placed my pen against the paper.

'I'm not going to sign anything, no way!'

'Relax. It's just for my reference.'

Guillot took three deep breaths. I handed him his glass and he swallowed the remaining few drops of the tea. 'What I know is this: Lacroix didn't kill the Nigerian. He hasn't got the balls for it.'

'Was it the Wolves?'

'Yes. Lacroix heard Adekanye was operating where he shouldn't. Small stuff, but it didn't matter. Lacroix leaned on a Vietnamese outfit to approach Adekanye with a proposal. The Vietnamese were supposed to make a pact with Adekanye, convince him to join forces with their lucrative empire and keep away from Lacroix's turf. If he refused to back off, they'd whistle and the Wolves would do their thing.'

'Their thing?'

'Kidnap him and slap him around a bit. Teach him a lesson.'

'They must have held him hostage the whole time he was missing.' That was from early October.

'It would appear so.'

'Holy shit. Do you know how he was treated?' I cursed myself for the umpteenth time for allowing the body to go missing; an autopsy would have revealed if Adekanye had been tortured while held captive.

'That I can't tell you. But I know it was them who overstepped the mark and killed him. Strung him up and made it look like a race crime by mutilating his body.'

A thought occurred to me: could the three "children" Rita and Kirill chased through the forest have been those Vietnamese students? The ones I'd seen around were short and slight of stature, so it was a possibility. Maybe they'd got wind of the crime and came for a look. I scratched my head. Something didn't make sense at all. 'How on Earth do you know all this, Laurent? Why would Lacroix reveal so much detail to you? You're hardly the gangster type.'

'He didn't tell me anything.'

'Who did then?'

'A woman called Pilar, a Bolivian student I know at the Gandhi University. She's a staunch communist like me, organises get-togethers for foreign students in the area. Pilar and I meet up to discuss politics once a week. She detests hypocrites like Lacroix.'

'Come off it!' This was getting more and more unbelievable. 'Why the hell would she share that information with you? And more importantly, why wouldn't she go directly to the authorities if she knew all this?'

'Pilar suspected he's got protection and *she* could end up in the shit. She might be a true believer in communism, but she doesn't trust the Soviet legal system.'

'Smart woman,' I chuckled. 'Neither do I. Still, I don't imagine she'd be happy for Lacroix to get away with murder, knowing the truth like she does.'

Guillot nodded slowly. 'She's not, but she's also terrified of getting involved personally. The message sent by Adekanye's...execution...was clear.'

'Understandable. So, my next question: How the hell does Pilar know all this?'

'She heard it from a friend of hers called Olga.'

I sat bolt upright, fumbled the pen. Could it be the mysterious woman Flora said had a romantic attachment with Adekanye? 'Tell me what you know about her.'

'She's a local girl in her early twenties, doesn't seem to have a job, hangs around the university, drops in here sometimes, too. She likes mixing with foreigners, has a thirst for knowledge about the world outside the Soviet Union.'

'Or she's looking to marry a foreigner and get the fuck out of this country.'

'A cynic might say that, yes,' he admitted reluctantly.

I lit a cigarette and drew deeply. 'How does Olga know all the details?'

'Pilar told me Olga had struck up a relationship with Adekanye and was concerned when he went missing. Not only that, Olga was seeing Lacroix.'

'What?'

'Yep. Unbelievable. The guy's famous for his charm, so it's not surprising, I guess.'

I rubbed my forehead. The dots were beginning to join themselves. 'It was only yesterday Olga revealed the truth to Pilar.'

'And Pilar told you.'

'Yes.'

'When?'

'Just a few hours ago. We were having a coffee in the little bar on the fifth floor of this building.' He glanced up at the ceiling.

'Didn't you suggest the two of you ought to act on this information? Even if you don't trust the legal system, you must have come up with...I don't know...some ideas!'

'Of course.'

'What?'

'I suggested we go to the press, leave an anonymous note at one of the bigger newspapers.' He rubbed his forehead. 'I thought an investigative reporter might take up the cause. Unfortunately, Pilar didn't like that idea.'

'Why the hell not? Sounds good to me.'

'She doesn't trust journalists either.'

'For goodness sake! Who does she trust?'

'No one.'

'Can't say I blame her. Where's Pilar now?' Getting her to give evidence, or better yet, tell me where I could find Olga, might obviate the need to travel to Lyubertsy. A trip I wasn't looking forward to. Even though it shouldn't, a Soviet citizen's evidence could be given more weight than a foreigner's. Given Laurent's reluctance to sign a statement, though, I had a feeling none of them would take the risk and put their name to paper.

'At the parade, where do you think?'

Of course she'd be there; so would Guillot if he could walk properly. We'd be travelling to Lyubertsy after all.

'I assume Lacroix felt safe telling Olga the truth because he trusted her implicitly.' I expelled a fat cloud of smoke. 'He boasted about his deeds to impress her.' I looked up from my notes; Guillot wore a faraway expression.

'That's exactly what happened, I'd say. He's obsessed with the idea of being the tough guy.'

The elevator door dinged in the hallway. Time was ticking, but I wanted to get as much information out of Guillot as I could. 'Tell me all you know about Olga's relationship with Aaron Adekanye.'

'Pilar said she'd seen Olga and Adekanye getting all cosy with each other on campus a week before he went missing, holding hands and staring into each other's eyes. At the time, Pilar thought he was just some random foreign guy Olga was targeting for a potential marriage partner, like you said before.'

'Go on.'

'Anyway, a few days later Pilar was in the city centre, strolling around the Arbat, when she spots Olga with Lacroix at a café, kissing and cuddling.'

'What a piece of work she is, leading on one man while she's sleeping with another.'

'No.' Guillot shook his head. 'It's not like that. Lacroix's an arsehole. He took advantage of Olga's good nature. She's a simple soul, eager to please everyone, not a slut. I think she's, you know,' Guillot pointed at his temple, 'touched, as they say. Lacroix exploited that.'

'In what way?'

'The obvious way. He used her for sex.'

'Disgusting.'

'Pilar told me two nights ago he got roaring drunk, went to Olga's flat for a tumble. When they were done he bragged about the horrible things he'd done. Apparently she barely held it together as he ranted about killing a Nigerian student who'd been trying to rip him off. Olga mightn't be too bright, but she was smart enough to keep her mouth shut to Lacroix about her own dalliance on the side.'

'What an ordeal for her to go through.' I imagined her heart pounding, wondering if Lacroix was baiting her to admit something he must have suspected.

'Yesterday, Olga poured her heart out to Pilar, begged her to do something with the information because she was too scared of Michel, but Pilar told her there was nothing she could do.'

I banged my fist on the table. 'Olga's too scared of him, Pilar's too scared of him.' I pointed my finger in his face. 'You're too scared of him.' I stood, zipped up my jacket. 'I'll tell you something. I'm not!' I folded up the piece of paper I'd been writing on. If I could get Lacroix to confess and have him charged, Laurent might change his mind and sign the damn thing.

'Where are you going now?' he asked timidly.

'Where do you think. To find Lacroix.'

'You won't tell him I said anything will you?'

'Of course not. You're lucky I'm one of a handful of cops in this city who always keeps his word.'

Chapter 29

I strode as fast as I could without looking like a second-rate competitor in a walking race. A quick glance inside the canteen – no Pronin. *Please be in the car already.*

I shoved open the big glass door to exit the institute when I spotted a blue and yellow Militsiya van bumping its way down the narrow driveway closely followed by a shiny black Volga. My initial thought – Shukhov had rumbled Pronin and called in the troops. Or someone in the institute recognised me and blabbed to the rector. That meant whoever was in those vehicles wasn't looking to buy me a drink. I pulled my collar up high, tugged the new beanie low over my ears, the touch of its soft wool a comforting caress. The northerly wind was picking up, flecks of sleet dotted my jacket sleeves. Visibility was deteriorating. Thoughts of the warmth of the Devyatka's interior drew me on like a magnet.

My heartrate was in the danger zone by the time I reached the meeting point. The sight of Pronin sitting calmly in the rear seat brought that vital down to almost normal. He stopped leafing through a sports magazine when I jumped into the car. As I'd hoped, the engine was purring and hot air was pouring out of the vents.

I glared at the driver. 'OK, Stepanchik. Let's go.'

'What's the problem?'

'The cops are onto us.'

His brow wrinkled in confusion. 'I thought *you* were–'

'Move!'

My neck nearly snapped as Stepan stomped on the accelerator. 'You got it, boss!' The spiv was enjoying this way too much for my liking. We soon came to a skidding stop at a T-junction. 'Where to now?'

My inclination was to head to Lyubertsy immediately, but I wanted a last word with Flora Madenge. 'Gandhi University.'

Pronin tried to talk me out of coming here; it was too big a risk. But it was a risk I was prepared to take. I would've loved an audience with rector Kuznetsov, to tell him what I knew and watch him squirm, but that was out of the question now. It was all about Flora; I wanted to tell her of my intention to confront Lacroix, force him to confess, do whatever necessary to get justice for Aaron; give her some reassurance and peace of mind.

'If those MVD cars were after you, they'll be heading here too once they come up empty at the Chekhov,' said Pronin. 'Shukhov will work it out in a second that I played him for a fool.'

'I don't care, Tolya. I'll be quick. And careful. If I don't find her within five minutes, we'll leave. OK?'

He shook his head. 'I've got a bad feeling about this.'

'Me too,' said Stepan.

'When I want your opinion, I'll ask for it.'

Stepan tucked his chin like a scolded child. Hamming it up again.

'Is everything a game to you?'

'Yeah, pretty much.'

I was done playing games with him. 'Wait here, don't move. Tolya, you stay here too.' I stepped out of the car, walked the 200 metres from a side street to the university's boom gate entrance.

The first three people I saw looked like Flora. They weren't, I just *wanted* them to be her. People were scarce on campus today, just like at the Chekhov Institute and all other places of study and work across the entire USSR. The holiday, the parade, any excuse for a day off. I stood in the middle of the cross, lit a cigarette and waited. If I couldn't find out where she was by the time I'd finished it, I'd leave.

After three puffs it was just me in the courtyard, feeling like a lone wolf in expansive tundra. Cold wind blew scraps of paper in a sad little tornado around my boots. Pronin was right. It was a waste of time.

A tap on the shoulder. Samuel, not Flora. 'I'm afraid you are too late.'

My heart dropped. 'Too late for what?'

'I assume you came to see Flora.'

I nodded frantically. 'You assume correctly.'

'Bad news.'

My first thought – she'd been attacked, killed. 'Don't make me guess, man! What the hell happened to her?'

'She was summoned to the embassy. She's being sent home.'

'When? Now?'

'No. She's got until Christmas to finish some of her subjects, but no continuation into next year. It's kind of a blessing though. Her father is sick, dying from cancer, so she will be there for his last days.'

I caught my breath. Hands on hips, I bent at the waist and sucked in a couple of big ones as supreme relief washed over me. 'Thank God for that.'

'You are happy her father is dying? You Russians are strange people.'

'No, Samuel. You misunderstand me. I'm happy she's OK.'

'She is not, she is grieving terribly.'

'No, I meant…never mind.'

I turned to leave. The job would be done in any case, whether Flora knew or not.

'Captain Voloshin?'

'Yes?'

The man did something I'll never forget. He wrapped two tree trunk arms around me and pulled me close. I thought I heard one of my ribs crack as he squeezed. 'Thank you for trying,' he whispered before letting me go. 'Thanks to you it was decided to call off the demonstration we had planned for the parade.'

'You did?'

'Of course, some radical elements may still proceed, but their numbers will be small and the protest ineffectual.'

This made no sense. 'Because of me?'

He nodded and smiled. 'Yes. Word has filtered through that you visited our embassy, that you are trying hard to discover who killed Aaron. Nothing else is being done about it. Nothing! Sir, if you ever come to Lagos, you will be greeted like a hero.'

'I think you're exaggerating.'

He laughed as I imagined giants do in fairy tales, deep and rich. 'Maybe a little. Please, because you are here now, I know you are still investigating. Have you got any closer to the truth?'

My hands fumbled inside my pockets, located cigarettes. Samuel eagerly accepted one, his face switching to pensive as he lit it.

'I have. The lead your friend Daniel gave me proved crucial.'

'Lacroix?'

I nodded.

'I think Daniel was wrong about Adekanye being a spy, though. Aaron was dabbling in the black market, did something that pissed off Lacroix and he ended up getting killed for his trouble. Aaron's claim about being a spy was the booze talking. If Aaron *was* reporting to the Americans, like Daniel said, I can't confirm or deny it. To be honest, I haven't even bothered checking.'

Samuel's eyes were downcast. 'Yes, we knew Aaron was up to his eyeballs in illegal trading.' He paused for a few seconds. 'We all are. Flora, my God, she got carried away with the success of her business, flaunted it too much.'

'She told me she agreed to stop. Promised to ask the institute to give her more modest accommodation.'

'Ha!' Samuel shook his head. 'I am not sure she would have followed up on that promise. She does enjoy her creature comforts.'

I smiled and nodded. 'A princess.'

'Correct, sir. We will miss her greatly; she was the best organiser us students could hope for, defended our rights.'

'What will you do? I know you and your friends were working for her, earning some extra cash on the side.'

'Maybe we will go straight. Living off a student stipend is very hard; unlike Flora, I shall make no promises.' He kicked a clump of snow off his boot, gathered his thoughts. 'We can trust you not to make trouble for us over a few dollars and jars of caviar, am I right?'

'Of course.' At that moment I couldn't have cared less if they made a million roubles each out of their business. 'Why did Daniel play up the "spy" angle?'

'To make you look harder for the killers. He thought the death of a petty criminal wouldn't get the same attention as that of a spy.'

'That's a fair assumption.' I stuck a hand inside my hat, scratched an itchy patch of scalp. 'Once I learned about Lacroix's activities, you must have realised Aaron's own scheme would come to light too.'

'Sure. We just wanted you to take it seriously.'

'I take all my work seriously. Most cops wouldn't give a fuck about your friend. Sadly for Lacroix, I'm not most cops.'

'You're going to arrest him? That is wonderful news!'

'The murder was carried out on Lacroix's order.' I coughed into my fist. 'But I have a huge problem.'

'What?'

'I have no solid proof I could use in court, or even to arrest him. Only accounts from people too scared to make official statements.'

'So what are you going to do now?'

I told Samuel of my plan, thanked him profusely for his vote of confidence. 'Don't lose heart. I'm going to do my utmost to bring this bastard to justice.'

We shook hands and went our separate ways.

Chapter 30

Stepan negotiated the gears from first to fourth before I'd put my seatbelt on properly. Some fancy clutch work at the corner onto Leninsky Prospekt, then a controlled fishtail onto the arterial highway. I thought for a fleeting moment how Yegor would've appreciated Stepan's erratic driving.

'Did you find her?' asked Pronin.

'No.'

'You look heartbroken. Are you sure you didn't have a thing for her?

'Sergeant, enough!'

Stepan jumped in his seat next to me. 'If you're going to yell, why don't you get in the back? You'll be more comfortable, and I'll feel like I'm chauffeuring a pair of VIPs. Win win.'

I took his advice, got him to pull over and switched seats. Stepan's head shake and furrowed frown told me the guy instantly regretted his suggestion; he wouldn't be able to earwig in on our every word.

'From what I hear, the Madenge woman is quite a beauty.' Pronin was a dog with a bone.

'Don't be impudent.' Pronin saw through my disingenuousness. I had indeed questioned my own feelings about her. 'She's leaving the country, and good luck to her.'

'Why's that, Viktor Pavlovich?'

'She'll end up in a world of trouble if she stays.' I could have done with a shot of vodka to settle my nerves, configure my brain. I fought the urge to ask Stepan to crack open the cognac. 'And her father's dying.'

Pronin set to gnawing his already well-chewed fingernails; must've sensed by my tone I didn't want to continue this conversation. We both stared out the window for a while, admired the ubiquitous fluttering hammer and sickle flags and assorted bunting in honour of the day. It grew thinner the further we drove from the centre, but there was always some of it in sight. I checked my watch; surely the big parade would be over by now.

We settled into a cruising speed of a comfortable twenty over the limit for ten minutes, then turned left at the south-western sleeper suburb of Tyoply Stan and merged onto the mighty MKAD, the Moscow Automobile Ring Road. We'd proceed in an easterly direction in a slight arc for another half hour before arriving at the Wolves' HQ. That's if we didn't get pulled over for speeding. Didn't matter, there was enough contraband in the boot of the car to bribe ninety-five percent of traffic cops in the capital.

I realised I'd been so preoccupied with the Africans, I'd forgotten to ask Pronin about his encounter with Shukhov. A faint rosy glow in Pronin's cheeks told me the rector must have treated him to a toddy or two. 'What did you learn from the prick?'

'I was wondering when you'd ask. You'll be pleased to know the rector was nothing but courteous and respectful.'

'The man was an absolute snake to me and Yegor. How did you get him to be civil?'

'I promised season tickets for him and his wife. Best seats to all the Dynamo games next year. You should have seen him grovel after that.'

Judging by the self-satisfied grin plastered across his face, Pronin revelled in the quick undercover job.

'Did he tell you where we might be able to find Lacroix?'

'At the parade.'

'Dammit!'

'Don't lose heart, Viktor Pavlovich. Apparently he was only interested in the military side of it and was heading to his pals in Lyubertsy for the afternoon.'

'Did you get anything else out of him?' I hoped like hell Shukhov had implicated himself in the murders, signed a confession and asked to be handcuffed and dragged to jail. Fat chance.

'Besides some single malt whiskey, you mean?'

'You lucky bastard. I had a bowl of disgusting soup and you get top-flight scotch.'

Pronin shrugged. 'What can I say?'

Stepan chuckled. 'You guys are hilarious.'

'Keep your comments to yourself, can you?' I said. He'd gone from being cheeky to plain annoying.

'Sure boss.'

I decided to ignore Stepan, not speak to him unless I needed something from him, keep my exchanges with Pronin to a whisper.

'He was determined to impress on a Dynamo official, aka me, what an exemplary fellow Lacroix was. A fine student, an example to all, intelligent, loyal to the cause of socialism, all that shit.'

'To be expected.'

'Yeah. I said we'd heard rumours the lad might be up to some extracurricular activities of an illegal nature and the ice hockey club was debating whether to end our association with him.'

'Brilliant, Pronin. Like I said before, I don't understand why you're satisfied languishing at the rank of Sergeant.'

'What's the difference? The pay's crap no matter what your rank, so there's no point seeking promotion. You and I know the only way to supplement your income is by taking bribes. Sometimes, the lower the rank, the closer you are to a steady source of said backhanders.'

'I'm going to pretend you didn't say that, Tolya. What else happened?'

'I told him I'd heard a rumour some people had been murdered in the local area. I used a real conspiratorial voice. You know, hush hush kinda thing. You should have seen his face start to twitch when I asked if it was a black student and a top cop.'

'He *is* implicated, the dirty son of a bitch.'

'Then he said something I didn't expect. Could be a red herring, but he suggested any criminal activities in the area had nothing to do with his students, the students at the Gandhi, and especially Michel Lacroix.'

'Who then?'

'Some gang I've never heard of. The Belyaevo Boys. That's the exact name, in English even, if you please.'

'Did he know anything else about them?'

Pronin gave a tiny nod. 'He had some first names – Slava, Leonid, Maxim.'

'Interesting.' I jotted down the names in my notepad.

'Shukhov claims they extort money from stall holders around the Belyaevo Metro Station; they only take small change but strut about like peacocks. He reckons they're wannabes who just might go too far to get a reputation as hard men.'

'Like murdering a student.'

'Like that. Shukhov reckons he told the CID his suspicions and they were probably acting on his information. He looked real proud of himself, like he was critical to solving the crime.'

'Might be worth checking out this Belyaevo Boys thing if we get nowhere today. Do you think it was legit?'

'I couldn't say for sure, Viktor Pavlovich. It sounded rehearsed, like he might have used the same story a few times.'

I gathered my thoughts for a moment. If Shukhov had trotted out that version before, it could have been in response to questioning by the CID, to take suspicion away from Lacroix and himself. 'If your hunch is right, I'd almost be inclined to rule out Militsiya or KGB involvement, at least in the Adekanye murder. With the District Medical Examiner, well, I'm all out of ideas on that one. I thought the shooter was aiming at me and hit Ivanov by mistake. Maybe the target was someone else altogether.'

'I disagree, Comrade Captain. I think the shooter was firing blind and any of us at the scene was the target; I wouldn't be surprised if Shukhov's story about the so-called Belyaevo Boys was provided to him by the CID to use if anyone asked awkward questions. Like a big-time hockey coach who dropped in out of the blue for a chat.'

Cracking knuckles was my only solace at this point. One by one until all fingers had popped to my satisfaction. Frustration didn't begin to describe how I felt. Then, as I gazed at the thousandth red flag, a light bulb lit up in my head. Pronin's theory made sense. The primary players in the double tragedy had learned their lines by heart and were ready to fend off any and all troublesome enquiries.

My sense of alienation from the decision makers was now complete. Imagine a lone man surrounded by a hundred others, machine guns pointed at him. I was that man, and all the security agencies that served this country – including some obscure branches no one apart from the people working for them have ever heard of – were the hundred others. With Yegor's life hanging by a thread, the only person I could trust was Pronin.

'Your thoughts, Viktor Pavlovich?'

'I think I'd rather be somewhere warm. The tropics, maybe our wonderful ally Cuba. I hear some Soviet citizens are allowed to go there if they're well behaved. I'd like to sit on a sun-drenched beach all day, sip cocktails and smoke the finest cigars. Jazz music in the evenings followed by more cocktails and the attention of a hot-blooded local lady keen to learn all there is to know about the life of a jaded Russian cop.'

'Not the answer I was expecting.' Pronin shot me a lopsided grin.

'Want to know my other thoughts? My initial pessimistic assessment that all are acting against us, determined for Lacroix to get away with his crime, for an empty coffin to be flown back to Nigeria, no questions asked, is turning out to be bang on the money.'

Stepan cut off our discussion. 'This is going to sound corny, but we've got company.' He craned his neck almost 180 degrees, gave me a bug-eyed stare. 'And I don't think it's an official escort.'

I spun in my seat to look out the back window. Pronin's breath burned hot on my cheek as he clutched the headrest, his body twisted like a piece of liquorice. An olive green UAZ-469 army vehicle was trundling along about 100 metres behind the Devyatka. Other than us and them, traffic was light; nothing ahead for a good 300 metres and the same behind the army car.

'I'm going 20 over the limit, and that sucker's gaining. He's been tailing me for a while.'

'Why didn't you say anything, dammit?'

222

'I thought you wanted me to keep quiet. This vehicle's got me a little worried, boss. Do you think it's a problem?'

'Not sure,' I pointed to a big sign ahead. 'Take that exit onto the Kashira Highway. Let's see if they follow.'

Pronin's mouth opened to say something, snapped shut in an instant. My own head rocked to one side a split second after my brain figured out we were accelerating. Fast. The engine roared as Stepan gunned the car towards its maximum speed. With the exit approaching fast, Stepan tugged the wheel hard left. Tyres screeched as he zipped across three lanes to make the exit of the MKAD into eastern Moscow. I looked around again, our tail gracelessly lurched in the same direction we were going.

No doubt any more.

We were being hunted.

At the first opportunity, Stepan swung the Devyatka right onto a two-laned minor road. Already back in suburbia, boilerplate identical apartment buildings blocked the sky. Up ahead loomed a red and white barrier marking off road works delayed by the holiday. No barrier to Stepan, he smashed through it at high speed and sent wood splinters flying.

'That's going to cost me a packet to get the scratches taken out,' he moaned.

'Better than a grenade through the window.'

He shrugged and battled with the steering wheel at the same time. 'Yeah, whatever. I'll be sending you the repair bill.'

'Shut up and drive!' Pronin's eyes were wider than the Bosporus.

'All right, all right,' Stepan screamed over his shoulder. 'It's still behind us. Their car handles rough roads better than the Devyatka. We should have stayed on the MKAD.'

A flash of something grey caught my eye as the muzzle of a weapon emerged out of the UAZ's passenger window. The gaping round hole of the gun took aim directly at middle of our rear windscreen. They were about 100 metres from us now and gaining.

'Tolya, look!'

'Dear mother of God.' His voice quavered.

'Do you know what that is?'

'Not sure, a rocket launcher. My guess is it's some kind of RPG.'

'Aren't they designed to take out tanks?'

'That's my understanding.'

I shook Stepan roughly by the shoulder. 'Can't you make this thing go any faster?'

'Hey! I'm doing my best weaving around these fucking great potholes.'

'Take the next turn. Anywhere.'

'Hold on tight.'

We made another right down a narrow driveway running beside an apartment block the size of the Roman colosseum. My stomach sank when I saw dozens of children out and about, playing on sleds and throwing snowballs at each other. If the soldiers were out to get us with that weapon… I shuddered to think of the collateral damage.

The driveway swept us in a semicircle to the rear of the building, from there hopefully back onto a minor arterial road and safety. It looked like we'd shaken the army truck; it must have continued on straight when we made the last turn. I glanced over my shoulder again – no. There it was, windscreen glinting as the sun poked through thick clouds. The driver and his passenger were clearly visible now, faces set and determined.

'Faster, Stepan!'

'Bad luck, I'm afraid.' I spun in my seat to face the front. 'Looks like we're trapped.'

There was no way out. A dead end loomed; a three-metre concrete fence topped with rusty barbed wire and scrawled with ugly graffiti. A fitting location to get blown to smithereens by a grenade. I saw Stepan in the rear view mirror sporting a tight grimace. 'Looks like we'll have to run for it, fellas. Go, go, go!'

'Fuck it,' said Pronin, fumbling with his seat belt 'Come on!' By the time I had my uncooperative buckle undone, Pronin and Stepan were nowhere to be seen. I flicked the door handle and rolled out commando style, laid face down on cold gritty asphalt. My heart galloped as I waited for the inevitable flash of light, the deafening boom. Under the chassis I clocked Tolya, also lying prostrate on the ground. He'd placed his hands over his ears, bracing himself for the apocalypse. It seemed a good idea, so I copied him.

I counted to ten.

Silence.

No explosions.

No flash of light.

Too late for me to make a bid for freedom; I'd have to deal with whatever came my way. Probably a hunting knife in the jugular or a bullet in the head. I made out the soft footsteps of one man running through slush. A hand reached under the car and tapped me on the upper arm.

'Excuse me, sir.'

I took my hands away from my ears. 'Don't shoot, I'm a cop!'

'Your brake lights aren't working.'

What the hell? I rolled away from the car and stood, fists bunched and ready to fight. My entire body shook. 'What the fuck did you say?' I showed him my ID to make sure he got the message we weren't ordinary citizens to be trifled with.

The slender young man stood smartly to attention, civility and deference personified. It dawned on me; these men were not out to kill us. 'I'm sorry, Comrade Captain. We saw your car turn on the MKAD back at Tyoply Stan and noticed the brake lights were on the blink.'

'Why were you following us? Busted brake lights is no reason for soldiers to tail people. Damn suspicious, if you ask me.'

The man shook his head. 'Nothing untoward, I assure you. We just happened to be going in the same direction as you. We thought we'd drive alongside and yell out to let you know the problem.' He gave a thin smile. 'In the spirit of Revolution Day.'

Pronin was on his feet again, arms spread across the roof of the Devyatka. 'That still doesn't explain why were you aiming an anti-tank gun at us, for fuck's sake!' he roared, face beetroot red.

The soldier shuffled his feet. 'It's not a gun, it's plastic plumbing pipe.'

'Excuse me?' I said.

'My father's renovating the family dacha in Shatura. I'm taking the pipe and some other gear for him to fix the–'

'Why were you pointing the damn thing at us?' Pronin had lit a nerve-calming cigarette but it was failing to do the job. 'We thought it was an RPG and you were going to shoot us, dammit.'

The lad was battling to stop himself from laughing. 'I'm very sorry, comrades.'

'Sorry! Is that all you can say? Sorry?'

'We're transporting some boxes of military equipment. Spare parts. We couldn't fit the plumbing pipe in the back so I had to stick it across my shoulder and out the window. I guess it might have looked a bit like a weapon.'

'It looked exactly like a fucking weapon!' Pronin appeared to be on the verge of a stroke.

The soldier driving the UAZ leapt from the cabin of the truck, trotted over and saluted us.

'Good day, comrades. Everything all right? Apologies for giving you a fright. We thought–'

'Yes, I know!' I said. I wasn't as livid as Pronin, but the difference was paper thin. 'Brake lights.'

Soldier Two nodded. 'Yes. And then when your car veered suddenly we thought maybe the driver was having a heart attack, so we followed you. And then when you smashed through the traffic barrier, we were sure–'

I held up my hand. 'We get it. A terrible misunderstanding. Now, if you don't mind, we need to get to Lyubertsy.'

'Sure.' The soldiers returned to their vehicle, its engine roared into action.

I turned to see Stepan's figure retreating into the distance, a good 200 metres away. He sprinted down a laneway and disappeared.

'Looks like you're driving the rest of the way, Tolya.'

'With pleasure, Viktor Pavlovich.' Not looking the least bit pleased, he nestled into the driver's seat, patted around the steering wheel, along the dashboard. 'Hmm, there's a problem.'

'What's wrong?'

'No keys.'

'And?'

'Sorry, Comrade Captain, but I can't drive without keys.'

'Don't you know how to hot wire a car?'

Pronin looked at me askance. 'No. Do you?'

I had to admit my ignorance on the matter. For some reason I thought Pronin would have the required knowledge.

The rumbling UAZ was reversing slowly out of the laneway. I leapt out of the car and ran towards it, waving my arms frantically, and the army vehicle came to a shuddering halt. Soldier One, who turned out to be a motor mechanic by trade, agreed to show us what to do. Tolya and I watched intently as he yanked a couple of wires from under the dash, touched them together and, like magic, sparked life into the Devyatka.

Although we'd nearly shat ourselves only minutes ago, our encounter with the two soldiers accomplished two things. First, it told me not all today's youth are selfish bastards and, second, it rid us of the irritating Stepan. For both of those things I gave silent thanks to the God I don't believe in.

Chapter 31

'I have to say, Tolya, I felt safer when Stepan was driving.'

'Me too.' Pronin nervously crunched the gears as we veered onto the MKAD exit that would take us, hopefully, to Lyubertsy. The man seemed to have no concept of speed; one minute we were flying, the next crawling along. His sense of direction was also off – from my passenger side seat it looked like he was about to ram us into the metal side guard at any moment.

'Even Yegor's got more road smarts than you.'

Pronin grunted and ground the gears again, probably on purpose this time.

'You're supposed to press your foot against the left pedal when you do that.' I instinctively planted my feet against the floor and braced hard as we missed an oncoming taxi by less than a metre. 'Pay attention, dammit!'

Pronin muttered something under his breath and the car kangaroo hopped to a juddering halt at a set of traffic lights.

'For God's sake, Tolya. Do you even have a licence?'

'Of course I do. Cut me some slack, Viktor Pavlovich, I haven't driven a car for a couple of years. I'm not familiar with these modern gear boxes.'

'I'll be speaking to Burov about refresher lessons. This level of incompetence is unacceptable.' To be fair, my skills would be no better but I wasn't admitting it. As long as Pronin got us to our destination in one piece I'd forgive him. The other skills in his armoury – shooting and unarmed combat – meant more to me today.

Several close shaves with other drivers later, Pronin parked the car a block from the Wolves' den. The temperature hovered around zero, but this town always felt colder to me. We cleared the chambers of our Makarovs, jammed two spare magazine clips each into our pants pockets, brass knuckles into jacket pockets. We quickly debated about taking the camera, but decided to save that for Lacroix. The Wolves would clam up entirely if we tried snapping photos in their den.

'Are you all right, Tolya?'

'Yes, Comrade Captain.' His face was flushed pink, brightest on his high cheekbones. 'To be perfectly honest, this has been the most interesting day in my entire Militsiya career.'

I held out my hand and he shook it. 'Sorry for complaining about your driving. A good effort.'

His lips dipped at the corners. 'I know it was pretty bad.'

'Nonsense. I have to thank you for backing me up on this when no one else was interested.'

'It's an honour to serve with you, Viktor Pavlovich. If I can in anyway help to avenge Yegor and the Nigerian, then...'

'Let's not get ahead of ourselves. First we have to find Lacroix.'

'Yes, Comrade Captain.'

'Coming here was probably a stupid move and we might get killed for our trouble.'

Pronin patted his pockets and smiled. 'No we won't sir. We've got all the help we need. I think we'll be all right.'

The padlock Yegor and I busted off the chain yesterday lay forlornly on the ground. Pronin and I pushed the heavy gate open and quickly made our way inside. We strode down the corridor, each with a brass-knuckled hand hidden in our left pockets, loaded pistols nestled in their holsters. I pounded on the door to the training hall. Ear pressed to the keyhole, I made out up-tempo martial music, snatches of conversation, bursts of laughter. Female voices as well as male. Absent, the sounds of men exercising.

'What's happening?' Pronin stood half a step behind, as ready to protect

229

me as Yegor had been on our recent visit.

'Sounds like their having a day off from training, having a wee party.' I rapped on the door again, this time with the heel of my gun, clip removed. I heard the sound of marching boots approaching. I slid the clip back in just as Aleksey Rybakin opened the door. He beamed like he was expecting his best friend. The grin became a scowl when he clocked it was me, but there was no repeat of yesterday's hostility.

'Captain Voloshin! Back so soon, and with a new deputy. What happened to the last one? Did he quit when he realised what a pathetic cop you are?' He chuckled and turned to his companions, who copied his derisive laughter. Rybakin's flippant reference to Yegor got my blood boiling. They'd beaten him almost to death, now they were scoffing. I suppressed an urge to pull out the Makarov and empty the magazine into Rybakin's brain.

A sweet pungent odour assaulted my nostrils. 'What have you been smoking? I thought you hated drugs.'

'Nothing. I'm high on life, comrade. What a joy today is! Seventy-five years of progress.'

'You're lying, Aleksey. I can smell something foul. Can you, Sergeant?'

'I sure can,' said Pronin. 'Marijuana, unmistakable. Let's book him.'

A deep chesty laugh bubbled out of Rybakin's thin-lipped mouth. 'Fair go, comrades. We aren't hurting anyone. Come in and have a drink and you can tell me why we're so popular with you big-city cops.' An undercurrent of menace flowed not far beneath Rybakin's welcoming façade. I knew his type well; chatty and friendly one minute, the cold blade of a knife pressed to your throat the next.

Two battered faux-leather couches were set at right angles in a corner, a brand-new colour TV sat on an upturned wooden crate. Numbers were down on yesterday's sweaty workout session. This must be the inner circle of dipshits. Kostya, Dima and Grisha. The men wore these same clothes: *telnyashka* singlets and blue chequered pants, the Lyuber uniform. They'd never wear jeans, a symbol of Western decadence and moral decay. No, only Soviet-made clothing would do, never mind they looked like buffoons. Squeezed in next to the men sat four women, all bottle blondes, so similar in appearance they could've been sisters.

The man we'd come to find wasn't there.

Rybakin pointed at a kitchen table. 'How about the three of us sit down and have a drink.' He clicked his fingers. 'Dima, bring us a bottle of vodka. Get a cold one from the freezer.'

An icy bottle and three shot glasses appeared, along with salt-dried *vobla* fish and some sunflower seeds. As Russian as it gets. All we needed to complete the picture was a balalaika band.

'No drinking for us, Rybakin.' I plucked a handful of sunflower seeds and started nibbling. 'We're looking for someone and I think you know exactly who I'm talking about.'

He shrugged. 'Suit yourself.' He poured himself a shot, tossed it back, then another. 'It's rare for us to touch hard liquor because we respect its significance. Okay for celebrations, unacceptable as part of daily life.'

'I'm not here to talk about the moral aspects of Russian drinking culture.' I slammed my fist on the table, making sure he got a good look at the gleaming knuckle dusters. His brow wrinkled, eyebrows formed arches.

'Whoa! What do we have here?' He was on his feet before I could blink. Stoned or not, this was an adversary I had to watch like a hawk. Within seconds, the three of us were squaring off, eyes darting left and right. The other lads had ditched their lady friends and were striding across the floor. The women screamed, one of them tucked her knees into her buxom chest and howled like a woman giving birth.

'Everyone stay calm!' I instinctively wrapped my fingers around the pistol grip. Aleksey and his goons yelled unintelligible obscenities that blended into one cacophonous screech.

Tolya pulled out his gun and waved it menacingly at the oncoming zombie cavalry. 'Stop! If you come any closer I'll shoot!' The Makarov jerked about in his trembling hand. All froze a metre away, hands raised in surrender.

Except for Grisha.

He must have drunk more vodka or smoked more weed than his pals. He tilted his head back and let out a derisive laugh then reverted to type: snarling guard dog. His eyes blazed as he took a wild swing at Pronin's head. For a horrible second I thought Pronin would pull the trigger and kill Grisha on the spot; to his credit he swayed to avoid the haymaker, gun pointed at the ceiling. He bent his knees and swivelled hard, unleashed a ripping blow to the thug's solar plexus. Grisha clutched at his stomach and hit the deck with a thump. He rolled around groaning as his mates looked on in silence, hands still in the air.

By this time I also had my gun drawn, pointed directly at Aleksey. I looked down the barrel, lined it up directly with the centre of his sweaty forehead. 'Tell your men we won't hesitate to shoot if there's a repeat of that stupidity. Seriously, where do you recruit these idiots from?'

Aleksey thrust out his jaw, his lips twitched as if he was searching for a clever rejoinder. He nodded at the two men still standing. 'You two, go look after the ladies. I'll take care of this.'

'Listen to your boss,' said Pronin. 'Piss off or you'll be joining your mate on the floor.'

Kostya and Dima slowly lowered their hands, skulked back to the women. I heard them whispering, probably boasting how they'd make sure to get us back for the humiliating shut down of their leader. I didn't care. Now Aleksey was going to take us seriously. We resumed our seats.

'Tell me where he is,' I demanded. Tolya kept a firm grip on his pistol, held it flat against the tabletop, barrel pointed in the region of Aleksey's chest. I slid the brassy from my hand and returned it to my pocket, stowed my gun.

'Who?'

'You know perfectly well who. I'm not playing games with you anymore.'

'Why should I tell you?' Rybakin snatched the vodka bottle and poured three shots, splashing plenty on the tabletop. This time Pronin and I made no objections; we damn well needed a drink. I can't vouch for Tolya, but my nerves were jangling after Grisha's foolish bravado. In my peripherals I saw him crawling back to the couch like a whipped dog.

'So you're admitting you know Lacroix, huh? Last time you flat out denied it.'

'You know I'm sick of you filth coming here uninvited, spoiling our fun.' I had to hand it to him – he knew how to change the subject. 'I'm going to

232

have to keep the gym door locked during the day.' He ripped a dried fish apart, picked at the flesh and popped tiny portions into his mouth. 'And, by the way, you can pay for a new padlock for the fucking gate.'

'I can't believe you've left the place wide open.' I shrugged. 'Not very security conscious.'

'Or smart.' Pronin sparked up a smoke and took a deep drag. I half expected Rybakin to make a fuss about the unhealthy cigarette smoke, but he held his tongue. A tarnished tin ashtray in the middle of the table contained four scraggly roach ends.

'People around here understand they'd get their arses kicked for dropping by uninvited.' Rybakin drummed his oddly well-manicured fingernails on the table. 'If you weren't armed cops you'd be picking your teeth off the floor right now.'

Pronin flashed his nearly perfect set of pearly white choppers, picked up his shot glass and drained it. He was smart enough to ignore Rybakin's bait.

'Speaking of respect,' I said. 'You know you're getting zero from your Canadian friend, don't you?'

'I told you I don't know the guy. Why are you persisting with this?'

'In case he decides to drop by at any stage...'

'I said I don't fucking know him. How many times do I have to repeat myself before it gets through your thick skulls?' A little twitch started in Aleksey's right eye, then in a cheek muscle.

'Listen, dipshit.' Pronin flicked his pistol with thumb and forefinger, set it in a blurring spin on the table. 'I've heard the whole story from the horse's mouth. Shukhov – you know the rector of the Chekhov Institute, don't you? Anyway, he kindly told me all about your association with Michel Lacroix, how he even introduced you to him.'

'Bullshit.'

'Not bullshit.' I was enjoying Pronin taking the lead. 'Late last year it was. Lacroix had barely stepped off the plane and breathed his first breath of Moscow air when Shukhov organised your little get together.'

The twitch was more noticeable now. Aleksey would be a shit poker player.

'Shukhov put two and two together,' Pronin continued, stopped the spinning Makarov with a slap of the palm, calmly returned it to its holster. 'You boys love hockey, as does Lacroix. Plus there's the other tie-in; the thing that unites you more than sport. No no, don't shrug, you worm, listen while I'm talking to you. It's your desire to rid Russia of foreign elements that binds you together. Funny that, him being a dirty foreigner himself.'

Rybakin stood, shaking his head. I shoved him back down into his seat. The man's acolytes stared at us open-mouthed from across the room, no idea what to do, their women silent. I sensed they wanted to help their leader but our guns were enough to stay them for the time being. 'My colleague is still speaking, Aleksey. Don't be so rude.'

A throat-clearing cough from Pronin. 'Thank you, Comrade Captain. Would you like to take over? I'm going to lose my temper with this dickhead if he keeps stalling. Empty a clip into his hideous face.' It looked like Rybakin was about to start crying; not because Tolya was threatening him with bullets, but because he was being humiliated. Pronin's bluster inspired more fear in criminals than Yegor ever could, yet I knew which one I'd prefer in a fight. Somehow Rybakin managed to hold back the tears.

'I would, thank you officer.' I focused my gaze on Rybakin. 'This philosophy of Lacroix's to keep Russia pure is bogus for two reasons. Can you guess what they are?'

Rybakin shook his head, confusion stamped on his face.

'The first one's obvious. Like Sergeant Pronin pointed out, he's a fucking foreigner. Now, you might like him because he's Aryan, a Russophile, or he says the right things to you, or whatever, that's your choice. Perhaps what you don't know is this: he's running a massive black market operation that nets him tens of thousands of roubles, money that should be going into the pockets of the ordinary man and woman on the street, the backbone of the nation. Instead of working for the betterment of the USSR, he's working against it.'

I waited. A short hush fell over the gathering, punctuated by crackles from the television.

'Bullshit.' Rybakin slammed another shot. His average yearly amount probably consumed in one day. 'He's solid. I've never heard anything to the contrary.'

'I'm afraid it's true,' said Pronin. 'We've gathered enough evidence to have him imprisoned for ten years, maybe twenty. Lots of people are prepared to testify against the bastard.' Rybakin gave an involuntary rapid one-two-three blink. Pronin's lie hit the mark. 'Unfortunately, too many influential people are protecting him. He'll never see the inside of a Russian jail.'

'I don't believe a word you're saying,' Rybakin scowled.

'You weren't born yesterday,' I said. 'Clothes a bit too flashy for a champion of the proletariat. Surely you suspected he was rotten.'

'Prove it!'

Time to lay it on the line. 'He's been seen buying and selling foreign currency. He even brags about it around the Chekhov Institute. You know one of his mates. A French kid who got his leg broken – by you – for daring to question Lacroix's motives.'

'Who? I never broke no one's fucking leg!'

'A little weasel called Laurent Guillot. He worships the CPSU, Marxism, all that nonsense. He's spilled the beans on Lacroix and his two-timing girlfriend Olga. Now he's probably sitting in his miserable little dorm room, suffering all alone. How ironic that Guillot's beliefs match yours more closely than Lacroix's, and what does he get for his trouble? A tyre lever to the leg.'

'Now you've got me really confused, Voloshin. I don't know any French kids.'

'Do you deny you or your men were responsible for inflicting serious injury on Guillot?'

'Of course I deny it. Are you kidding me?' Was there a ring of honesty in Rybakin's protestation this time? Maybe what Shukhov told Pronin about the emergence of the other gang was true.

'Maybe this will spur you along. When I was here yesterday, I mentioned some skinheads had told me you've got a girlfriend called Klavdia, which you outright rejected.' I gestured towards the silent spectators on the couches. 'I'm sure if I asked to see the young ladies' passports, one of them's going to be the mysterious Klavdia Tereshkova. Am I right?'

An attractive brunette in a tight sweater that accentuated her generous bust was shaking like a leaf. I pointed at her. 'Are you Klavdia?'

She gave a guilty nod.

'You see, Aleksey? It's not that hard to be honest with the Militsiya. Klavdia there is a fine example of a Soviet citizen doing her duty and telling the truth. You could learn a lot from her.'

Rybakin glared. 'I hate fucking skinheads.'

A flash of inspiration. 'Shukhov's ready to finger you for everything. Pronin here snuck under his defences, got him to open up. He's so enamoured of Lacroix, he's prepared to sacrifice you in order to save him. I'll be frank, skinheads are the last of your worries.'

Rybakin dropped his head into his hands. If he didn't believe Lacroix was a black marketeer, appealing to his sense of group loyalty might make him turn against the man.

'You seem to have this crazy notion your Canadian friend's out there promoting the socialist message, the Soviet ideal. You couldn't be more wrong. He's recruiting spies for the fucking KGB. Turning kids against their own countries. Against their families and friends.'

'So what? They'd be better off living like us. Their societies are rotten and crumbling. Western culture? Huh! Give me a break. America, Europe, you name it, they're full of degenerates. The values they respect are greed, materialism and envy, all the shit the Great Revolution rid us of! If Michel is doing that, more power to him.'

'So, it's Michel now, is it? Pretty stupid you denying all knowledge of him earlier.'

'That was before you started throwing these allegations around, wasn't it? I know the man like a brother, and he's nothing like what you're describing.'

'He's pulled the wool over your eyes, Aleksey. I hate to be the bearer of bad news.' Pronin's tone verged on sympathetic. 'But we've got sworn statements from half the students at the Chekhov and Gandhi Institutes, rival criminals, the Nigerians in particular.'

Rybakin put his hands to his ears. 'Don't tell me about the fucking

Nigerians, please! Dirty scum.'

'You're a fine piece of work, Aleksey.' A foul bitter taste in my mouth made me want to spit.

'They're rubbing our faces in it.' He looked up, as if seeking my understanding. 'They parade around like kings, like they're better than us, our beautiful Russian women draped across their arms.'

'Why is that a problem for you?' I said. 'Surely it's none of your damn business what people do in their spare time.'

'Because it's not natural, it's fucking disgusting. Isn't it lads?'

The three men on the couch offered garbled shouts of agreement.

'Is it disgusting enough for you to kill a black man?' I challenged.

Rybakin's eyes grew wide; did he realise we knew of this gang's involvement in killing Adekanye? That we weren't there just to track down Lacroix?

Pronin rose from his seat. 'And is it disgusting enough to beat a man – a white man like you, a fellow Russian – almost to death to make a point?'

'I, ah…'

'Shut the fuck up!' Pronin had the gun drawn and pointed at Rybakin's nose.

'Who the hell is Adekanye, anyway?'

BANG!

The shot echoed like thunder in the warehouse. The bullet sizzled past Rybakin's left ear and embedded itself in the brickwork behind him. 'Stop it! Pronin screamed. 'We never mentioned his name! You murder an innocent man simply because he's black. Then you nearly kill my friend, a cop.' Pronin set his legs at shoulder width, re-aimed the pistol at Rybakin's face. I quickly checked what the goons were doing. Cowering in the corner, posing zero threat to us now Pronin had shown his hand – we weren't to be trifled with. Rybakin himself was close to catatonic, the colour drained from his face and his eyes blinked at a hundred miles an hour. In his career as a hooligan he may have been in countless scrapes, but I doubt a shot had ever been fired next to his head. A small wet patch appeared on Rybakin's upper thigh, spread out and down towards his knee.

'You're getting no more chances, arsehole.' Pronin took a step towards

Rybakin, raised the gun again. 'Next shot's not going to miss.'

'You can kill me if you like, but I ain't saying another word.' Rybakin had stopped blinking, was breathing more or less normally. That chin of his, again sticking out like a sore thumb, was begging to be hit with something. I couldn't resist; the brass knuckles somehow wriggled their own way back onto my fingers. I leaned to the right, let loose with a savage right cross that connected with the point of Rybakin's chin before he realised what was happening. The crunch on impact sounded like a canon crash in Tchaikovsky's famous overture. Rybakin's head snapped back then rolled forward as if he'd been in a head on collision. I ploughed my fist into the same spot again. This time I felt bone give way – I'd broken his jaw just under the two front teeth. Blood cascaded from his mouth and he spat out a tooth. My revenge for the one he knocked out of me two years ago.

'We *might* kill you,' I said. 'But not until we've had some fun. Tolya, keep your weapon pointed at that human swill over there while I do a bit of training. You like training, don't you Aleksey?' He mumbled something that got lost in the bubbling red mass that poured from his swelling lips. 'Sorry, didn't quite catch that, maybe you need another drink.' I poured some vodka into the ashtray and tossed the stinking contents at his mouth. He spluttered and held his hands up.

'Had enough?'

'Yes,' he whispered. His chest rose and fell with a gurgling rattle.

'I disagree.' It wasn't a wise decision to continue the onslaught, but I couldn't help it. His head was a magnet for my fists. I belted him with a flurry of blows, an eight-punch combination to the nose. I stood back to assess the damage but Rybakin didn't give me long to admire my work. He teetered and wobbled for a second, then crashed to the ground. The sound of his head smashing onto the concrete made my guts turn over.

'Help me get him up, Tolya.'

Back in his chair, Rybakin looked more like a Picasso portrait than a real human being. A wave of shame swept over me; I'd sunk to their level. But it was too late, there was no turning back.

Chapter 32

'I'll try again, Aleksey. Where is he?'

A blank stare.

'It looks like you're struggling to articulate, comrade. I admit I may've been too rough. You can't blame me though, can you? Let's try this: one blink for yes, two for no. Do you understand?'

Aleksey's eyes remained wide open, no blinks. I repeated the request, loud and slow, my Makarov pointed at his stomach. His eyes now flickered uncontrollably. Perhaps a shot to the guts and walking away would be my best option.

'I think you're playing games with me. One last time before I pump all the bullets into you.'

He mumbled something incoherent, bestial, coughed up a mix of phlegm and blood. It made a right mess of his singlet. I had to act fast before he passed out. I grabbed the bottle of vodka and drained the remaining alcohol in three steady gulps.

'If you fail to tell me where Lacroix is, I'll have no choice but to do to you what you did to Adekanye. Fair's fair, right?'

A louder grunt, laced with terror.

'You know exactly what I'm talking about, don't you?'

He whimpered, shook his head a fraction.

This was no good. I berated myself for overstepping the mark. Rybakin was useless to me now. Surely one of the others knew where the Canadian was holed up. 'Any of you pricks know where Lacroix is? Speak up now or

239

your friend dies. I only want the Canadian. Tell me where he is and he'll take the fall for the crime. I guarantee you immunity, just give me him!' If they believed I'd spare them justice, they were bigger idiots than I imagined.

The smallest of the thugs, Kostya, raised his hand. He eyes blazed. I guessed he didn't want to rat out Lacroix, but Aleksey, a Russian and a fellow Lyuber, was dearer to his bitter heart. 'I think I know where he might be.'

'Good lad,' I said. Rybakin could sit there suffering for all I cared. As a parting gesture I delivered a vicious front kick to his stomach. He reeled backwards in the chair; his arms waved about comically as if it might help him regain his balance. He hit the ground and fell silent. After a few seconds he let out a pathetic groan. I would've enjoyed playing knock-'em-downs with Aleksey all day, but there was work to be done.

As we strode across the room, Pronin and I levelled our weapons at the six people quivering on the couches, waved them from side to side as menacingly as we could. Abject fear blended with hatred bulged their eyes. Perfect. The lot of them must have thought Tolya and I had completely lost our minds. I was starting to get the same feeling. Total focus was now on finding Lacroix and getting him to sign a confession. What happened after that, I'd play by ear.

'Before you tell us where he is, I want you to tell me exactly what happened,' I said to Kostya.

'What do you mean?'

The lightning-fast left-handed slap Pronin delivered to Kostya's face made him cry out and me jump.

'Hey, what did you do that for? I'm co-operating, for fuck's sake.'

This time Pronin jabbed him square in the mouth, luckily for Kostya it was only a half-strength punch with a bare fist. Droplets of blood dripped onto the man's chequered pants. Kostya touched his fingertips to his lips. 'OK, you can stop hitting me.'

I instructed Pronin to fetch the camera from the car; I wanted souvenir photos of this interrogation, even if they never saw the light of day in a court of law. Upon Pronin's return, I dragged Kostya off the couch, sat him roughly on a wooden crate; then I grabbed a chair, spun it round and positioned myself a metre from Kostya. Pronin remained standing, camera at the ready, the rest of the ensemble cast almost motionless. I could hear everyone's breathing, punctuated by the occasional low moan from Rybakin across the room.

'Tell me how Aaron Adekanye ended up dead. Then you tell me where Lacroix is. Then we leave,' I said. 'Deal?' I wanted to hear this version of the story before I grilled Lacroix. Something told me the truth would come from the Lyubers, not the Canadian.

He nodded. 'Deal.' A flash of the Magicube accompanied Pronin's first snapshot.

'Start talking.'

'Michel showed us photographs of a white girl with Adekanye. They were embracing, kissing, holding hands. It was disgusting. I can't believe a Russian woman would degrade herself with a...' Kostya's thin lips curled downwards '...dirty black–'

Pronin delivered a combination of left-right open hand slaps to Kostya's cheeks, blood and sweat sprayed in all directions. 'No opinions, right Comrade Captain?' I gave a nod of agreement. 'Just facts. Otherwise I'm gonna break some bones next time.'

'Continue,' I said to Kostya. 'We haven't got all day.'

Breaths were hard to come by for Kostya, bruises were appearing all over his face. He ploughed on, speaking quickly as if inspired to get the whole nasty business over with. 'He told us the Nigerian was going to be waiting for some Vietnamese guys at the Central Tourist hotel on Leninsky Prospekt. Lacroix had paid them to offer some kind of "deal" that was too good to resist. Early October it was. First big snowfalls. They walked with him through the forest. A bunch of us lay in ambush, grabbed the bla–, the African.'

'Were you and the rest of your friends here a part of this kidnapping?'

'Who else? We're the main crew.'

I thought his friends would be aghast at his frank admission of their guilt, instead they wore proud smirks.

'Didn't he resist? He's a big man.'

'Yeah, I'll give him his due. Fought back like a bear, even though he'd been drinking for hours. Amazing, really. The Vietnamese made sure he was pretty sozzled, but still capable of walking. If he'd collapsed, they'd have had no hope of carrying him. Once we subdued him, we transported him in a van Lacroix had rustled up from somewhere. We brought him back here, used him as a punching bag for a couple of weeks.' The hooligan's eyes shimmered, savouring the recollection. 'Sometimes we untied him for sparring sessions, to make it a bit more sporting. We fed him regular, though. Starving someone to death is too cruel. We've all seen pictures of the concentration camps from the Great Patriotic War, hey Comrade Captain?' My God, what he thought was fair and right was a perversion. 'Last Wednesday night we took him back to the woods and strung him up.'

I felt like vomiting. The casual manner in which Kostya narrated the tale defied belief. Yegor had been right: these bastards don't equate non-whites as being human. They'd imprisoned him like an animal, kept him alive for "sport".

'What about the castration, the cross carved into his back?'

An eerie laugh burst from Kostya's lips. 'Man, if you think *we're* bad people, we've got nothing on Lacroix. We did the heavy lifting, he did all that extra decorating.'

The other monsters on the couch chuckled at Kostya's "joke". I wanted to murder them all, the females included. I jotted down all the details, my hand quivering as I struggled to write on the notepad.

Time to throw the grenade.

'Did you realise the white woman in the photos, long-range so you couldn't identify her, is Olga?' I saw a collective sea of raised eyebrows. 'That's right, Lacroix's own girlfriend. He was willing to use her to get you clowns to do his dirty work. He's played you for a chump.' I pushed my face right up into Kostya's. 'You might also be surprised to learn he'll happily do business with black folks as long as they don't step on his toes. The "hit" you helped him with was purely business.'

'Tell him where the prick is, Kostya. The cop's right, he played us for fools!'

242

It was Igor. 'We've treated him like an honoured guest, and he's spat in our face. Tricking us to do his dirty work.'

And that was all it took. One dissenter and they all rolled over to squeal. I jotted down everyone's name and address, promising them complete immunity from prosecution for testifying before a court if I could somehow get the public prosecutor to play ball.

'So you'll tell us where he is?'

Igor shook his head. 'Better than that, Comrade Captain.' *Where did this respect come from?* 'I'll take you to him. It's only a couple of blocks away.'

Chapter 33

A mattress on the floor butted up against a discoloured radiator; surprisingly good quality bedding for a dirty old squat. The clean white sheets looked new. Lacroix's ill-gotten pocket money obtained luxuries I could only dream of. He lay on his back, fast asleep, a rake-thin raven-haired woman tucked up next to him, deflated right breast exposed. A needle sat in a tiny puddle of translucent liquid in a dirty saucer, other drug paraphernalia lay on the floor beside them. A half-full bottle of expensive vodka within arm's reach. Some gnawed black bread and pickled cucumbers.

'Wake up motherfucker!' Igor pushed past me and Pronin. He slapped Lacroix across the face before spitting in it. 'You've got some explaining to do before I kill you!'

The sleeping man moaned softly, turned onto his side. The Lyuber had struck him hard, but the drugs must've dulled the Canadian's senses. I'd only seen him fleetingly at the hockey stadium and didn't get a proper look. Up close the man was cherubic. I struggled to comprehend the evil mind inside his pretty head.

The woman's eyes opened, her body juddered. The flicker of recognition when she saw Igor quickly changed to alarm. A friend and ally turned savage. *Why did you hit our esteemed guest?* her eyes seemed to say. Eager fingers grabbed the bedsheet and pulled it up to her neck. I scruffed Igor by the collar before he could land any more blows on Lacroix. 'You, stand by the door. Don't touch the suspect again.'

Igor shuffled out of the way, chastened but sporting a vengeful grin. He jumped around by the doorway like a flea. Watching the Lyuber bouncing about made me nervous. Lacroix would be more inclined to spill his guts if Igor wasn't there. I pointed at the woman. 'You! Get your clothes on.' I turned to Igor. 'And you. Take her with you and wait outside, sit on the staircase.'

'But it's cold,' the woman, now rugged up, protested.

'I don't care.'

In an act of gallantry that surprised me, Igor gently took the woman by the arm and ushered her out. With them gone, the air somehow felt cleaner. But only marginally.

'Tolya.' I pointed at Lacroix's semi-comatose figure. 'Take some photos of him lying there, the drug gear, everything.'

With Igor and the woman gone and a new roll of film in the camera, I set about waking up sleeping beauty. The abandoned flat was mostly empty, but there was some cutlery, basic furniture, enamel cups and a kettle in the kitchen. The cord was so frayed you couldn't turn the kettle on without fear of electrocution. Luckily I only needed cold water. I filled the kettle and tipped the contents over Lacroix's face. He woke with a start, spluttering and coughing. I knelt beside him, dodging water droplets and saliva.

'How are you, Michel?' I tried to sound as benign as a kindergarten teacher greeting a nervous new child. 'I've been dying to meet you. I must say, I'm surprised you're having a private party instead of celebrating Revolution Day with your patriotic pals, though. Rather selfish, don't you think?'

'What?' he said. Then something else in English which I interpreted as *Who the hell are you?*

'I know you speak Russian, sonny. So how about you get dressed, then come into the kitchen for a nice little chat with me and my colleague. OK?'

He began shaking the second he sat down, bewilderment clouded his eyes, pink from whatever he'd injected into himself. I passed him a cup of water. He gulped it down, gingerly handed the cup back to me.

'Please tell me what's going on.' The reports were true, his Russian was flawless, the accent imperceptible.

'I won't beat around the bush. You are in a whole world of trouble.' I stared at him unflinchingly.

A smile twisted his mouth. The effects of the drugs were wearing off fast. 'You must be joking. Who are you anyway? Amateur gangsters?' He glanced at Pronin. 'Nice cashmere jumper, by the way. Where'd you get it? Wouldn't mind one myself.' Nonchalant, carefree.

I calmly produced my ID and the cocky attitude vanished.

'Not all cops are bums. Some of us like to dress nicely when we work under cover.'

I saw a glimmer of hope brighten Lacroix's expression. The faint scent of an out. 'Listen, fellas. If it's quality threads you're after, then–'

I grabbed the lad by the collar of his t-shirt, dragged his face close to mine. His features may have been angelic, but his breath emanated from the pits of hell. I winced, edged back a few inches. 'Listen, I'm not like all the corrupt filth you deal with.' I gestured towards Pronin, his face partially obscured by the camera. The room lit up as he pressed the button. 'And nor is my colleague. If you think bribing us to look the other way is going to save your skin, think again.'

Lacroix took a huge breath. 'Is it about the drugs? If it is, I can tell you who's stealing it from the pharmaceutical factories, distributing it, the works.'

'What is it, Promedol?' I asked.

Lacroix nodded. 'Yeah. Otherwise known as Trimeperidine.'

I scribbled something in my notebook. 'I know what it is.' An addictive morphine-like drug developed right here in the USSR. 'Thanks for that admission, son. I'll add it to the other charge.'

'What other charge?' Alarm clearly in his voice now.

'Double homicide.' I flicked the page over, pretended to read the names from the page. 'Aaron Adekanye, Nigerian medical student. Pyotr Ivanov, District Medical Examiner of the Moscow Public Prosecutor's Office.'

He closed his eyes tight as he began to take rapid, shallow breaths. Pronin seized the moment to capture his discomfiture. *Flash.*

'Wow, I've got to hand it to you guys.' Lacroix squinted. 'You've got quite an imagination.'

'Is this also imagined?' I hit him under the jaw with a right uppercut, complemented the blow with a left cross. He reeled sideways, smacked his head on the parquet floor with a sickening thwack.

Pronin set down his camera, stepped up to the body on the floor and delivered a kick to the kidney area. 'And that's for my friend you got beaten up, you son of a bitch.' Lacroix screamed, rolled around clutching the small of his back. Pronin waited a moment for the lad to settle, grabbed him under the armpits and hefted him back onto the chair. Blood streamed from the side of Lacroix's mouth, terror filled his eyes.

I ripped a pillowslip from one of the pillows on the floor, soaked it in water from the kitchen and cleaned up his face as best I could. I let the lad stew for a minute, then lit two cigarettes, handed him one. 'A peace offering.' He smoked like he had no desire for it but feared a refusal might elicit more punches to the head. It very well might have, such was my loathing for him.

'Let's get down to the nitty gritty.' I listed the students from both institutes who'd testify against him, invented a couple of extra names. Told him rector Kuznetsov from the Gandhi University had evidence against him, too. 'To stop them denouncing you, all you have to do is confess. Simple. You'll get thirty years in a Siberian jail. Better than the firing squad, don't you think?'

'Not going...to happen.' He could barely speak. 'Shukhov will...protect me.'

I handed him my notebook and pen. 'Initial each page and sign at the end.'

Lacroix silently read what I'd already prepared for him. A full admission of his guilt in organising the lynching of Adekanye and his personal role in defiling the body. Also acknowledgement of his responsibility for the attack on Yegor.

He shook his head. 'Not...signing...it. Fuck...your...mother.'

'This is such a shame, you not co-operating with us. Pronin, go and fetch Igor, will you?'

'Yes, Comrade Captain.'

I've seen vicious guard dogs, German shepherds tied to chains, teeth barred and snarling, spittle flying. Igor looked exactly like that. I gestured towards

Lacroix. 'Help yourself.'

Lacroix leapt to his feet, rather effeminately put his hands up to protect himself as Igor advanced, fists balled and yelling obscenities.

'Wait!' I pointed my Makarov at Igor. 'Stand still!'

The Lyuber stopped dead in his tracks, bewildered. 'I thought you wanted me to finish him off?'

I ignored his words, addressed Lacroix, who sought refuge huddled against the window, shivering and hyperventilating like he had the ague. 'Last chance. If there's anything you want to say in your defense, say it now.'

'It was Shukhov. He told me to join the Lyubers. Said they'd have no worries doing any dirty work I required. They're the ones who wanted to hang the Nigerian. You should have seen them laughing!'

'You mutilated him, you fucking freak. Not us.' Pronin fought to restrain Igor, who struggled like a madman to get to Lacroix. 'All of this is down to you!'

'I tend to agree with Igor, here,' I said. 'You need to own up to what you've done. Sign the document *now*, or Comrade Pronin and I walk away and leave you to your lovely friends. I'm sure their boss Aleksey would like to say a few last words to you before he cuts your throat.'

'OK, OK, I'll sign it.'

'Nice, legible handwriting, now.'

Lacroix's shaking hand scribbled frantically. When he was done, I made him hold it under his chin while Pronin snapped a couple of photos.

'Good boy,' I said, tucking the notebook into my pocket. 'And I guess that wraps up proceedings. Although I do have a couple of questions for you before we go.'

'You can't leave me here alone with these animals? They'll kill me.'

'Keep telling me what you know and I'll see you get treated appropriately.'

He nodded slowly. My ambiguous assurance seemed to calm him.

'Who killed Ivanov?'

'Who?'

'The District Medical Examiner.'

'How the hell would I know? Nothing to do with me. That's another level of power altogether. KGB probably.'

'Did you arrange for Yegor to be attacked?' Pronin asked.

Lacroix shook his head feverishly. 'Who the fuck's Yegor?'

'My friend, that's who.' Pronin grabbed Lacroix's testicles and twisted hard.

'Please, let go! I'll tell you,' Lacroix screeched. Pronin released his grip and Lacroix bent double. 'Whatever you're talking about was done by Shukhov,' he wheezed. 'Once he'd learned what happened to Adekanye, he said he'd take care of all the shit that would come afterwards. To protect me.'

What happened to Adekanye. As if he wasn't even part of it. The man was in complete denial.

'What do you know about the men who picked up Adekanye's body? Was it a couple of Lyubers pretending to be Militsiya? Or members of the Belyaevo Boys?'

He shook his head, nearly laughed. 'It was Shukhov, obviously. Do you think I'd be capable of despatching a couple of spare cops at a moment's notice?'

My god, those men were real Militsiya, not imposters. If Shukhov had the power to do that, I'd never be able bring him or Lacroix to justice. At least not via official channels. That's if Shukhov didn't get to me first.

There was nothing more for us to do here; Lacroix's fate was sealed.

'Looks like it's not your day, Michel.' I stood, gathered my hat and coat from the hallway rack. 'Come on, Tolya. I'm keen to watch the Revolution Day parade highlights on TV.'

The screams that echoed in the stairwell as Pronin and I trotted past the shivering Lyuber woman and down to the building's exit will haunt my dreams for all the years I have left on Earth.

Chapter 34

Six weeks later

Six weeks later

Flora took hold of the 10x15 cm colour photo of Lacroix holding up his confession.

'Can I keep it? I'd like to show Aaron's family.' She squinted as she examined the picture more closely. 'Are you sure he signed it voluntarily? He looks rather stressed. Is that bruising on his cheek?'

I snatched the photo back from her grasp. 'I'll be keeping that.'

'Why?'

'The guilty party's been punished. There's nothing to be gained by circulating this image. Aaron has been avenged.'

She puffed furiously on a cigarette, jittery as an aspen leaf. We were back at the lobby of the Intourist Hotel. 'Did you see the newspaper article?' she asked before tipping a large measure of cognac down her throat.

I nodded. The official MVD-plus-KGB report supplied to the press stated Michel Lacroix had been set upon and murdered by unknown assailants in the city of Lyubertsy and his body disposed of in Chernoye Lake. The Canadian-Soviet Friendship Society hailed him as a model student who would be sorely missed. The gruesome details of the killing remained confidential, but one of my old Militsiya contacts in Lyubertsy told me the true story over the phone. The victim had been stabbed over fifty times and was subjected to barbaric torture over a prolonged period. Talk about karma.

'At least he got some column inches in *Izvestiya*,' Flora's tone was loaded with sarcasm. 'Aaron got nothing. It's an absolute disgrace.'

'It is.' I sipped hot, sweet coffee. I hadn't touched a drop of alcohol since Pronin and I returned from our trip to Lyubertsy. Not sure it wasn't a hyperactive imagination, but I had an acute sense of being under observation. Being only half-aware of the world around me wasn't going to cut it anymore, not now my name was on lists I'd rather it wasn't. I had Ksenia to think about. Flora was my immediate concern, however, and she required appeasing. 'You have to be pleased Lacroix didn't get away with his crime, right?'

'Yes. But his accomplices did.' Her volume rose noticeably. 'Those racist hooligans, the ones who actually killed Aaron, got off scot-free!'

I leaned across the table. 'Keep your voice down or I'll arrest you for disturbing the peace.'

'What peace?'

'Mine.'

She smiled, a moment of levity in a tragedy of Shakespearean proportions. 'I acknowledge you did all you could in a system designed to produce a version of justice that's merely a convenience. Doesn't alter the reality of the situation, though.'

'Elegantly put, my dear.' She had a way with words I could only hope to emulate.

'My fellow students and I are grateful for your efforts.' Her hand reached across the table, rested on top of mine. 'At least we know Aaron wasn't murdered in a random racist attack.'

'Still...'

'Still what?'

Fire seemed to transfer to me from her fingers. Suddenly self-conscious, I pulled my hand away. 'There are elements in our society that aren't as tolerant as the propaganda would have everyone believe. So, my advice is – be careful at all times.'

She stubbed out her cigarette with a flourish. 'Now, Comrade Captain, will you please hail a taxi to take me to the airport?'

Chapter 35

hristmas Eve

C I couldn't leave it alone. The piece of paper drew my eyes like a magnet. I re-read it for the tenth time. A job offer with a secretive private security company. I was aware such organisations existed in Moscow, but their legal status was cloudy, to say the least. This company's founders were relatives of Yegor's Georgian friend, Irakli. I'd called around to the markets last week to see how things were going with troublemakers. Irakli was pleased to report there'd been precisely zero incidents since Yegor and I collared the skinheads. After some sad conversation about Yegor, the big Georgian gave me his golden grin, said I'd be better off quitting the Militsiya and joining his cousin Zurab's clandestine outfit as an investigator. Better money, for one thing. *Twenty times the salary*, he said. *You'll be able to afford my oranges*, he said. *I'll think about it*, I said. This morning I dropped by the market again and Irakli handed me an envelope. Inside – the offer.

The call came from Burov at 9:30pm. I was watching ice-hockey, a sport I now appreciated for its artistry, courage and brutality.

'It's Yegor.' The boss's voice was flat.

My heart stopped. It had to be bad news; we'd heard nothing of Yegor's condition for many days.

'Are you there, Viktor Pavlovich?'

'Yes.' I wasn't sure any sound came out of my dry mouth.

'He's on the mend.'

'I beg your pardon?'

'It's some kind of miracle. I don't understand all the medical terms, but the doctor told me the swelling on Yegor's brain has reduced and he's making noises that sound remarkably like words. In fact, they are words.'

'What has he said?'

A cigarette sparked up on the other end of the line. Along with giving up the booze, I'd not smoked for a month. I craved tobacco so much I felt my mouth water as I heard the Colonel inhale. 'I hate to burst your bubble, but it wasn't your name. He asked for Tolya. I had no idea Yegor and Pronin were close friends, did you?'

I swallowed hard. 'No. None at all.'

'Just goes to show, doesn't it?'

'Goes to show what?'

'You never know people as well as you think you do.'

'You can say that again, Yevgeny Nikolaevich.'

After we exchanged our good-nights, I watched the end of the match, yelled myself hoarse when the Soviet Wings' forward slipped the puck between the Dynamo goalie's legs with two seconds left on the clock.

Tomorrow I'd give Irakli's cousin a call.

* * *

Extract from Mikhail Gorbachev's speech given on 2 November 1987 on the occasion of the 70th Anniversary of the October Revolution

It is 70 years since the unforgettable days of October 1917, those legendary days that started the count of the new epoch of social progress, of the real history of humankind.

The past—its heroism and drama—cannot fail to thrill our contemporaries. Our history is one, and it is irreversible. Whatever emotions it may evoke, it is our history, and we cherish it. Today we turn to those October days that shook the world. We look for and find in them both a dependable spiritual buttress and instructive lessons. We see again and again that the socialist option of the October Revolution has been correct.

Like Marx and Engels, Lenin was convinced that the defense force of the revolution would be a people's militia. But the concrete conditions prompted a different solution. The Civil War and the intervention from outside, imposed on the people, called for a new approach. A worker-peasant Red Army was formed by Lenin's decree. It was an army of a new type which covered itself with undying glory in the Civil War and in repulsing the foreign intervention. Those years brought severe trials for the newly established Soviet Republic. It had to settle the elementary and crucial question of whether socialism would or would not be.

Other Books by Blair Denholm

The Fighting Detective Series
  Fighting Dirty (prequel – e-book always FREE on Amazon)
  Kill Shot (Book 1)
  Shot Clock (Book 2)
  Trick Shot (Book 3)

Game Changer Series
  SOLD (Book 1)
  Sold to the Devil (Book 2)

About the Author

A bit about me

BLAIR DENHOLM is an Australian fiction writer and translator who has lived and worked in New York, Moscow, Munich, Abu Dhabi and Australia. He once voted in a foreign election despite having no eligibility to do so, was almost lost at sea on a Russian fishing boat, and was detained by machine-gun toting soldiers in the Middle East.

When not writing novels, he works as a Russian language specialist for an international conservation organisation.

He currently resides in the wilds of Tasmania with his partner, Sandra, and two crazy canines Max and Bruno.

You can connect with me on:

- https://blairdenholm.com
- https://twitter.com/blairdenholm
- https://www.facebook.com/blairdenholm

Printed in Great Britain
by Amazon

74482103R00153